EVERY SUMMER AFTER

EVERY SUMMER AFTER

Carley Fortune

Berkley
NEW YORK

BERKLEY
An imprint of Penguin Random House LLC
penguinrandomhouse.com

Copyright © 2022 by Carley Fortune
Readers Guide copyright © 2022 by Carley Fortune
Penguin Random House supports copyright. Copyright fuels creativity,
encourages diverse voices, promotes free speech, and creates
a vibrant culture. Thank you for buying an authorized edition
of this book and for complying with copyright laws by not
reproducing, scanning, or distributing any part of it in any form
without permission. You are supporting writers and allowing
Penguin Random House to continue to publish books for every reader.

BERKLEY and the BERKLEY & B colophon
are registered trademarks of Penguin Random House LLC.

ISBN: 9780593638460

The Library of Congress has catalogued the Jove trade edition of this book as follows:

Names: Fortune, Carley, author.
Title: Every summer after / Carley Fortune.
Description: First edition. | New York: Jove, 2022.
Identifiers: LCCN 2021045380 (print) | LCCN 2021045381 (ebook) |
ISBN 9780593438534 (trade paperback) | ISBN 9780593438541 (ebook)
Subjects: LCGFT: Romance fiction.
Classification: LCC PR9199.4.F678 E94 2022 (print) |
LCC PR9199.4.F678 (ebook) | DDC 813/.6—dc23/eng/20211006
LC record available at https://lccn.loc.gov/2021045380
LC ebook record available at https://lccn.loc.gov/2021045381

Printed in the United States of America
1   3   5   7   9   10   8   6   4   2

Book design by Ashley Tucker

To my parents, for taking us to the lake
And to Bob, for letting me go back

1

Now

THE FOURTH COCKTAIL HAD SEEMED LIKE A GOOD IDEA. SO did the bangs, come to think of it. But now that I'm struggling to unlock my apartment door, I'm guessing I might regret that last spritz in the morning. Maybe the bangs, too. June told me breakup bangs were almost always a very bad choice when I sat in her chair for a cut today. But June wasn't going to her friend's engagement celebration, newly single, that night. Bangs were in order.

It's not that I'm still in love with my ex; I'm not. I never was. Sebastian is kind of a snob. An up-and-coming corporate lawyer, he wouldn't have lasted one hour at Chantal's party without scoffing at her choice of signature drink and referencing some pretentious article he read in the *New York Times* that declared Aperol spritzes "over." Instead, he would pretend to study the wine list, ask the bartender annoying questions about *terroir* and acidity and, regardless of the answers, go with a glass of the most expensive red. It's not that he has exceptional taste or knows a lot about wine; he doesn't. He just buys expensive stuff to give the impression of being discerning.

Sebastian and I were together for seven months, giving our relationship the distinction of being my longest-lasting one yet. In the end, he said he didn't really know who I was. And he had a point.

Before Sebastian, the guys I picked were up for a good time and didn't seem to mind keeping things casual. By the time I met him, I figured being a serious adult meant I should find someone to get serious about. Sebastian fit the bill. He was attractive, well read, and successful, and despite being a bit pompous, he could talk to anyone about almost anything. But I still found it hard to share too many pieces of myself. I'd long ago learned to tamp down my tendency to let random thoughts spew unfiltered from my mouth. I thought I was doing a good job of giving the relationship a real chance, but in the end Sebastian recognized my indifference, and he was right. I didn't care about him. I didn't care about any of them.

There was only the one.

And that one is long gone.

So I enjoy spending time with men, and I appreciate how sex gives me an escape ladder out of my mind. I like making men laugh, I like having company, I like taking a break from my vibrator once in a while, but I don't get attached, and I don't go deep.

I'm still fumbling with my key—*seriously, is something wrong with the lock?*—when my phone buzzes in my purse. Which is weird. No one calls me this late. Actually, no one ever calls me, except for Chantal and my parents. But Chantal is still at her party and my parents are touring Prague and won't be awake yet. The buzzing stops just as I get the door open and stumble into my small one-bedroom apartment. I check the mirror by the entrance to find my lipstick mostly smudged off but my bangs looking pretty phenomenal. *Suck it, June.*

I begin to unfasten the strappy gold sandals I'm wearing, a dark sheet of hair falling over my face, when my phone starts up again. I dig it out of my purse and, one shoe off, make my way toward the couch, frowning at the "unknown name" message on the screen. Probably a wrong number.

"Hello?" I ask, bending to take off the second sandal.

"Is this Percy?"

I stand upright so fast I have to hold on to the arm of the couch to steady myself. *Percy.* It's a name nobody calls me anymore. These days I'm Persephone to almost everyone. Sometimes I'm P. But I'm never Percy. I haven't been Percy for years.

"Hello . . . Percy?" The voice is deep and soft. It's one I haven't heard in more than a decade, but so familiar I'm suddenly thirteen years old and slathered in SPF 45, reading paperbacks on the dock. I'm sixteen and peeling off my clothes to jump into the lake, naked and sticky after a shift at the Tavern. I'm seventeen and lying on Sam's bed in a damp bathing suit, watching his long fingers move across the anatomy textbook he's studying by my feet. Blood rushes hot to my face with a *whoosh*, and the steady, thick pumping of my heart invades my eardrums. I take a shaky breath and sit, stomach muscles seizing.

"Yes," I manage, and he lets out a long, relieved-sounding breath.

"It's Charlie."

Charlie.

Not Sam.

Charlie. The wrong brother.

"Charles Florek," Charlie clarifies, and begins explaining

how he tracked down my number—something about a friend of a friend and a connection at the magazine where I work—but I'm barely listening.

"Charlie?" I interrupt. My voice is high-pitched and tight, one part spritz and two parts shock. Or maybe all parts total disappointment. Because *this* voice does not belong to Sam.

But of course it doesn't.

"I know, I know. It's been a long time. God, I don't even know how long," he says, and it sounds like an apology.

But I do. I know exactly how long. I keep count.

It's been twelve years since I've seen Charlie. Twelve years since that catastrophic Thanksgiving weekend when everything between Sam and me fell apart. When I tore everything apart.

I used to count the number of days until my family would head up to the cottage so I could see Sam again. Now he's a painful memory I keep hidden deep beneath my ribs.

I also know I've gone more years without Sam than I spent with him. The Thanksgiving that marked seven years since I'd spoken to him, I had a panic attack, my first in ages, then drank my way through a bottle and a half of rosé. It felt monumental: I'd officially been without him for more years than we'd had together at the lake. I'd cried in ugly, heaving sobs on the bathroom tiles until I passed out. Chantal came over the next day with greasy takeout and held my hair back as I puked, tears streaming down my face, and I told her everything.

"It's been forever," I tell Charlie.

"I know. And I'm sorry to call you so late," he says. He sounds so much like Sam it hurts, as if there's a lump of dough lodged in my throat. I remember when we were fourteen and it was almost impossible to tell him apart from Charlie on the phone. I remember noticing other things about Sam that summer, too.

"Listen, Pers. I'm calling with some news," he says, using the name he used to call me but sounding much more serious than the Charlie I once knew. I hear him breathe in through his nose. "Mom passed away a few days ago, and I . . . well, I thought you'd want to know."

His words slam into me like a tsunami, and I struggle to fully understand them. Sue's dead? *Sue was young.*

All I can get out is a ragged-sounding "What?"

Charlie sounds exhausted when he replies. "Cancer. She'd been fighting it for a couple of years. We're devastated, of course, but she was sick of being sick, you know?"

And not for the first time, it feels like someone stole the script to my life story and wrote it all wrong. It seems impossible that Sue was sick. Sue, with her big smile and her denim cutoffs and her white-blond ponytail. Sue, who made the best pierogies in the universe. Sue, who treated me like a daughter. Sue, who I dreamed one day might be a mother-in-law to me. Sue, who was sick for years without me knowing. I should have known. I should have been there.

"I'm so, so sorry," I begin. "I . . . I don't know what to say. Your mom was . . . she was . . ." I sound panicked, I can hear it.

Hold it together, I tell myself. *You lost rights to Sue a long time ago. You are not allowed to fall apart right now.*

I think about how Sue raised two boys on her own while running the Tavern, and about the first time I met her, when she came over to the cottage to assure my much older parents that Sam was a good kid and that she would keep an eye on us. I remember when she taught me how to hold three plates at once and the time she told me not to take crap from any boy, including her own two sons.

"She was . . . everything," I say. "She was such a good mom."

"She was. And I know she meant a lot to you when we were kids. That's sort of why I'm calling," says Charlie, tentative. "Her funeral is on Sunday. I know it's been a long time, but I think you should be there. Will you come?"

A long time? It's been twelve years. Twelve years since I've made the drive north to the place that was more like home to me than anywhere else has been. Twelve years since I dove, head-first, into the lake. Twelve years since my life crashed spectacularly off course. Twelve years since I've seen Sam.

But there's only one answer.

"Of course I will."

2

Summer, Seventeen Years Ago

I DON'T THINK MY PARENTS KNEW WHEN THEY BOUGHT THE cottage that two adolescent boys lived in the house next door. Mom and Dad wanted to give me an escape from the city, a break from other kids my age, and the Florek boys, who went unsupervised for long stretches of the afternoons and evenings, were probably as big a surprise to them as they were to me.

A few of the kids in my class had summer homes, but they were all in Muskoka, just a short drive north from the city, where the word *cottage* didn't seem quite right for the waterfront mansions that lined the area's rocky shores. Dad flat-out refused to look in Muskoka. He said if we bought a cottage there, we might as well stay in Toronto for the summer—it was too close to the city and too full of Torontonians. So he and Mom focused their search on rural communities further northeast, which Dad declared too developed or too overpriced, and then further still until finally they settled on Barry's Bay, a sleepy, working-class village that transformed into a bustling tourist town in the summer, sidewalks bursting with cottagers and European sightseers on their way to camp or hike in Algonquin Provincial Park. "You'll love it there, kiddo," he promised. "It's the *real* cottage country."

I would eventually look forward to the four-hour drive from our Tudor in midtown Toronto to the lake, but that first trip spanned an eternity. Entire civilizations rose and fell by the time we passed the "Welcome to Barry's Bay" sign, Dad and I in the moving truck and Mom following behind in the Lexus. Unlike Mom's car, the truck had neither a decent sound system nor air-conditioning, and I was stuck listening to the monotonous hum of CBC Radio, the backs of my thighs glued to the vinyl bench and my bangs plastered to my clammy forehead.

Almost all the girls in my seventh-grade class got bangs after Delilah Mason did, though they didn't suit the rest of us as well. Delilah was the most popular girl in our grade, and I considered myself lucky to be one of her closest friends. Or at least I used to, but that was before the sleepover incident. Her bangs formed a neat red valance over her forehead while mine defied both grav-ity and styling products, jutting out in odd poufs and angles, making me look every bit the awkward thirteen-year-old I was, rather than the mysterious dark-eyed brunette I wanted to be. My hair was neither straight nor curly and seemed to change its personality based on an unpredictable number of factors, from the day of the week to the weather to the way I slept the night before. Whereas I would do anything I could to make people like me, my hair refused to fall in line.

~~~

WINDING DOWN THE bushland on the western shore of Ka-maniskeg Lake, Bare Rock Lane was a narrow dirt road that lived up to its name. The drive Dad turned down was so over-grown that branches scraped the sides of the small truck.

"Smell that, kiddo?" Dad asked, rolling down his window as we bumped along in the truck. Together we inhaled deeply, and the scent of long-fallen pine needles filled my nostrils, earthy and medicinal.

We pulled up to the back door of a modest wood A-frame cabin that was dwarfed by the white and red pines that grew around it. Dad shut off the engine and turned to me, a smile below his graying mustache and eyes crinkling under dark-rimmed glasses, and said, "Welcome to the lake, Persephone."

The cottage had this incredible smoky-wood smell. Some-how it never faded, even after years of Mom burning her expensive Diptyque candles. Each time I returned, I'd stand at the entrance, breathing it in, just like I did that first day. The main floor was a small open space, covered floor to ceiling in pale planks of knotted wood. Massive windows opened onto an almost obnoxiously stunning view of the lake.

"Wow," I murmured, spotting a staircase leading from the deck and down a steep hill.

"Not bad, huh?" Dad patted me on the shoulder.

"I'm going to check out the water," I said, already darting out the side door, which closed behind me with an enthusiastic *thwack*. I fled down dozens of steps until I reached the dock. It was a humid afternoon, every inch of sky carpeted by thick gray clouds that were mirrored in the still, silver water below. I could barely make out the cottages that dotted the far shore. I wondered if I could swim across it. I sat on the edge of the dock, legs dangling in the water, shocked at how quiet it was, until Mom yelled down for me to help unpack.

We were tired and cranky from moving boxes and fighting

off mosquitoes by the time we unloaded the truck. I left Mom and Dad to get the kitchen organized and headed upstairs. There were two bedrooms; my parents forfeited the lakeside one to me, saying that since I spent more time in my room, I'd make better use of the view. I unpacked my clothes, made the bed, and folded a Hudson's Bay blanket at the end. Dad didn't think we needed such heavy wool blankets in summer, but Mom insisted on having one for each bed.

"It's Canadiana," she explained in a tone that said that should have been obvious.

I arranged a perilously high stack of paperbacks on one nightstand and tacked up a *Creature from the Black Lagoon* poster above the bed. I had a thing for horror. I watched a ton of scary movies, my parents having long ago given up on censoring them, and hoovered classic R.L. Stine and Christopher Pike books, as well as newer series about hot teens who turned into werewolves during full moons and hot teens who hunted ghosts after cheerleading practice. Back when I still had friends, I'd bring the books to school and read the good bits (as in anything gory or remotely sexy) aloud. At first, I just loved getting a reaction from the girls, loved being the center of attention but with the safety net of someone else's words as the entertainment. But the more horror I read, the more I grew to love the writing behind the story—how the authors made impossible situations believable. I liked how each book was both predictable and unique, comforting and unexpected. Safe but never boring.

"Pizza for dinner?" Mom stood at the doorway, eyeing the poster but saying nothing.

"They have pizza?" Barry's Bay hadn't looked big enough to have delivery. And, it turned out, it wasn't, so we drove to the takeout-only Pizza Pizza, located in a corner of one of the town's two grocery stores.

"How many people live here?" I asked Mom. It was seven p.m., and most of the businesses on the main drag looked closed.

"About one thousand two hundred, though I expect it's probably triple that in the summer with all the cottagers," she said. With the exception of a crowded restaurant patio, the town was pretty much deserted. "The Tavern must be *the* place to be on a Saturday night," she commented, slowing down as we passed.

"It looks like it's the *only* place to be," I replied.

By the time we got back, Dad had the small TV set up. There was no cable, but we had packed our family DVD collection.

"I was thinking *The Great Outdoors*," said Dad. "Seems appropriate, don't you think, kiddo?"

"Hmm . . ." I crouched down to inspect the contents of the cabinet. "*The Blair Witch Project* would also be appropriate."

"I'm not watching that," Mom said, setting out plates and napkins next to the pizza boxes on the coffee table.

"*The Great Outdoors* it is," said Dad, popping it into the player. "Classic John Candy. What could be better?"

The wind had picked up outside, moving through the pine boughs, and waves were now traveling across the lake's surface. The breeze coming through the windows smelled like rain.

"Yeah," I said, taking a bite of my slice. "This is actually pretty great."

～～～

A BOLT OF lightning zigged through the sky, illuminating the pines and the lake and the hills of the far shore, like someone had taken a flash photo with a giant camera. I watched the storm, transfixed, from my bedroom windows. The view was so much bigger than the wedge of sky I could see from my room in Toronto, the thunder so loud it seemed to be right above the cottage, as though it had been custom ordered for our first night. Eventually the deafening claps faded into distant rumbles, and I slipped back into bed, listening to the rain pelting the windows.

Mom and Dad were already downstairs when I woke the next morning, momentarily confused by the bright sun coming through the windows and ripples of light moving across the ceiling. They sat, coffees at the ready, reading materials in hand—Dad in the armchair with an issue of *The Economist*, scratching his beard absentmindedly, and Mom on a stool at the kitchen counter, flipping through a thick design magazine, her oversized red-framed glasses balancing on the tip of her nose.

"Hear that thunder last night, kiddo?" Dad asked.

"Kinda hard to miss," I said, grabbing a box of cereal from the still mostly empty cupboards. "I don't think I got a lot of sleep."

After breakfast, I filled a canvas tote with supplies—a novel, a couple of magazines, lip balm, and a tube of SPF 45—and headed down to the lake. Though it had poured the night before, the dock was already dry from the morning sun.

I placed my towel down and slathered sunscreen all over my face, then lay on my stomach, face propped on my hands. There wasn't another dock for maybe another 150 meters on one side, but the one in the other direction was relatively close. There was a rowboat tied to it and a raft floating further out from shore. I pulled out my paperback and picked up from where I left off the night before.

I must have fallen asleep because I was suddenly jerked awake by a loud *splash* and the sound of boys yelling and laughing.

"I'll get you!" one shouted.

"Like you could!" a deeper voice taunted.

Splash!

Two heads bobbed in the lake next to the neighbor's raft. Still lying on my belly, I watched them climb onto the raft, taking turns launching themselves off in flips and dives and flops. It was early July, but they were both bronzed already. I guessed they were brothers and that the smaller, skinny one was probably close to my age. The older boy stood a head above him, shadows hinting at lean muscles running along his torso and arms. When he tossed the younger one over his shoulder into the water, I sat up laughing. They hadn't noticed me until then, but now the older boy stood looking in my direction with a big smile across his face. The smaller one climbed up on the raft beside him.

"Hey!" the older boy shouted with a wave.

"Hi!" I yelled back.

"New neighbor?" he called over.

"Yeah," I hollered.

The younger boy stood staring until the older one shoved his shoulder.

"Jesus, Sam. Say hi."

Sam raised his hand and stared at me before the older boy pushed him back into the lake.

~~~~~

IT TOOK EIGHT hours for the Florek boys to find me. I was sitting on the deck with my book after washing the dinner dishes when I heard a knock at the back door. I strained my neck but couldn't see who Mom was talking to, so I tucked my bookmark into the pages and pushed myself out of the folding chair.

"We saw a girl on your dock earlier today and wanted to come say hi." The voice belonged to a teenage boy, deepish but young sounding. "My brother doesn't have anyone his age nearby to play with."

"Play? I'm not a baby," a second boy replied, his words cracking in irritation.

Mom looked at me over her shoulder, eyes narrowed in question. "You've got visitors, Persephone," she said, making it clear she wasn't exactly pleased about that fact.

I stepped outside and closed the screen door behind me, looking up at the tawny-haired boys I'd seen swimming earlier in the day. They were clearly related—both lanky and tanned—but their differences were just as plain. Whereas the older boy was smiling wide, scrubbed clean and clearly knew his way around a bottle of styling gel, the younger one was staring at his feet, a wavy tangle of hair falling haphazardly over his eyes. He wore baggy cargo shorts and a faded Weezer T-shirt that was at least one size too big; the older boy was dressed in jeans, a fitted white crew neck and black Converse, the rubber toes perfectly white.

"Hi, Persephone, I'm Charlie," the bigger one said, with deep dimples and celery-green eyes dancing across my face. Cute. Boy-band cute. "And this is my brother, Sam." He put his hand on the younger boy's shoulder. Sam gave me a reluctant half grin from under a swoosh of hair, then looked down again. I figured he was tall for his age, but all that length made him gangly, his arms and legs twiggy sticks, and his elbows and knees sharp as jagged rocks. His feet looked like tripping hazards.

"Uh . . . hey," I started, looking between them. "I think I saw you guys down at the lake today."

"Yup, that was us," said Charlie while Sam kicked at pine needles. "We live next door."

"Like, all the time?" I asked, giving oxygen to the first thought that came into my head.

"Year-round," he confirmed.

"We're from Toronto, so this," I said, waving around at the surrounding bush, "is pretty new for me. You're lucky to live here."

Sam snorted at that, but Charlie went on, ignoring him.

"Well, Sam and I would be happy to show you around. Wouldn't we, Sam?" he asked his brother, not pausing for the answer. "And you're welcome to use our raft anytime. We don't mind," he said, still smiling. He spoke with the confidence of an adult.

"Cool. I definitely will, thanks." I gave him a shy smile back.

"Listen, I have a favor to ask you," said Charlie conspiratorially. Sam groaned from under his mop of sandy hair. "Some friends of mine are coming by tonight, and I thought Sam could hang out with you here while they're over. He doesn't have much of a social life, and you look about the same age," he said, giving me a once-over.

"I'm thirteen," I replied, glancing at Sam to see if he had an opinion on this proposal, but he was still examining the ground. Or maybe his submarine-size feet.

"Perrrrfect," Charlie purred. "Sam's thirteen, too. I'm fifteen," he added proudly.

"Congratulations," Sam muttered.

Charlie continued, "Anyway, Persephone . . ."

"Percy," I interrupted with a burst. Charlie gave me a funny look. I laughed nervously and spun the friendship bracelet I wore around my wrist, explaining, "It's Percy. Persephone is . . . too much name. And a bit pretentious." Sam straightened up and looked at me then, scrunching his eyebrows and nose momentarily. His face was kind of ordinary, no feature especially memorable, except for his eyes, which were a shocking shade of sky blue.

"Percy it is," Charlie agreed, but my attention was still on Sam, who watched me with his head tilted. Charlie cleared his throat. "So as I was saying, you'd be doing me a huge favor if you'd entertain my little brother for the evening."

"Jesus," Sam whispered at the same time I asked, "Entertain?" We blinked at each other. I shifted my weight on my feet, not sure what to say. It had been months since I'd offended Delilah Mason so fantastically that I no longer had any friends, months since I'd spent time with someone my age, but the last thing I wanted was for Sam to be forced to hang out with me. Before I could say so, he spoke up.

"You don't have to if you don't want." He sounded apologetic. "He's just trying to get rid of me because Mom's not home." Charlie belted him across the chest.

The truth was I wanted a friend more than I wanted my bangs to behave. If Sam was willing, I could use the company.

"I don't mind," I told him, adding with false confidence, "I mean, it is a huge imposition. So you can show me how to do one of those somersaults off the raft as payback." He gave me a lopsided grin. It was a quiet smile, but it was a great smile, his blue eyes glinting like sea glass against his sunny skin.

I did that, I thought, a thrill running through me. I wanted to do it again.

3

Now

MY TEENAGE SELF WOULDN'T BELIEVE IT, BUT I DON'T OWN a car. Back then, I was determined to have my own set of wheels so I could head north every weekend possible. These days, my life is confined to a leafy area in Toronto's west end, where I live, and the city's downtown core, where I work. I can get to the office, the gym, and my parents' condo by either walking or public transit.

I have friends who haven't ever bothered getting their license; they're the kind of people who brag about never going north of Bloor Street. Their whole world is confined to a stylish little urban bubble, and they're proud of it. Mine is, too, but sometimes I feel like I'm suffocating.

The truth is, the city hasn't really felt like home since I was thirteen and fell in love with the lake and the cottage and the bush. Most of the time, though, I don't let myself think about that. I don't have time to. The world I've built for myself bursts with the trappings of urban busyness—the late hours at the office, the spin classes, and the many brunches. It's how I like it. An overstuffed calendar brings me joy. But every so often I catch myself fantasizing about leaving the city—finding a small place on the water to write, working at a restaurant on the side to pay the bills—and my skin starts feeling too tight, like my life doesn't fit.

This would surprise pretty much everyone I know. I'm a thirty-year-old woman who mostly has her shit together. My apartment is the top floor of a big house in Roncesvalles, a Polish neighborhood where you can still find a decent enough pierogi. The space is striking, with exposed beams and slanting ceilings, and, sure, it's tiny, but a full one-bedroom in this part of the city doesn't come cheap, and my salary at *Shelter* magazine is . . . modest. Okay, it's crap. But that's typical of media jobs, and while my pay may be small, my job is a big one.

I've worked at *Shelter* for four years, climbing steadily up the ranks from lowly editorial assistant to senior editor. That puts me in a position of power, assigning stories and overseeing photo shoots at the country's biggest decor magazine. Thanks in large part to my efforts, we have amassed a dedicated following on social media and a huge online audience. It's work that I love and that I'm good at, and at *Shelter*'s fortieth-anniversary bash, the magazine's editor in chief, Brenda, credited me with bringing the publication into the digital era. It was a career highlight.

Being an editor is the kind of job that people think is extremely glamorous. It looks fast and flashy, though if I'm being honest, it mostly involves sitting in a cubicle all day, googling synonyms for *minimalist*. But there are product launches to attend and lunches to be shared with up-and-coming designers. It's also the kind of job that hotshot corporate lawyers and social-climbing bankers swipe right on, which has proved useful in finding dates to join me on the cocktail party circuit. And there are perks, like press trips and open champagne bars, and an obscene amount of free stuff. There's also an endless flow of industry gossip for Chantal and me to chew over, our favorite way to pass a Thursday evening. (And my mom never tires of seeing Persephone Fraser in print on the magazine's masthead.)

Charlie's phone call is an ax through my bubble, and I'm so anxious to get north that as soon as I hang up, I book a car and a motel room for tomorrow, even though the funeral is a few days from now. It's like I've woken from a twelve-year coma, and my head throbs in anticipation and terror.

I'm going to see Sam.

~~~~~

I SIT DOWN to write an email to my parents to tell them about Sue. They haven't been regularly checking their messages on this European vacation of theirs, so I don't know when they'll get it. I also don't know whether they were still in contact with Sue. Mom kept in touch with her for at least a few years after Sam and I "broke up," but each time she'd mention any one of the Floreks, my eyes would well up. Eventually she stopped giving me updates.

I keep the note short and when I'm done, I throw some clothes into the Rimowa suitcase I couldn't afford but bought anyway. It's now well after midnight, and I have an interview for work in the morning and then a long drive, so I change into pj's, lie down, and shut my eyes. But I'm too wired to sleep.

There are these moments I come back to when I'm at my most nostalgic, when all I want to do is curl up in the past with Sam. I can play them in my mind as if they're old home videos. I used to watch them all the time in university, a bedtime routine as familiar as the pilled Hudson's Bay blanket I'd taken from the cottage. But the memories and the regrets they carried with them chafed like the blanket's wool, and I would lose nights imagining where Sam was at that precise moment, wondering if there's a chance he might be thinking of me. Sometimes I felt sure he was—like there was an invisible, unbreakable string that ran between us, stretching vast distances and keeping us joined. Other times, I dozed off in the midst of a movie only to wake in the middle of the night, my lungs feeling like they were on the verge of collapse, and I'd have to breathe my way through the panic attack.

Eventually, by the end of school, I'd managed to shut off the nightly broadcasts, filling my brain instead with looming exams and article deadlines and internship applications, and the panic attacks began to subside.

Tonight I have no such restraint. I cue up our firsts—the first time we met, our first kiss, the first time Sam told me he loved me—until the reality of seeing him starts to sink in, and my thoughts become a swirl of questions I don't have answers for. How will he react to my showing up? How much has he changed? Is he single? Or, *fuck*, is he married?

My therapist, Jennifer—not Jen, never Jen—I made the mistake once and was sharply corrected. The woman has framed quotes on the wall ("Life begins after coffee," and "I'm not weird I'm limited edition"), so I'm not sure what kind of gravitas she thinks her full name adds. Anyway, Jennifer has tricks for coping with this kind of anxious spiraling, but deep belly breaths and mantras don't stand a chance tonight. I started seeing Jennifer a few years ago, shortly after the Thanksgiving I spent puking up rosé and spilling my guts to Chantal. I didn't want to talk to a therapist; I thought that panic attack had just been a blip on an otherwise (fairly successful!) path to pushing Sam Florek out of my heart and mind, but Chantal was insistent. "This shit is above my pay grade, P," she'd told me with trademark blunt force.

Chantal and I met as interns at the city magazine where she is now the entertainment editor. We bonded over the peculiar business of fact-checking restaurant reviews (*So the halibut is coated in a pine nut dust, not a pistachio crust?*) and the editor in chief's farcical obsession with tennis. The moment that solidified our friendship was during a story meeting that the editor literally began with the words, "I've been thinking a lot about tennis," and then turned to Chantal, who was the only Black person in the entire office, and said, "You must be great at tennis." Her face remained perfectly composed when she replied that she did not play, while at the same time I blurted, "Are you kidding?"

Chantal is my closest girlfriend, not that there's much competition. My reluctance to share embarrassing or intimate parts of myself with other women makes them suspicious of me. For instance: Chantal knew I grew up with a cottage and that I hung around with the boys next door, but she had no idea about the extent of my relationship with Sam—or how it ended in a messy explosion that left no survivors. I think the fact that I'd kept such a fundamental piece of my history from her was more shocking than the story of what happened all those years ago.

"You do understand what it means to have friends, right?" she'd asked me after I told her the horrible truth. Considering that my two closest friends no longer speak to me, the answer probably should have been *Not really*.

But I have been a good friend to Chantal. I'm the person she calls to bitch about work or her future mother-in-law, who is continually suggesting Chantal relax her hair for the wedding. Chantal has no interest in wedding-y things, except for having a big dance party, an open bar, and a killer dress, which, fair, but since the event needs to come together somehow, I've become the default planner, putting together Pinterest boards with decor inspo. I'm reliable. I'm a good listener. I'm the one who knows what cool new restaurant has the hottest chef. I make excellent Manhattans. I am fun! I just don't want to talk about what keeps me awake at night. I don't want to reveal how I'm beginning to question whether climbing the ladder has made me happy, how sometimes I long to write but can't seem to find the courage, or how lonely I sometimes feel. Chantal is the only person who can pull it out of me.

Of course, my reluctance to discuss Sam with Chantal has nothing to do with whether or not I think about him. Of course I do. But I try not to, and I don't stumble very often. I haven't had a panic attack since I started seeing Jennifer. I like to think I've grown over the last decade. I like to think I've moved on. Still, every once in a while, the sun will shimmer off Lake Ontario in a way that reminds me of the cottage, and I'm right back on the raft with him.

~~~~~

MY HANDS ARE shaking so badly when I fill out the forms at the rental car counter that I'm surprised the clerk hands over the keys. Brenda was understanding when I called to ask for the rest of the week off—I told her there had been a death in the family, and while it was technically a lie, Sue *was* like family. At least she had been at one time.

I probably hadn't needed to stretch the truth, though. I have taken precisely one day off this year for an extended Valentine's spa weekend with Chantal—we have marked the holiday together since we were both single, and no boyfriend or fiancé will put an end to the tradition.

I briefly consider not telling Chantal where I'm going, but

then I have visions of getting in an accident and no one knowing why I was on the highway far from the city. So I write a quick text from the rental car lot, adding a few *I'm totally fine* exclamation points before I hit send: Your party was so much fun!!! (Too much fun! Shouldn't have had that last spritz!) Heading out of town for a few days for a funeral. Sam's mom.

Her text buzzes seconds later: THE Sam??? Are you OK?

The answer is no.

I'll be fine, I write back.

My phone starts vibrating as soon as I hit send, but I let Chantal's call go to voicemail. I'm so low on sleep, I'm running purely on adrenaline and the two vats of coffee I drank at this morning's interview with a full-of-himself wallpaper designer. I really don't want to talk.

In the time it takes me to navigate through the city streets and onto the 401, my bowels are in such tight knots that I need to pull into a Tim Hortons off the highway for an emergency bathroom break.

I'm still shaky when I get back in the car, bottle of water and raisin-bran muffin in hand, but a surreal kind of calm comes over me as I drive further north. Eventually, rocky outcrops of Canadian Shield granite erupt from the land, and roadside signs for live bait and chip trucks emerge from the scrub. It's been so long since I've traveled this route, yet it's all so familiar—like I'm driving back into another part of my life.

The last time I made this trip was Thanksgiving weekend. I was alone then, too, racing up in the used Toyota I'd bought with my tip money. I didn't stop the entire four-hour drive. It had been three agonizing months since I'd seen Sam, and I was desperate for him to wrap his arms around me, to feel enveloped by his body, to tell him the truth.

Could I have known how that weekend would give me both the greatest and most terrible moments of my life? How rapidly things would go very, very badly? That I would never see Sam again? My mistake had come months earlier, but could I have prevented the aftershocks that caused the most severe destruction?

My stomach takes a roller-coaster ride as soon as I spot a glimpse of the lake's southern end, and I take deep breaths *iiiiin one, two, three, four* and *ooouuuut one, two, three, four* all the way to the Cedar Grove Motel on the outskirts of town.

It's late afternoon by the time I check in. I buy a copy of the local paper from the elderly man at the lobby desk and move the car in front of room 106. It's clean and nondescript. A generic print of a deer in a forest hanging over the bed and a frayed polyester quilt that was probably burgundy at the beginning of its long life are the only doses of color.

I hang up the black sheath dress I've brought for the funeral and sit on the edge of the bed, tapping my fingers on my thighs and looking out the window. The north end of the lake, town dock, and public beach are just visible. I feel itchy. It seems wrong to be so close to the water but not go to the cottage. I've packed my bathing suit and towel so I could walk over to the beach, but all I want to do is dive off the end of my dock. There's just one problem: It's not my dock anymore.

4

Summer, Seventeen Years Ago

I'D NEVER HAD A BOY IN MY BEDROOM UNTIL THAT FIRST
evening when Charlie dropped Sam off on the doorstep of our
cottage. As soon as we were alone, I was tongue-tied with nerves.
Sam didn't seem to have the same problem.

"So what kind of name is Persephone?" he asked, stuffing a
third Oreo into his mouth. We were sitting on the floor, door
open at Mom's insistence. Given how sullen he was when we
met, he was a lot chattier than I expected. Within minutes I
learned he had lived next door all his life, he was also starting
eighth grade in the fall, and that he liked Weezer well enough,
but the shirt was actually a hand-me-down from his brother.
"Almost all my clothes are," he explained matter-of-factly.

Mom hadn't looked happy when I asked if Sam could stay for
the evening. "I don't know if that's the best idea, Persephone,"
she said slowly, *right in front of him,* then turned to Dad for his in-
put. I think it was less about Sam's boy-ness and more that Mom
wanted to keep me away from other teenagers for at least two
months before we went back to the city.

"She needs to have a friend, Diane," he replied, to complete my mortification. Letting my hair fall across my face, I grabbed Sam by the arm and pulled him toward the stairs.

It took five minutes for Mom to check on us, holding a plate of Oreos like she did when I was six. I was surprised she didn't bring glasses of milk. We were munching on the cookies, chests speckled with dark crumbs, when Sam asked about my name.

"It's from Greek mythology," I told him. "My parents are total geeks. Persephone is the goddess of the underworld. It doesn't really suit me."

He studied the *Creature from the Black Lagoon* poster and the stack of horror paperbacks on my bedside table, then fixed his gaze on me, one eyebrow raised.

"I dunno. Goddess of the underworld? Seems like it suits you. Sounds pretty cool to me . . ." He trailed off, his expression turning serious. "Persephone, Persephone . . ." He rolled my name around in his mouth like he was trying to figure out how it tasted. "I like it."

"What's Sam short for?" I asked, my hands and neck heating. "Samuel?"

"Nope." He smirked.

"Samson? Samwise?"

He jerked his head back like I'd surprised him.

"*Lord of the Rings*, nice." His voice cracked over the *nice*, and he gave me an off-kilter grin that sent another thrill zipping through my chest. "But, nope. It's just Sam. My mom likes one-syllable names for boys—like Sam and Charles. She says they're stronger when they're short. But sometimes, when she's really pissed, she calls me Samuel. She says it gives her more to work with."

I laughed at this, and his grin turned into a full-blown smile, one side slightly higher than the other. He had this easy way about him, like he wasn't trying to please anyone. I liked it. I wanted to be just like that.

I was polishing off a cookie when Sam spoke again. "So what did your dad mean downstairs?"

I feigned confusion. I'd been hoping he somehow hadn't heard. Sam squinted and added quietly, "About you needing to have a friend?"

I winced, then swallowed, not sure of what to say or how much to tell him.

"I had some"—I made air quotes with my fingers—"'issues' with a few of the girls at school this year. They don't like me anymore." I fidgeted with the bracelet on my wrist while Sam pondered this. When I peered up at him, he was looking right at me, brows drawn like he was working out a math problem.

"Two girls in my class were suspended for bullying last year," he finally said. "They were getting the boys to ask this one girl out as a prank, and then they'd tease her for believing it."

As much as she despised me, I don't think Delilah would have gone that far. I wondered if Sam was part of the prank, and as if he could see my mind churning, he said, "They wanted me to get in on it, but I wouldn't. It seemed mean and kind of messed up."

"It's totally messed up," I said, relieved.

Keeping his blue eyes trained on me, he changed the subject. "Tell me about this bracelet you keep playing with." He pointed to my wrist.

"This is my friendship bracelet!"

Before I was a social outcast, I was known for two things at school: my love of horror and my friendship bracelets. I wove them in elaborate patterns, but that was secondary to picking just the right colors. I carefully chose each palette to reflect the wearer's personality. Delilah's was pinks and deep reds—feminine and powerful. My own was a trendy mix of neon orange, neon pink, peach, white, and gray. Delilah had always been the prettiest, most popular girl in our class, and even though the other kids liked me, I knew my status was due to my proximity to her. When I got requests for bracelets from every girl in our class and even a few of the eighth graders, I felt like I finally had my own thing aside from being Delilah's funny sidekick. I felt creative and cool and interesting. But then one day, I found the bracelets I'd made for my three best friends cut up in little pieces in my desk.

"Who gave it to you?" Sam asked.

"Oh . . . well, no one did. I made it myself."

"The pattern is really cool."

"Thanks!" I perked up. "I've been practicing all year! I thought the neons and the peach were kind of funky together."

"Definitely," he said, leaning closer. "Could you make me one?" he asked, looking back up at me. He wasn't kidding. I hopped up and dug out the embroidery floss kit from my desk. I placed the small wooden box with my initials carved on top on the floor between us.

"I've got a bunch of different colors, but I'm not sure if I have anything you'll like," I said, pulling out the rainbow loops of thread. I'd never done one for a boy before. "But tell me what you're into, and if I don't have it, I can get Mom to take me into town to see if we can find it. Usually I know people a little better before I make them. It might sound silly, but I try to match the colors to their personality."

"That doesn't sound silly," he said. "So what do those colors say about you?" He reached out and tugged on one of the strings dangling from my wrist. His hands were like his feet, too big for his body. They reminded me of the oversized paws of a German shepherd puppy.

"Well . . . these don't really mean anything," I stammered. "I just thought it was a sophisticated palette." I returned to organizing the embroidery floss, lining them up in a tidy row from light to dark on the wood floor between us. "Maybe I could make it in blues to match your eyes?" I said, thinking aloud. "I don't have a ton of blue, so I'll just need to get a few more shades." I glanced at Sam to see what he thought, except he wasn't looking at the floss; he was staring right at me.

"That's okay," he said. "I want it to be just like yours."

～～～

THE NEXT MORNING I scarfed down breakfast, then raced to the water with my kit. I sat cross-legged on the dock and fastened the bracelet to my shorts with a safety pin to work on it while I waited for Sam.

When his footsteps tramped across the dock next door, it was almost like they were right beside me. He was wearing the same navy shorts as yesterday; it looked like they might fall off his narrow hips at any moment. I waved at him, and he raised his hand and then dove off the end of the dock and paddled toward me. He was in the water in front of me in under a minute.

"You're fast," I said, impressed. "I've taken swimming lessons, but I'm nowhere near as good as you."

Sam gave me the crooked grin, then hauled himself out of the water and plopped down next to me. Water dripped off his hair and ran in rivulets down his face and his chest, which was almost concave in form. If he was at all self-conscious about being half-naked next to a girl, I wouldn't have known it. He pulled on the strands of embroidery floss I was working on.

"Is that my bracelet? It looks great."

"I started it last night," I told him. "They don't actually take that long to make. I should be able to finish it for you tomorrow."

"Awesome." He motioned to the raft. "Ready to collect your payment?" Sam had agreed to show me how to do a flip off the raft in exchange for the bracelet.

"Definitely," I said, taking off my Jays hat and slathering copious amounts of SPF all over my face.

"You're really into sun safety, huh?" He picked up the hat.

"I guess. Well, no. It's more that I'm not into freckles, and the sun gives me freckles. They're okay on my arms and stuff, but I don't want them all over my face." What I wanted was a creamy, unblemished complexion like Delilah Mason's.

Sam shook his head, baffled, then his eyes lit up. "Did you know that freckles are caused by an overproduction of melanin that gets stimulated by the sun?"

My jaw dropped.

"What?" he said. "It's true."

"No, I believe you," I said slowly. "It's just a really random fact for you to know."

He grinned. "I'm going to be a doctor. I know a lot of"—he made air quotes—"'random facts,' as you call them."

"You already know what you want to be?" I was blown away. I had no clue what I wanted to do. Not even close. English was my best subject, and I liked to write, but I never really thought about having a grown-up job.

"I've always wanted to be a doctor, a cardiologist, but my school kind of sucks. I don't want to be stuck here forever, so I learn stuff on my own. My mom orders used textbooks for me online," Sam explained.

I took this in. "So . . . you're smart, huh?"

"I guess." And then he stood, a stack of arms and legs and pointy joints, and hauled me up by my arms. He was surprisingly strong for someone so weedy. "And I'm an awesome swimmer. C'mon, I'll show you how to do that somersault."

Countless belly flops, a few dives, and one semi-successful somersault later, Sam and I lay outstretched on the raft, faces to the sky, the already-hot morning sun drying our bathing suits.

"You're always doing that," Sam said, looking over at me.

"Doing what?"

"Touching your hair."

I shrugged. I should have listened to Mom when she told me bangs wouldn't work for my hair type. Instead, one spring evening while my parents were marking papers, I took matters—and Mom's good sewing shears—into my own hands. Except that I couldn't get the bangs to lie evenly, and every snip just made things worse. In less than five minutes, I had totally butchered my hair.

I crept downstairs to the living room, tears running down my face. Hearing my sniffles, my parents turned to see me standing with scissors in hand.

"Persephone! What on earth?" My mother gasped and flung herself at me, checking my wrists and arms for signs of damage, before hugging me tightly, while Dad sat agape.

"Don't worry, honey. We'll get this fixed," Mom said, stepping away to make an appointment at her salon. "If you're going to have bangs, they need to look intentional."

Dad gave me a weak smile. "What were you thinking, kiddo?"

My parents had already put in an offer on a lakeside property in Barry's Bay, but seeing me clutching those scissors must have

sent them over the edge, because the next day Dad called the
Realtor and told her to up the offer. They wanted me out of the
city as soon as the school year ended.

But even today I think my parents were probably overreacting. Diane and Arthur Fraser, both professors at the University
of Toronto, doted on me in a way particular to older, upper-
middle-class parents with just one child. My mom, a sociology
scholar, was in her late thirties when they had me; my father,
who taught Greek mythology, was in his early forties. My every
request for a new toy, a trip to the bookstore, or supplies for a
new hobby was met with enthusiasm and a credit card. Being a
child who preferred earning gold stars to causing trouble, I didn't
give them much need for discipline. In turn, they gave me a very
long leash.

So when the three girls who formed my closest circle of
friends turned their backs on me, I was unaccustomed to dealing
with any sort of adversity and I had no idea how to cope except
to try my hardest to win them back.

Delilah was our group's uncontested ruler, a position we be-
stowed upon her because she possessed the two most important
requirements for teenage leadership: an exceptionally pretty face
and total awareness of the power it gave her. Since it was Delilah
whom I angered, and Delilah whom I needed to win back, my
attempts to gain readmittance to the group were targeted at her.
I thought cutting my bangs like hers would demonstrate my loy-
alty. Instead, when she saw me at school, she raised her voice in
an exaggerated whisper, and said, "God, does everyone have
bangs these days? I think it's time to grow mine out."

Every morning I dreaded the school day—sitting alone at re-
cess, watching my old friends laugh together, wondering if it was
me they were laughing about. A summer away from everything,

where I could read my books without worrying about being called a freak and swim whenever I wanted to, felt like heaven.

I looked over at Sam.

"Where's your brother today?" I asked, thinking of how they'd goofed around in the water the day before. Sam turned onto his stomach and propped himself up on his forearms.

"Why do you want to know about my brother?" he asked, his brows knitted together.

"No reason. I just wondered. Is he having friends over tonight?" Sam looked at me from the corner of his eye. What I really wanted to know was if Sam wanted to hang out again.

"His friends were over really late," he said finally. "He was still asleep when I came down to the lake. I don't know what's going on tonight."

"Oh," I said limply, then decided to take a risk. "Well, if you want to come over again, that'd be cool. Our TV's kind of small, but we have a big DVD collection."

"I might just do that," said Sam, his forehead relaxing. "Or you could come over to our place. Our TV is pretty decent. Mom's never home, but she wouldn't mind you being there."

"You guys are allowed to have friends over when she's not there?" My parents were by no means strict, but they were always home when I had people over.

"One or two is okay, but Charlie likes to have parties. Just small ones, but Mom gets mad if she comes home and there's, like, ten kids in the house."

"Does that happen a lot?" I'd never been to a real teenager party. I crawled to the edge of the raft and dangled my feet in the water to cool off.

"Yeah, but mostly they're pretty boring, and Mom doesn't find out." Sam came and sat beside me, plunging his shoestring legs into the lake, kicking them back and forth. "I usually stay in my room, reading or whatever. If he has a girl over, then he tries to get rid of me like last night."

"Does he have a girlfriend?" I asked. Sam pushed back the hair that had fallen over his eye, and gave me a suspicious sideways glance. I'd never had a boyfriend, and unlike a lot of girls in my class, getting one wasn't high on my priority list. But I'd also never been kissed and would have given my right arm for someone to think I was pretty enough to kiss.

"Charlie always has a girlfriend," he said. "He just doesn't have them for very long."

"So," I said, changing the subject. "How come your mom's not around a lot?"

"You ask a lot of questions, you know that?" He didn't say it harshly, but his comment sent a prickle of fear down my neck. I hesitated.

"I don't mind," he said, nudging me with his shoulder. I felt my body relax. "Mom runs a restaurant. You probably don't know it yet. The Tavern? It's our family's place."

"I do know it, actually!" I said, remembering the packed patio. "Mom and I drove past. What kind of restaurant is it?"

"Polish . . . like pierogies and stuff? My family's Polish."

I had no idea what a pierogi was, but I didn't let on. "It looked really busy when we went by."

"There aren't many places to eat here. But the food's good. Mom makes the best pierogies ever. But it's a lot of work, so she's gone most days from the afternoon on."

"Doesn't your dad help?"

Sam paused before responding. "Uh, no."

"Okaaaay," I said. "So . . . why not?"

"My dad's dead, Percy," he said, watching a Jet Ski roar by.

I didn't know what to say. What I should have said was nothing. But instead: "I've never met anyone with a dead dad before." I immediately wanted to scoop the words up and shove them back down my throat. My eyes went wide with panic.

Would it make things more or less awkward if I jumped in the lake?

Sam turned to me slowly, blinked once, stared straight into my eyes, and said, "I've never met anyone with such a big mouth before."

I felt like I was caught in a net. I sat there, mouth hanging open, my throat and eyes burning. And then the straight line of his lips curled up at one corner, and he laughed.

"Just kidding," he said. "Not about my dad being dead, and actually you do have a big mouth, but I don't mind." My relief was instant, but then Sam put his hands on my shoulders and gave them a little shake. I stiffened—it was like all the nerve endings in my body had moved to beneath his fingers. Sam gave me a funny look, squeezing my shoulders gently. "You okay there?" He shifted his head down to meet my eyes. I took an unsteady breath.

"Sometimes things just come out of my mouth before I think about how they sound or even what I'm really saying. I didn't mean to be rude. I'm sorry about your dad, Sam."

"Thanks," he said softly. "It happened a bit over a year ago, but most of the kids at school are still weird about it. I'll take your questions over the pity any day."

"Okay," I said.

"No more questions?" he asked with a smirk.

"I'll save them for later," I said, standing on shaky legs. "Want to show me that somersault again?" He jumped up beside me, a crooked smile on his mouth.

"Nope."

And then in a flash, he grabbed my waist and pushed me into the water.

~~~

WE FELL INTO an easy routine that first week of summer. There was a narrow path by the shore that ran through the bush between our two properties, and we went back and forth several times a day. We spent the mornings swimming and jumping off the raft, then read on the dock until the sun got too hot, and then we'd hit the water again.

Despite how often she was at the restaurant, it took Sue just a few days to figure out that Sam and I were spending more time together than apart. She showed up on our doorstep, Sam in tow, holding a large Tupperware container of homemade pierogies. She was surprisingly young, like, way younger than my parents, and dressed more like me than a grown-up, in denim cutoffs and a gray tank top, her pale blond hair pulled back into a swishy ponytail. She was small and soft, and her smile was wide and dimpled like Charlie's.

Mom put on a pot of coffee and the three adults sat out on the deck chatting while Sam and I eavesdropped from the couch. Sue assured Mom and Dad that I was welcome at her house anytime, that Sam was a "freakishly responsible kid," and that she'd keep an eye on us, at least when she was home.

"She must have had those boys right out of high school," I heard Mom telling Dad that evening.

"It's different up here," was all he said.

Sam and I ended up spending most of our time in the water or at his place. On the days when the sun was too hot, we'd head up to the house, which was built in the style of an old farmhouse, painted white. A basketball net hung above the garage door. Sue hated air-conditioning, preferring to keep the windows open to feel the breeze off the lake, but the basement was always cool. Sam and I would flop down at either end of the cushy red plaid sofa and put on a movie. We were starting to make our way through my horror collection. Sam had seen just one or two, but it didn't take long for him to catch my enthusiasm. I think half the fun for him was correcting any (and every) scientifically un-sound detail he picked up on—the unrealistic amount of blood being his favorite sticking point. I'd roll my eyes and say, "Thanks, Doc," but I liked how closely he paid attention.

We took turns picking what to watch, but according to Sam, I "went all weird" when he wanted to watch *The Evil Dead*. I had my reasons—the movie was why my three best friends no longer spoke to me. I ended up telling Sam the entire story, which in-volved a sleepover at my house and an ill-advised screening of the bloodiest, raunchiest film in my collection.

Because Delilah, Yvonne, and Marissa liked the horror sto-ries I read at school, I had assumed *The Evil Dead* was a no-brainer. We huddled around the TV in nests of blankets and pillows, wearing our pajamas, with bowls of popcorn in hand, and watched a group of hot twentysomethings head to a creepy cabin in the woods. During the most disturbing scene, Deli-lah covered her face, then sprang from the sofa and ran to the bathroom, leaving a wet spot behind on the Ultrasuede fabric. The girls and I looked at each other wide-eyed, and I hur-ried to the cupboard to get paper towels and a bottle of cleaning spray.

I hoped Delilah would forget about the whole peeing-her-pants thing by the time we returned to school. She did not. Not even close. If she had, I would have been spared the next few months of torture.

"That was pretty disgusting," Sam said when the credits were rolling. "But also awesome?"

"Right?!" I said, jumping onto my knees to face him. "It's a classic! I'm not weird for liking it, right?" His eyes popped at my sudden display of energy. Did I sound nuts? I think I probably did.

"Well, I can see why that Delilah girl was so freaked out by it—I don't think I'm going to sleep tonight. But she's a jerk, and you're not weird for liking it," he said. I slumped back down onto the couch, satisfied. "You're just weird in general," he added, holding back a grin, and I lobbed a cushion at him. He raised his hands and laughed, "But I like weird."

I would have been thankful for any friend that summer, but finding Sam was like winning the friendship lottery. He was nerdy in a good way and sarcastic in a hilarious way, and he liked to read almost as much as I did, though he was more into books about wizards and magazines about science and nature. There was a whole shelf of *National Geographic* magazines in his basement, and I think he'd read all of them.

Sam was fast becoming my favorite person. And I'm pretty sure he felt the same—he always wore the bracelet I made him. He once pulled it down to show me the pale ring of skin underneath it. Sometimes he'd leave for an excruciatingly long morning or afternoon to hang out with his friends from school, but when he was home, we were almost always together.

By midsummer, a smattering of freckles dotted my nose, cheeks, and chest. As if they had somehow escaped my notice, Sam leaned in close to my face one day when we were lying on the raft, and said, "I guess SPF 45 wasn't strong enough."

"I guess not," I growled. "And thanks for reminding me."

"I don't understand why you hate your freckles so much," he said. "I like them." I stared at him, unblinking.

"Seriously?" I asked.

Who in their right mind likes freckles?

"Yeaaaah." He drew the word out and gave me a *Why are you being so weird?* look, which I chose to ignore.

"Swear on it?"

"Swear on what?" he asked, and I hesitated. "You said swear on it," he explained. "What do you want me to swear on?"

"Umm . . ." I hadn't meant it literally. I looked around, my eyes landing on his wrist. "Swear on our friendship bracelet." His brows furrowed, but then he reached over and hooked his index finger under my bracelet, giving it a gentle tug.

"I swear," he vowed. "Now you swear that you'll drop this weird freckle obsession." A small smile played on his lips, and I let out a little laugh before reaching over and curling my finger around his bracelet, tugging on it like he had.

"I swear." I rolled my eyes, but secretly I was pleased. And I didn't worry too much about my freckles after that.

~~~~

HALLOWEEN IN AUGUST was the official name Sam and I gave to the week we devoted to bingeing the entire *Halloween* franchise. We had just put on the fourth movie when Charlie loped down the basement stairs in his boxers and launched himself over the couch between us. Charlie, I had learned, was always wearing a smile and rarely a shirt.

"Could you get any further away from her, Samuel?" he chuckled.

"Could you get any more naked, Charles?" Sam deadpanned.

Charlie's face split into a toothy smile. "Sure!" he cried, jumping up and hooking his thumbs into the waistband of his boxers.

I yelped and covered my eyes.

"Jesus, Charlie. Cut it out," Sam yelled, his voice cracking.

Both the Florek boys liked to tease; whereas I was the object of Sam's gentle ribbing, Sam was subjected to Charlie's relentless digs about his scrawniness and sexual inexperience. Sam rarely talked back, and the only sign of his irritation was the red stain on his cheeks. At the lake, Charlie pushed Sam into the water at every possible chance, to the point that even I found it annoying. "He does it more when you're around," Sam told me one day.

Charlie laughed and plunked back down on the couch. He elbowed my side and said, "Your neck's all blotchy, Pers." He pulled my arms away from my face and put his hand over my knee and squeezed. "Sorry, I didn't mean to upset you." I glanced at Sam, but he was staring at Charlie's hand on my leg.

We were interrupted by Sue calling us up for lunch. A platter of cheese and potato pierogies waited for us on the round table in the kitchen. It was a sunny space with cream cabinets, windows overlooking the lake, and a sliding glass door onto the deck. Sue stood at the sink in her denim cutoffs and a white T-shirt, her hair pulled back into her usual ponytail, washing up a large pot.

"Hi, Mrs. Florek," I said, sitting down and helping myself to three massive dumplings. "Thanks for making lunch."

She turned around from the sink. "Charlie, go put on some clothes. And you're welcome, Percy—I know how much you like my pierogies."

"I love them," I said, and she gave me one of her toothy, dimpled smiles. Sam told me pierogies had been his dad's favorite and Sue had stopped making them at home before I came around.

After I finished my serving, I piled more onto my plate along with a large dollop of sour cream.

"Sam, your girlfriend eats like a horse," Charlie laughed. I winced at the g-word.

"Cut it out, Charlie," Sue snapped. "Never comment on how much a woman eats, and don't tease them. They're too young for any of that, anyway."

"Well, I'm not too young," Charlie said, wiggling his eyebrows in my direction. "Want to trade up, Percy?"

"Charlie!" Sue barked.

"I'm just messing around," he said and stood up to clear his plate, knocking his brother across the back of the head.

I tried to catch Sam's eye, but he was scowling at Charlie, his face the color of a field tomato.

~~~~

AS THE LAST week of summer vacation came to an end, I began dreading heading back to the city. I had dreams about going to school naked and finding Sam's bracelet cut up into orange and pink pieces in my desk.

We were lying on the raft the afternoon before I was leaving. I had tried my best all day not to be a downer, but apparently I wasn't doing a very good job because Sam kept asking if I was okay. Suddenly, he sat up and said, "You know what you need? One last boat ride." The Floreks had a small 9.9 motor on the back of their rowboat that Sam had taught me how to drive.

I grabbed my book, and Sam gathered his rod and tackle box. We folded our towels across the benches and set off in our damp bathing suits and bare feet. I drove to a reedy bay, which Sam claimed was a good spot for fishing, and cut the engine. I'd been watching him cast off the front of the boat when he started talking.

"It was a heart attack," he said, his eyes on his rod. I swallowed but stayed quiet. "We don't talk about him much at home," he added, reeling the line in. "And definitely not with my friends. They could barely look at me at the funeral. And even now, if they mention something about one of their dads, they look at me like they've accidentally said something super offensive."

"That sucks," I said. "I can tell you all about my dad if you want. But I warn you: He's totally boring." He smiled, and I went on. "But seriously, you don't have to talk with me, either. Not if you don't want to."

"That's the thing," he said, squinting into the sun. "I do. I wish we'd talk about him more at home, but it makes Mom sad." He set down his rod and looked up at me. "I'm starting to forget stuff about him, you know?" I climbed into the middle bench, closer to him.

"I don't really know. I don't know anyone with a dead dad, remember?" I nudged his foot with my toe, and he huffed out a laugh. "But I can imagine. I can listen." He nodded once and ran his hand through his hair.

"It happened at the restaurant. He was cooking. Mom was at home and someone called to tell us that Dad had fallen and that the ambulance had taken him to the hospital. It only took us ten minutes to get there—you know how close the hospital is—but it didn't matter. He was gone." He said it quickly, like it hurt to get the words out.

I reached out and squeezed his hand, then twisted his bracelet around so the best part of the pattern faced up. "I'm sorry," I whispered.

"Explains the whole doctor thing, huh?" I could tell he was trying to sound upbeat, but his voice was dull. I smiled but didn't reply.

"Tell me what he was like . . . when you're ready," I said instead. "I want to hear all about him."

"Okay." He picked up the rod again. Then added, "Sorry for going all emo on your last day."

"Suits my mood, anyway." I shrugged. "I'm kind of depressed about summer ending. I don't want to go home tomorrow."

He bumped my knee with his. "I don't want you to go, either."

5

Now

SUE'S FACE IS STARING AT ME, HAIR PULLED BACK, SMILE SO wide it's beckoned her dimples. There are fine lines fanning out from her eyes that didn't used to be there, but even on the local paper's smudged newsprint, you can see determination in the slight upward tilt of her chin and the hand that rests on her hip. She's standing in front of the Tavern in the photo, which runs under the headline "Tribute to a Beloved Barry's Bay Business Leader."

I've become skilled at warding off the loneliness that threatened to pull me under in my early twenties. It's a formula that involved throwing myself into work, no-strings sex, and overpriced cocktails with Chantal. It took years to perfect. But sitting in the motel room with Sue's obituary in my hands and the lake sparkling in the distance, I can feel it in every part of my body—the twisting of my gut, the ache in my neck, the tightness in my chest.

I could talk to Chantal. She's sent three more texts, asking me to call her, asking me when the funeral is, asking whether I want her to come. I should at least text her back. But Thanksgiving breakdown aside, I haven't spoken to her about Sam too often. I tell myself I don't have the energy to get into it right now, but it's more that if I start talking about him, about how monumental it feels to be here, how scary, I may not be able to hold it together.

What I really need is a bottle of wine. My stomach gurgles. And maybe some food. I haven't eaten anything except for the raisin-bran muffin from my emergency Tim Hortons stop. It's a blistering late afternoon, so I throw on the lightest thing I've packed: a sleeveless poppy-colored cotton dress that hits above the knees. It has large buttons down the front and a belted waist. I fasten my gold sandals and head out the door.

It takes about twenty minutes to walk to the center of town. My bangs are stuck to my forehead by the time I get there, and I hold my hair in a dense pile on top of my head to cool my neck down. Other than a new café with a sandwich board advertising lattes and cappuccinos (neither of which you could get in town when I was a kid), the family businesses on the main street are pretty much the same. Somehow I'm not prepared for the wallop of seeing the butter-yellow building and the red sign painted with Polish folk art flowers. I stand in the middle of the sidewalk, staring. The Tavern is in darkness, the green patio umbrellas folded shut. This is probably the first time since the restaurant opened that it's been closed on a Thursday evening in July. There's a small sign taped to the front door, and without thinking, I move toward it.

It's a short message, written with black marker: *The Tavern is closed until August to mourn the loss of owner Sue Florek. We thank you for your support and understanding.* I wonder who wrote it. Sam? Charlie? Butterflies swarm my stomach. I lean into the glass door with my hands cupped around my face and notice a light on inside. It's coming from the windows that lead into the kitchen. Someone's in there.

As if drawn by a magnetic force, I head around to the back of the building. The heavy steel door that leads into the kitchen is propped open a few inches. The butterflies become a flock of flapping gulls. I pull the door wider and step inside. And then I freeze.

At the dishwasher stands a tall, sandy-haired man, and although his back is turned to me, he is as unmistakable as my own reflection. He's wearing sneakers, a blue T-shirt, and navy-and-white-striped board shorts. He's still slim but there's so much more of him. All golden-brown skin and broad shoulders and strong legs. He's scrubbing something in the sink, a tea towel over one shoulder. I watch the muscles clench in his back as he lifts a platter into the washer rack. The sight of his large hands sends blood rushing to my ears so loudly it's like waves are crashing inside my head. I remember when he knelt over me in his bedroom, running those fingers along my body like he had discovered a new planet.

His name slides softly from my lips.

"Sam?"

He turns, a look of confusion across his face. His eyes are the clear blue skies they always were, but so much else is different. The edges of his cheekbones and jaw are harder, and the skin underneath his eyes is tinged purple, as if sleep has eluded him for nights on end. His hair is shorter than he used to wear it, cropped close on the sides and only a little floppy on top, and his arms are thick and corded. He was beautiful at eighteen, but adult Sam is so devastating I could cry. *I missed him becoming this.* And the grief of that loss—of seeing Sam grow into a man—is a fist squeezing around my lungs.

Sam's gaze moves across my face and then drops down my body. I can see the flint of recognition that sparks when his eyes make their way back up to mine. Sam always kept a snug-fitting seal on his feelings, but I spent six years figuring out how to pry

it off. I devoted hours to studying the subtle movement of emo-
tions across his features. They were like rain that traveled from
the far shore and across the water, unassuming until it was right
there, pelting the cottage windows. I memorized his shimmers
of mischief, the distant thunder of his jealousy, and the whitecaps of his ecstasy. I knew Sam Florek.

His eyes lock on to mine. Their hold is as unrelenting as ever.
His lips are pinched into a flat line, and his chest expands in slow,
steady breaths.

I take a hesitant step forward as if I'm approaching a wild
horse. His eyebrows shoot up, and he shakes his head once like
he's been startled from a dream. I halt.

We stand staring at each other silently, and then he takes
three giant strides toward me and wraps his arms around me so
tight it's like his large body is a cocoon around mine. He smells
like sun and soap and something new that I don't recognize.
When he speaks, his voice is a deep rasp that I want to drown in.

"You came home."

I squeeze my eyes shut.

I came home.

~~~~

SAM PULLS BACK from me, his hands on my shoulders. His eyes
ping around my face in disbelief.

I give him a small smile.

"Hi," I say.

The lopsided grin that curves his mouth is a drug I've never
kicked. The faint crinkles at the corners of his eyes and the stubble on his face are new and so . . . sexy. Sam is sexy. So many
times I've wondered about what he'd be like all grown up, but the
reality of thirty-year-old Sam is so much more solid and dangerous than what I could have imagined.

"Hi, Percy." My name passes from his lips and straight to my bloodstream, a sudden injection of desire and shame and a thousand memories. And just as quickly, I remember why I'm here.

"Sam, I'm so sorry," I say, my voice cracking. I'm so raw with grief and regret that I can't stop the tears that roll down my cheeks. And then Sam is holding me again, whispering, "Shhh," into my hair while he moves one hand up and down my back.

"It's okay, Percy," he whispers, and when I peer up at him, his forehead is wrinkled in concern.

"I should be comforting you," I say, wiping my cheeks. "I'm sorry."

"Don't worry about that." His voice is soft as he pats my back and then takes a step back, running his hand through his hair. The familiar gesture tugs a frayed string inside me. "She was sick for years. We had a long time to come to terms with it."

"I can't imagine any amount of time being long enough. She was so young."

"Fifty-two."

I inhale sharply, because that's even younger than I had guessed. And I can imagine how this must gnaw at Sam. His dad was young, too.

"I hope it's okay that I came," I say. "I wasn't sure you'd want me here."

"Yeah, of course." He says it as if it hasn't been more than a decade since we spoke. As if he doesn't hate me. He turns back to the dishwasher, emptying a tray of side plates and stacking them on the counter. "How did you know?" He glances at me and squints when I don't immediately reply. "Ah."

He's already figured out the answer, but I tell him anyway. "Charlie called me."

His face darkens. "Of course he did," he says flatly.

There are serving dishes and chafing trays lined up on the

counters—the kind of equipment needed to cater a big function. I move beside him at the dishwashing station and begin putting some dusty serving utensils in a rack to run through the washer. It's the same machine from when I worked here. I've run it so many times I could do it with my eyes closed.

"So what's all this for?" I ask, keeping my eyes on the sink. But I don't get a response. I can tell from the quiet that Sam has stopped emptying dishes. I take a deep breath, *in one, two, three, four* and *out one, two, three, four,* before looking over my shoulder. He's leaning against the counter, arms crossed, watching me.

"What are you doing?" he asks, voice rough. I turn to face him straight on, taking another deep breath, and from some deep forgotten place, I find Percy, the girl I used to be.

I lift my chin and give him an incredulous look, putting a hand on my hip. My hand is soaking wet, but I ignore that as well as the swooping in my stomach.

"I'm helping you out, genius." The water seeps through my dress, but I don't budge. I don't look away. A muscle in his jaw twitches and his frown loosens just enough that I know I've stuck a knife under his sealer lid. A smile threatens to ruin my poker face, and I bite my lip to hold it back. His eyes flash to my mouth.

"You were always a shit dishwasher," I say, and he bursts out laughing, the rich bellow bouncing off the kitchen's steel surfaces. It is the most magnificent sound. I want to record it so I can listen to it later, again and again. I don't know the last time I've smiled this widely.

His blue eyes sparkle when they find mine, then drift down to the wet spot my hand has left on my hip. He swallows. His neck is the same golden brown as his arms. I want to stick my nose at the curve where it meets his shoulder and inhale a hit of him.

"I see your trash talk hasn't improved," he says with affection, and I feel like I've won a marathon. He motions to the dishes on the counter and sighs. "Mom wanted to have everyone here for a party after she passed. The idea of people standing around with crustless egg salad sandwiches in the church basement after her funeral horrified her. She wants us to eat and drink and have fun. She was very specific." He says it with love, but he sounds tired. "She even made the pierogies and cabbage rolls she wanted served months ago, when she was still well enough, and put them in the freezer."

My eyes and throat burn, but I stay strong this time. "That sounds like your mom. Organized and thoughtful and . . ."

"Always stuffing people full of carbs?"

"I was going to say, 'feeding the people she loves,'" I reply. Sam smiles, but it's a sad one.

We stand there in the quiet, surveying the tidy array of equipment and plates. Sam pulls the tea towel off his shoulder and sets it down on the counter, giving me a long look as if he's deciding something.

He points to the door. "Let's get out of here."

~~~

WE'RE EATING ICE cream and sitting on the same bench we used to as kids—not far from the center of town on the north shore. I can see the motel across the bay in the distance. The sun has dipped low in the sky, and there's a breeze coming off the water. We haven't spoken much, which is okay with me because sitting beside Sam feels unreal. His long legs are spread out beside mine, and I'm fixated on the size of his knees and his leg hair. Sam grew out of his stringy phase after he hit puberty, but he is so thoroughly *a man* now.

"Percy?" Sam asks, breaking my focus.

"Yeah?" I turn toward him.

"You might want to eat that a little faster." He points to the pink and blue trail of ice cream dripping down my hand.

"Shit!" I try to catch it with a napkin, but a blob lands on my chest. I dab at it, but it only seems to make matters worse. Sam watches from the corner of his eye with a smirk.

"I can't believe you *still* eat cotton candy. How old are you?" he teases.

I motion to his waffle cone with two massive scoops of Moose Tracks, the same flavor he used to order as a kid. "You're one to talk."

"Vanilla, caramel, peanut butter cups? Moose Tracks is classic," he scoffs.

"No way. Cotton candy is the best. You just never learned to appreciate it."

Sam raises one brow in an expression of absolute trouble, then leans over and runs his tongue flat over my scoop of ice cream, biting off a hunk from the top. I let out an involuntary gasp, my mouth hanging open as I stare at his teeth marks.

I remember the first time Sam did that when we were fifteen. The glimpse of his tongue shocked me speechless then, too.

I don't look up until he elbows me in the side.

"That always freaked you out," he chuckles in a soft baritone.

"Menace." I smile, ignoring the pressure building in my lower belly.

"I'll give you a taste of mine to be fair." He tilts his cone to me. *This is new.* I wipe away the beads of sweat forming above my lip. Sam notices, giving me a crooked grin as though he can read every dirty thought that's running through my mind. "I promise it's good," he says, and his voice is as dark and smooth as coffee.

I'm not used to this Sam—one who seems fully aware of his effect on me.

I can tell he doesn't think I'll do it, but that just spurs me on. I take a quick taste of his cone.

"You're right," I say, shrugging. "It's pretty good." His eyes flash to my mouth, and then he clears his throat.

We sit in awkward silence for a minute.

"So how have you been, Percy?" he asks, and I hold my hands up helplessly.

"I'm not sure where to start," I laugh, nervous. How do you even begin after so much time has passed?

"How about three updates?" He nudges me, his eyes glinting.

It was a game we used to play. We went for long stretches apart, and whenever we'd see each other again, we'd tell each other our three biggest pieces of news in rapid fire. *I have a new draft of my story for you to read. I'm training for the four-hundred-meter freestyle. I got a B on my algebra exam.* I laugh again, but my throat has gone dry.

"Umm . . ." I squint out at the water. It's been more than a decade, but has that much really happened?

"I still live in Toronto," I start, taking a bite of ice cream to delay. "Mom and Dad are well—they're traveling around Europe. And I'm a journalist, an editor, actually—I work at *Shelter*, the design magazine."

"A journalist, huh?" he says with a smile. "That's great, Percy. I'm happy for you. I'm glad you're writing."

I don't correct him. My work involves little writing, mostly headlines and the odd article. Being an editor is all about telling other people what to write.

"And what about you?" I ask, returning my focus to the water in front of us—the sight of Sam sitting beside me is too jarring. I'd looked him up on social media years earlier, his profile picture was a shot of the lake, but never took the step of adding him as a friend.

"One, I'm a doctor now."

"Wow. That's . . . that's incredible, Sam," I say. "Not that I'm surprised."

"Predictable, right? And, two, I specialized in cardiology. Another shocker." He's not bragging at all. If anything, he sounds a bit embarrassed.

"Exactly where you wanted to be."

I'm happy for him—it's what he was always working toward. But somehow it also hurts that his life continued without me as planned. I made my way through my first year of university in a fog, struggling through my creative writing classes, not able to focus on much of anything, let alone character development. Eventually a professor suggested I give journalism a shot. The rules of reporting and story structure made sense to me, gave me an outlet that didn't feel so personal, so connected to Sam. I abandoned my dream of being an author, but I eventually set new goals. There's speculation that when it's time for a new editor in chief at *Shelter*, I'll be at the top of the list. I created a different path for myself, one that I love, but it stings that Sam managed to follow his original one.

"And three," he says, "I'm living here. In Barry's Bay." I jerk my head back, and he laughs softly. Sam was as determined to leave Barry's Bay as he was to become a doctor. I assumed after he left for school he'd never move back.

From the moment we were together-together, I dreamed of what our life would be like when we finally lived in the same place. I imagined moving to wherever he was doing his residency after my undergrad. I would write fiction and wait tables until our incomes were steady. We'd come back to Barry's Bay whenever we could, splitting our time between the country and the city.

"I stayed in Kingston for my residency," he explains, as if reading my mind. Sam attended med school at Queen's University in Kingston, one of the top schools in the whole country. Kingston was nowhere near as large as Toronto, but it sat on Lake Ontario. Sam was meant to be near water. "But I've been here for the last year to help Mom. She was sick for a year before that. We were hopeful at first . . ." He looks out over the water.

"I'm sorry," I whisper, and we sit quietly for a few minutes, finishing our cones and watching someone fish off the town dock.

"After a while, it didn't seem like things were going to get any better," he says, picking up from where he left off. "I had been driving back and forth between here and Kingston, but I wanted to come home. You know, go to the treatments and all the appointments. Help out around the house and at the restaurant. It was too much for her even when she was healthy. The Tavern was always meant to be her and Dad."

The thought of Sam being here for the past year, living in that house down on Bare Rock Lane, without me knowing, without me being here to help, feels monumentally wrong. I put my hand over his briefly and squeeze before returning it to my lap. He tracks its movement.

"What about your work?" I ask, my voice hoarse.

"I've been working at the hospital here. A few shifts a week." He sounds tired again.

"Your mom must have really appreciated you coming back," I say, trying to sound upbeat instead of how bruised I feel. "She knew you didn't want to stay here."

"It's not so bad," Sam says, sounding like he means it, and for the second time this evening my jaw drops. "I'm serious," he promises with a small grin. "I know I ragged on Barry's Bay when I was a kid, but I missed it a lot when I was away at school. I'm lucky to have this," he says, nodding to the water.

"Who are you and what have you done with Sam Florek?" I joke. "But no, that's great. It's so amazing that you came to help your mom. And that you don't hate it here. I've missed this place so much. Every summer I get cabin fever in the city. All that concrete—it feels so hot and itchy. I'd do anything to jump into the lake."

He studies me, a serious look coming over his face. "Well, we'll have to make that happen." I give him a small smile, then look out over the bay. If things had turned out differently, would I have been living here for the past year? Keeping Sue company at her appointments? Helping with the Tavern? Would I have kept writing? I would have wanted to. I would have wanted all of that. The loss squeezes at my lungs again, and I have to focus on my breath. Without looking, I can feel Sam's attention on the side of my face.

"I can't believe you were here all that time," I murmur, pushing the hair off my forehead.

He prods my leg with his foot, and I tilt my head to him. He's wearing the biggest smirk, his eyes crinkled at the corners. "I can't believe you got bangs again."

6

Summer, Sixteen Years Ago

EIGHTH GRADE DIDN'T SUCK.

It didn't suck, but it was weird. I (finally) got my period. Kyle Houston touched my butt at the spring dance. And by the end of September, Delilah Mason and I were best friends again.

She had clomped up to me in a pair of white cowboy boots and a short denim skirt on the first day of school and complimented my tan. I told her about the cottage, trying to play it as cool as possible, and she filled me in on the equestrian camp she attended in the Kawarthas. There was a horse named Monopoly and an embarrassing period story involving white shorts and a daylong riding trip. (Delilah got her period *and* her boobs when we were eleven, naturally.)

After a few days of niceties and shared lunches, I asked about Marissa and Yvonne. Delilah curled her lip in disgust. "We went on a group date with my cousin and his friends, and they were *such* babies."

It's not that I had forgotten what happened the year before, but I was willing to look past it. Having Sam meant I didn't feel the same kind of pressure to please Delilah, didn't take her quite so seriously, although I was determined never to be *such* a baby. Besides, being friends with Delilah meant no more lunches alone, no more feeling like a complete loser. And while I wouldn't ever describe her as nice, Delilah was funny and smart.

She chose crushes for both of us, saying that high school boys were much cuter, but we needed practice before we got there. Mine was Kyle Houston, who had both the coloring and personality of mashed potatoes. (For his part, Kyle didn't seem too interested, either. That is, until he copped a feel at the dance.)

~~~

SAM AND I had a never-ending email chain, but it wasn't until Thanksgiving that I saw him in the flesh again. Sue had invited us to join them for turkey dinner, and my parents had happily accepted. They may not have been sure about Sue when they first met her, but I could tell they'd warmed up to her. They had her over for coffee a couple of times the previous summer, and I heard Mom telling Dad about how impressed she was that Sue was raising "those two nice boys" on her own and how she "must have a keen business sense" to have made the Tavern such a big success.

Sam warned me that his mom tended to overdo it for holidays ever since his dad passed away. She wouldn't hear of my parents bringing any food, either. So we showed up carrying wine and brandy and a bouquet of flowers Mom and I had picked out at the grocery store. The sun was low in the sky and the Floreks' house looked like it was glowing from within. The smell of turkey wafted out to us as we stepped onto the porch, and the door swung open before we even knocked.

Sam stood in the doorway, his thick shag of hair combed into submission and parted to one side.

"I could hear your footsteps on the gravel," he said, seeing the surprised expressions on our faces. Then he added an uncharacteristically chirpy, "Happy Thanksgiving!" and held the door open with one arm, stepping to the side to let us in.

"May I take your coats, Mr. and Mrs. Fraser?" he asked. He wore a white button-down shirt tucked into khaki pants, which made him look like a busboy at my parents' favorite French restaurant.

"Certainly. Thank you, Sam," Dad said. "But Diane and Arthur will do just fine."

"Hey, guys! Happy Thanksgiving!" Sue greeted my parents, her arms held wide, while I put the gifts I was holding on the floor and took off my coat.

"May I take that, Persephone?" Sam asked with exaggerated graciousness, extending his arm for my coat.

"Why are you talking like that?" I whispered.

"Mom gave us a big speech about being on our best behavior. She even played the 'make your dad proud' card. He was big on manners," he said quietly. "You look lovely, this evening, by the way," he added in an overly enthusiastic tone. I ignored his comment, though I had made extra effort, brushing my hair out so it shone and wearing my crushed-velvet burgundy dress with the puffed sleeves.

"Well, cut it out," I said. "That voice you're using is giving me the creeps."

"Got it. No weird voice." He smirked, then crouched to pick up the bottles and flowers from the floor. When he stood, he leaned closer and said, "I mean it, though. You do look nice."

His breath on my cheek made me blush, but before I could

respond, Sue had me in a hug. "It's so good to see you, Percy. You look beautiful." I thanked her, still reeling from Sam's comment, and waved at Charlie, who stood behind her.

"Red's your color, Pers," he said. He had on a pair of black dress pants and a shirt that matched the pale green of his eyes.

"I didn't realize you knew how to fully dress yourself," I replied.

Charlie winked, and then Sue ushered us into the living room, where a fire crackled in the stone hearth. While Sue finished in the kitchen, Sam passed trays of cheese and bowls of nuts, and Charlie took drink orders, offering Mom a gin and tonic and asking Dad if he wanted red ("it's a pinot noir") or white wine ("sauvignon blanc"). My parents looked both impressed and amused. "Restaurant kid" was all Charlie said by way of explanation.

Sue joined us when everything was just about ready and had a drink with my parents. She was more made up than usual, in a fitted black turtleneck and capri pants. She had her blond hair down around her shoulders and wore a rose-colored lipstick. It had the effect of making her look both older and more beautiful. My own mom wasn't unattractive—she kept her dark straight hair in a neat bob and had strange rust-colored eyes—and she was fashionable. But Sue was *pretty* pretty.

By the time we sat down for dinner, our faces were flushed from the fire and the overlapping conversations. Charlie and Sam brought out platters and dishes and bowls of sides and sauces, and Sue carried the turkey to the head of the table and carved it herself. The boys dug in with impressive speed, manners abandoned, and my parents watched, slack-jawed.

"You should see my grocery bills," Sue laughed.

I sat next to Sam, and when I reached for a second helping of potato casserole, he gave me a stunned look.

"You're not wearing your bracelet," he said quietly, his fork suspended midway to his mouth, a piece of dark meat speared on the end.

"Uh, no," I replied, watching the hurt flicker in his eyes. I felt self-conscious wearing it around Delilah, but I couldn't say that right now. "I still have it, though. It's in my jewelry box at home."

"You're cold, Pers. Sam *never* takes his off!" Charlie cut in, and the chatter that had been swirling around us stopped. "He freaked when Mom wanted to wash it. Thought it would get ruined in the washing machine."

"It would have," Sam said flatly, streaks of crimson painting his cheeks.

"We hand washed it, and it was fine," Sue said, either not picking up on the tension between the two boys or ignoring it altogether. She went back to chatting with my parents.

"Jerk," Sam mumbled under his breath, looking down at his plate.

I leaned in closer and whispered, "I'll wear it next time. I promise."

~~~~

MOM AND DAD let me invite Delilah to the cottage for the first week of the summer. On the last day of June, the four of us rode up in my parents' new overstuffed SUV. My knees were bouncing with anticipation by the time we turned down Bare Rock Lane, and there was a huge, stupid smile across my face. The cottage needed more work before we visited in winter, so I hadn't seen Sam since Thanksgiving, seven months ago.

"What's with you?" Delilah whispered across a stack of luggage. "You look deranged."

I had sent Sam an IM with our estimated time of arrival the

night before we left, another when we were packing the car, and another just before we pulled out of the driveway. He hated IMs and responded to precisely none of them. Still, I knew he'd be waiting for us when we arrived. But I wasn't prepared to see two very tall figures standing outside the cottage.

"Is that them?" Delilah hissed, pulling a tube of lip gloss out of her pocket.

"Yeah?" I said, not totally believing it. Sam was *tall*. Like really tall.

I was out the door before Dad shut off the engine, and flung myself at him, stretching my arms around his slim torso. His wiry arms came around me, and I could feel him shake with laughter.

I pulled back with a big smile.

"Hi, Percy," he said, his eyebrows raised high under his uncombed hair. I paused at the sound of his voice. It was different. It was deep. I quickly pushed aside my shock and grabbed his arm.

"Update one," I said, holding my wrist next to his, lining up our bracelets side by side. "Haven't taken it off since after Thanksgiving," I added.

We grinned at each other like lunatics.

"This way we'll have something to swear on," I said.

"Thank god. It was my number one concern." Sarcasm oozed from Sam's words like caramel from a chocolate egg. He was pleased.

"Hey, Pers," Charlie said from over Sam's shoulder, then called to my parents, "Mr. and Mrs. Fraser, Mom sent us over to help unload."

"Appreciate it, Charlie," Dad hollered, his head in the trunk of the SUV. "But drop the Mr. and Mrs. thing, okay?"

"I'm Delilah," said a voice behind me. Whoops. I had completely forgotten my friend. A small part of me—okay, fine, a rather large chunk—didn't want to introduce Delilah to Sam. She was so much cuter than me, and her boobs had gotten *huge* this year while I remained flat chested. I knew it wasn't like that between Sam and me, but I didn't want it to be like that between them, either.

"Sorry, I'm being totally rude," I apologized. "Sam, this is Delilah. Delilah, Sam." They exchanged hellos, though his was noticeably cold.

Sam had replied with exactly three words when I emailed him about my rekindled friendship with Delilah: *Are you sure?* I was, but evidently, Sam was not.

"You must be Charlie," Delilah called out, homing in on him like a fox on a baby chick.

"Yeah, hey," Charlie said as he walked by carrying a box of groceries, paying her zero attention. Unruffled, she turned back to Sam, her big blue eyes twinkling. She was wearing the tiniest pair of coral shorts and a skintight yellow tube top that showed off her boobs and stomach.

"Percy didn't mention how cute you are," she said, lavishing upon him one of her signature beaming smiles, all glossy pink lips and fluttering lashes.

Sam's face scrunched up and his eyes darted to mine.

"Sorry," I mouthed, then grabbed Delilah's arm and pulled her toward the car as she giggled.

"Can you come over later?" Sam asked after we finished unloading. "I've got something I want to show you. It's updates one, two, and three." The way he spoke, like Delilah wasn't there, filled my chest with helium.

"You haven't told her about the boat yet?" Charlie asked. Sam rubbed his face and pushed his hair off his forehead in one movement of controlled agitation.

"No, it was *going to be* a surprise."

"Shit, sorry, man," Charlie said, and to his credit, he sounded like he meant it.

"Well, fill us in," Delilah piped up, her hands on the race-track curves of her hips.

"We fixed up Dad's old boat," said Sam in a baritone of pride. His voice would take some getting used to.

"And he means *old*," Charlie added.

"It used to be our granddad's, and Dad fixed it up and kept it going until . . ." Sam's sentence hung there.

"It's just been sitting in the garage," Charlie cut in. "Mom always promised I could use it once I turned sixteen, but it needed a bunch of work. Granddad helped repair it this spring when they got back from Florida. Even got this guy helping out." Charlie bumped Sam with his elbow.

"You've got to see it, Percy," said Sam with a crooked smile. "It's classic."

Delilah tossed her hair behind a pale shoulder. "We'd love to."

~~~

"OHMYGOD, PERCY!" DELILAH squealed as soon as we took our suitcases up to my bedroom. "Why did you not tell me how hot Charlie is? I would have worn something way cuter than this!"

I laughed. Delilah had become seriously boy crazy over the past year.

"Sam's not as good-looking, but he's cute, too," she said, staring up at the ceiling as though in careful thought. "I bet he'll be just as hot when he gets older." The taste of jealousy was bitter on my tongue. I didn't want her thinking Sam was cute. I didn't want her thinking about Sam at all.

"He's okay, I guess." I shrugged.

"Let's pick our outfits for when we go over this afternoon!" She was already opening her suitcase.

"It's just Sam and Charlie. Trust me, they don't care how we're dressed," I said, but now I wasn't entirely sure that was true. She looked at me skeptically. "I'll be wearing my bathing suit and my shorts if it makes any difference to you," I added.

We changed into our swimsuits after unpacking our things. Delilah put on a black string bikini, impossibly held together with flimsy ties, and wiggled into a pair of fresh white denim cutoffs so short the smile of her ass cheeks grinned out the bottom.

"What do you think?" She turned around, and I tried not to stare at her chest, but it was kind of impossible, considering the ratio of breast to bathing suit.

"You look insane," I said. "Good insane." I meant it, but the acid burn of envy was spreading down my throat. Mom refused to let me wear a string bikini, but she had allowed a two-piece— neon orange with wide buckled straps on the top. I thought it was cool at the store, but now I felt childish, and my jean shorts seemed entirely too full bottomed.

We padded down the stairs to the lake. The sky was clear and the water was blue-blue, rippling from a breeze coming from the southeast.

There was a bright yellow motorboat at the Floreks' dock, and the tops of Charlie's and Sam's heads were visible as they poked around inside.

"Nice boat!" I yelled, and they sprung up like meerkats, both shirtless and bronzed. The perks of living by the lake.

"I can see Charlie's muscles from here," Delilah shrieked.

I shushed her. "Sound carries easily on the water." But she was right. Charlie had filled out, and there was more definition to his arms, chest, and shoulders.

"Wanna come see?" Sam yelled back.

"Do we ever," Delilah purred, and I elbowed her and raised my hand in a thumbs-up.

We cut through the trail between our properties, emerging from the woods a few meters from their dock.

"Isn't it great?" Sam beamed at me from the boat.

"Isn't *she* great," Charlie corrected.

"It's awesome!" I said, and meant it. The boat had a rounded nose with brown vinyl benches in the front and room for six more in the back.

"Totally retro," Delilah enthused as we walked onto the dock.

"Whoa, whoa, Pers." Charlie held his hands up. "Your bathing suit plus this boat? I was going to take us for a drive, but I'm not sure I'll be able to see." I scowled at him.

"Hilarious," Sam said, then ran his eyes over me. "That suit's really cool. Matches the orange in the bracelet. Hop in."

Sam reached out his hand to help me, and a hot current of electricity buzzed from my fingers to my neck.

What was that?

"We call it the Banana Boat, for obvious reasons," Sam said, unaware of the zap he'd sent up my arm.

"We haven't even shown you the best part." Charlie pushed down on the wheel and a loud *aaaah-whoooo-gaaaaah* sounded from the horn. Delilah and I jumped and then cackled with laughter.

"Oh my god! This is a horny-sounding boat!" she cried.

"Gives new meaning to the name Banana Boat, huh?" Sam grinned at her, and the electricity that had been running up and down my arm faded.

Once we got the okay from my parents, who were already sitting on the deck with glasses of wine in hand, Charlie drove us south to a little cove and cut the motor.

"This, ladies, is the jumping rock," he declared, dropping an anchor into the water and removing his T-shirt. I was trying very hard not to stare at his new stomach muscles. I was failing.

"It's totally safe to jump," Sam said. "We've been doing it since we were kids."

"Who's in?" asked Charlie.

"I'll do it!" Delilah said, standing to unbutton her shorts. I had been too distracted to notice the rocky cliff we'd pulled in front of. I blanched.

"You don't have to," Sam said to me. "I'll stay in the boat with you."

I stood and took off my shorts. I would not be a baby.

We dove off the end of the boat and swam toward shore, Delilah and me following Sam and Charlie up the side of the cliff. I screamed when Charlie sprinted toward the edge and jumped over without warning.

We crept up to the edge to see his head bobbing in the water, his dimples clear even from this height.

"Who's next?" he called.

"I'm going," Delilah announced, and Sam and I stepped back to give her space. She moved back from the edge and then took three huge strides before jumping off. She came out of the water laughing.

"That was amazing. You've gotta try it, Percy!" she yelled.

My stomach twisted. It seemed *a lot* higher from up here than it did from the boat. I looked behind me, thinking that maybe I'd just walk down.

"Want to go back the way we came?" Sam asked, reading my mind.

I scrunched my mouth up. "I don't want to be a chicken," I

admitted, looking back over the lake and down to Charlie and Delilah.

"No, I get it, it's *really* high," Sam said, surveying the water below. "We could go together. I'll hold your hand, and we'll jump on the count of three."

I took a deep breath.

"Okay."

Sam threaded his fingers through mine.

"Together, on three," he said, squeezing my hand tight.

"One, two, three . . ." We dropped like concrete, our hands separating when we crashed through the surface. I was pulled down, down, down like an anvil was tied to my ankle, and for a fraction of a second, I worried I wouldn't make it back up. But then the downward momentum stopped and I kicked, swimming up to the light overhead. I came out gasping for air at the same time Sam emerged, spinning around to look for me. He wore a full toothy smile.

"You okay?"

"Yeah," I gasped, trying to catch my breath. "But I am never doing that again."

"What about you, Delilah?" Charlie asked. "Want to go again?"

"Definitely," she said. As if there would be another answer.

Sam and I swam back to the boat, using the little ladder at the back to haul ourselves up. He passed me a towel and we sat on the benches at the front across from each other, drying off.

"Delilah's not as bad as I thought," he said.

"Oh, really?"

"Yeah, she seems kind of . . . silly? But I still have my eye on her. If she says one mean thing to you, I will have to exact my revenge." His hair dripped onto his shoulders, which didn't look quite as bony as they used to. "I've been plotting it since you told me about her. It's all planned out."

I laughed. "Thanks for defending my honor, Sam Florek, but she's not like that anymore." He eyed me silently, then moved to the bench beside me, our thighs pressed together. I wrapped my towel around my shoulders, very aware of how my skin prickled where it met his. I barely registered the splashes of Charlie and Delilah's second jumps.

"What's in your hair?" he asked, reaching for the section I had wrapped in embroidery floss.

"Oh, I forgot that was there," I said. "I did it to match the bracelet. Do you like it?" When he turned his focus from my hair to my face, I was caught off guard by how stunning the blue of his eyes was. It wasn't like I hadn't noticed before. Maybe it was that I hadn't seen them this close up? He looked different from the last time I saw him, his cheekbones more prominent, the space below them hollower.

"Yeah, it's cool. Maybe I'll grow my hair out this summer and you can do it to match my bracelet, too," he said. He searched my face, and the prickling where his leg pressed against mine became a campfire blaze. He tilted his head and pursed his lips. The bottom one was fuller than the top, a faint crease bisected the pink crescent. I hadn't noticed *that* before.

"You look different," Sam murmured, squinting while he examined me. "No more freckles," he said after a few seconds.

"Don't worry, they'll be back," I said, looking up at the sun. "Probably by the end of the day." One corner of his lip rose slightly, but his brows remained furrowed.

"No more bangs, either," he said, giving the embroidered section of hair a gentle pull. I blinked back at him, my heart pounding.

What is even happening right now?

"No, and *they* won't be back—ever," I replied. I lifted my hand to tuck my hair behind my ear, realized it was shaking, and wedged it safely under my thigh. "You know, you're the only boy I've met who pays such close attention to hair?" I tried to sound calm, but the words came out wearing a straitjacket.

He grinned. "I pay attention to a lot of things about you, Percy Fraser."

~~~

THE CANADA DAY fireworks were an impressive display for such a small town. They were lit from the town dock, explosions illuminating the night sky and glittering on the inky water below.

"Do you think Charlie's friends are as cute as he is?" Delilah asked, tossing clothes all over the floor while we got ready. The plan was for Charlie, Sam, and Charlie's friends to pick Delilah and me up in the Banana Boat at dusk so we could watch from the lake.

"Knowing Charlie, I think his friends are probably all girls," I replied, pulling on a pair of sweatpants.

"Hmm . . . then I'll have to go all out." She held up a red halter top and a black miniskirt. "What do you think?"

"I think you'll be cold. It can get chilly when the sun goes down."

She gave me a devilish grin. "I'll risk it."

Thus clad—she in club wear, me in a navy U of T sweatshirt Dad bought at the university gift shop—we made our way to the water. We stopped dead as soon as we got to our dock and looked over at the Floreks'. Charlie and another boy were helping three girls into the boat. I took comfort in the fact that they were dressed more like me than Delilah, in leggings and pullovers.

Charlie brought the boat up to the end of our dock so we could climb aboard and introduced us to the group. Delilah's face fell when he referred to Arti as his girlfriend, but she quickly collected herself and planted her butt on the bench next to Sam. I sat across from them, my eyes sticky-glued to where Delilah's leg pressed against his.

Charlie parked just out from the town beach, where dozens of boats drifted on the water and cars lined the shore all around the bay. Charlie's friend Evan cracked a couple of cans of beer and passed them around as we waited. Both Charlie and Sam declined, but Delilah took a sip, puckering at the taste.

"You won't like it, Percy," she said, handing it back to Evan.

I took advantage of the dimming light to study Sam. He was listening to Delilah talk about her summer plans: horse riding in the Kawarthas and suntanning at a resort in Muskoka. His hair was thick and unruly, as usual, and he kept pushing it back only for it to fall over his eye again. He had a good mouth, I decided. His nose was the exact right size for his face, not too small or too big. It was kind of weirdly perfect. I already knew he had the best eyes. His whole face was nice, really. He was skinny, but his elbows and knees didn't look as stabby as they did last summer. Delilah was right; Sam was cute. I just hadn't realized before now.

I sat quietly with my revelation as he nodded along to Delilah's description of the resort pool, large hands wrapped around his knees, thighs squished against hers.

"You cold?" he asked her.

"A bit," she admitted. She was shivering, I could see that, but when Sam unzipped his black hoodie and passed it to her, it felt like a blade had been plunged into my belly.

It struck me like a bus: I had no idea how much time Sam spent with other girls during the year. I didn't think he had a girlfriend, but then again, the topic hadn't come up. And Sam was *cute*. And smart. And thoughtful.

"You okay, Percy?" he asked, catching me staring wide-eyed. Delilah shot me a funny look.

"Uh-huh!" It came out of my mouth as an odd squeak. I needed a diversion. "Hey, Evan? I wouldn't mind a sip of that," I said, pointing to his beer.

"Yeah, sure." He passed me the can, and *nope!* I did not like beer. I gave Evan a smile after my first gulp, then forced back two more before handing it back. Sam leaned toward me, his lips pinched together.

"You drink beer?" he asked with clear disbelief.

"Love it," I lied.

He frowned. "Swear on it?" He held up his wrist.

"Not a chance." He shook his head and laughed, and the sound brought a smile to my face.

Delilah's gaze ping-ponged between us, and when the fireworks started, booms echoing around the bay, she moved onto the seat beside me, linked her arm through mine, and whispered in my ear, "Your secret's safe with me."

〰〰

THE WEATHER HAD been perfect for Delilah's visit: clear skies, not a drop of rain, hot but not muggy, as if Mother Nature had known Delilah was coming, and put on her most impressive outfit. To Delilah's great disappointment, Charlie wasn't as cooperative, spending most of his time working at the Tavern or hanging out at Arti's house in town.

Her last day at the lake was what Dad called a scorcher, and when we could no longer walk on the dock without burning our feet, we headed to the Floreks' basement.

"What's Charlie up to?" Delilah asked as the three of us trudged down the stairs with sodas and a bag of salt-and-vinegar chips.

"Sleeping, probably," said Sam, grabbing the remote. "What do you feel like watching?" He and I took our usual spots at the opposite ends of the couch.

"I've got a better idea," Delilah said with a toss of red hair. "Let's play truth or dare."

Sam groaned.

"I don't know . . ." I hesitated, feeling uneasy. "I'm not sure we have enough people to play."

"Of course we do! You can play with just two people and there are *one, two, three* of us." Sam eyed Delilah like she was a poisonous snake. "C'mon! It's my last day. Let's do something *fun*."

"Just for a little while?" I directed my question at Sam.

"Okay, sure," he sighed heavily.

Delilah clapped her hands and positioned us in a circle on the sisal carpeting. "We don't have a bottle, so let's just spin the remote to see who goes first. Whoever the top end is facing starts," she directed. "Sam, why don't you go for it?"

"If I must," he said from under a swoop of tawny hair. He spun the remote, which pointed vaguely in Delilah's direction.

"Delilah: truth or dare?" Sam asked with the enthusiasm of a dead trout.

"Truth!"

Sam locked his blue eyes on her like a missile: "Have you ever bullied anyone?" I shot him a warning glance, but Delilah was oblivious.

"That's a weird question," she said, her bubblegum lips in a twist. "But, no, I haven't." Sam raised one eyebrow, but let it slide.

"Okay, my turn to ask one," she said and rubbed her hands together. "Sam: Do you have a girlfriend?"

"I do not," he replied, sounding utterly bored and a bit condescending. I fought back a smile that started in my fingertips, and let out the breath I'd been holding since the night of the fireworks.

After fifteen otherwise dull minutes of answering truth questions, Sam rubbed his face and moaned, "Can we put an end to this if I choose dare?"

Delilah considered this until a look of evil victory fell across her creamy face. "Great idea, Sam." She pretended to think, her index finger on her chin. Then she narrowed her eyes at him. "I dare you to kiss Percy."

My jaw slowly dropped. I'd been trying to figure out how I felt about Sam for days. But the glare he was giving Delilah, like he wanted to chop her up in itty-bitty pieces, was a flashing billboard that read *I would only kiss Percy Fraser if she were the last girl in the galaxy, and maybe not even then.* My stomach lurched.

"What, don't you think she's cute enough for you?" Delilah asked, her voice as sweet as aspartame, just as footsteps came down the stairs.

"Who's not cute enough for you, Samuel?" Charlie asked, stalking over to us in a pair of black track pants. He stretched up into a yawn that drew attention to his naked torso.

"No one," Sam replied as Delilah said, "Percy."

Charlie tilted his head toward her, his green eyes twinkling with delight. "Oh?"

"I dared him to kiss her but he obviously wasn't going to. I'd be insulted if it were me," she said, like I wasn't sitting right beside her.

"Is that right?" Charlie smirked. "How come, Samuel?"

"Get lost, Charles," he muttered, a high tide of blood red rising past his neck.

"Well, I wouldn't want Percy to feel bad just because *you* don't have the balls to kiss her," Charlie said. He bent down, took my face in his hands, and moved his mouth over mine before I had a chance to react. His lips were soft and warm and tasted of orange juice, and he pressed them to me long enough that I felt awkward with my eyes open. Then it was over. He pulled back a few inches, his hands still on my face.

"You snooze, you lose, Sam," Charlie said, looking at me with his cat eyes. He winked and straightened to full height, then headed back upstairs, leaving behind the spicy-sharp smell of his deodorant.

"Whoa, Percy!" Delilah grabbed my arm. I ran my tongue over my lips, the citrus tang lingering on them. "Earth to Persephone!" she giggled. Sam watched me silently, pink to the tips of his ears. I blinked away and bent my head, covering my face in a dark force field of hair.

I'd just had my first kiss, but my mind was stuck on the fact that Sam didn't want to kiss me. Not even on a dare.

~~~

MOM DROVE DELILAH back to the city the next morning. Delilah gave me a hug, saying she had the "best time ever" and was going to miss me "so much." I was relieved she was gone. I wanted Sam to myself so things could go back to normal, and I could forget about Charlie kissing me and Sam very much not kissing me.

The going-back-to-normal part was easy. We swam. We fished. We read. We made our way through eighties horror movies. Forgetting about the kissing stuff? Not so much. At least not for me. For Charlie, it wasn't a problem. I'm not sure he remembered putting his lips on mine at all—it's possible he was half-asleep or sleepwalking at the time—because he didn't mention it.

I was sitting in the Banana Boat mulling all this over while Charlie and Sam dried off from our latest trip to the jumping

rock (I stayed in the boat in a more supervisory capacity). It's
not that I wanted Charlie to mention the kiss again. I just kind
of wanted some reassurance that I wasn't a completely crappy
kisser. I was studying Charlie's mouth when I felt a tug on my
bracelet. It was Sam, and I was busted.

When we got back to the Floreks', Sam and I swam out to the
raft while Charlie went to get ready for his shift at the restaurant.
As soon as we climbed on, Sam lay down with his hands behind
his head and face to the sun, closing his eyes without a word.

What the hell?

He'd barely spoken to me since he caught me leering at his
brother, and suddenly I was irrationally annoyed. I backed up to
give myself a running start and cannonballed into the water next
to where he was lying. His legs were covered in droplets when I
emerged, but he hadn't moved an inch.

"You're quieter than usual," I said, once I'd climbed back
onto the raft, standing over him so water dripped onto his arm.

"Oh yeah?" His voice was dispassionate.

"Are you mad at me?" I glared at his eyelids.

"I'm not mad at you, Percy," he said, slinging one arm over
his face. *Okaaaaay.*

"Well, you seem kinda mad," I barked. "Did I do something
wrong?" No response. "I'm sorry for whatever it was," I added
with an edge of sarcasm. *Because—reminder!—he was the one who
rejected me.*

Still nothing. Frustrated, I sat down and pulled the arm from
his face. He squinted at me.

"Percy, I'm not. Seriously," he said. And I could tell he meant
it. I could also tell that something wasn't right.

"Then what's going on with you?"

He pulled his arm out of my hand and hoisted himself up, so

that we were both sitting cross-legged across from each other, knees touching. He tilted his head just slightly.

"Was that your first kiss?" he asked.

I stammered at the sudden change of topic. Kissing was not something we had discussed before.

"The other day. Charlie?" he prodded.

I looked over my shoulder for an escape route out of this conversation. "Technically," I murmured, still looking at the water behind me.

"Technically?"

I sighed and faced him again, cringing. "Do we have to talk about this? I know fourteen is old for a first kiss, but . . ."

"Charlie is such a dick," he interrupted with unusual sharpness.

"It's not a big deal," I said quickly. "It's just a kiss. It's not like it matters or anything," I lied.

"Your first kiss is a big deal, Percy."

"Oh my god," I groaned, looking down to where our knees were touching. "You sound like my mom." I studied the light hair that sprinkled his shins and thighs.

"Do you have your period?"

My eyes popped up to his. "You can't ask me that!" I screeched. He'd said it so casually, as if he'd asked *Do you like butternut squash?*

"Why not? Most girls menstruate around twelve. You're fourteen," he said matter-of-factly. I wanted to jump off the raft and never come up for air.

"I can't believe you just said 'menstruate,'" I muttered, my neck burning.

My period had arrived smack-dab in the middle of a school day. I stared at the red stain on my floral underwear for a full minute before pulling Delilah into the bathroom stall. For as much as I had obsessed about getting my period, I had no idea what to do. She ran to her locker and brought back a zippered pouch with pads and long tubes wrapped in yellow paper. Tampons. I couldn't believe she used them. She showed me how to put on the pad, then said, "You're going to have to do something about these granny panties. You're a woman now."

"So, do you?" Sam asked again.

"Do *you* have wet dreams?" I snapped.

"I'm not telling you that," he said, his cheeks turning a deep magenta.

I dug in. "Why not? You asked me about periods. I can't ask you about wet dreams?"

"It's not the same," he said, and his eyes flashed to my chest. We stared at each other.

"I'll answer your question if you'll answer mine," I hedged after several long seconds passed.

He studied me, his lips pressed together. "Swear on it?" he asked.

"I swear," I promised and tugged on his bracelet.

"Yeah, I have wet dreams," he said quickly. He didn't even break eye contact.

"What do they feel like? Does it hurt?" The questions sprang from my lips without my say-so.

He smirked. "No, Percy, it doesn't hurt."

"I can't imagine not having control of my body like that."

Sam shrugged. "Girls don't have control of their periods, either."

"That's true. I'd never thought about that."

"But you have thought about wet dreams." He eyed me closely.

"Well, they sound pretty gross," I lied. "Though not as gross as periods."

"Periods aren't gross. They're part of human biology, and they're actually pretty cool if you think about it," he said, his eyes wide with sincerity. "They're basically the foundation of human life." I gaped at him. I knew Sam was smart—I'd peeked at the report card that was tacked to the Floreks' fridge—but sometimes he said things like *Periods are the foundation of human life* that made me feel years behind.

"You are *such* a nerd," I scoffed. "Only you would say periods are cool, but believe me, they're gross."

"So you do have your period," he confirmed.

"Your deduction skills are outstanding, Doc," I said, lying down on my back and closing my eyes to put an end to the conversation.

But after a few seconds he spoke again. "They don't feel the same every time." I peered up at him, but his face was silhouetted by the sun. "Sometimes I can feel it happening during a dream, and sometimes I wake up and it's already happened."

I shielded my eyes with my hand, trying to make out his face. "What do you dream about?" I whispered.

"What do you think, Percy?"

I had a general sense of what boys found sexy. "Blondes with big boobs?"

"Sometimes, I guess," he said. "Sometimes girls with brown hair," he added quietly. The way he looked down at me made my insides feel like hot honey.

"What was your first kiss like?" I asked. The answer suddenly felt urgent.

He didn't speak for several long seconds, and when he did, it came out on a soft exhalation. "I don't know. I haven't kissed anyone yet."

~~~

THE RUMOR AT Deer Park High was that Ms. George was a witch. The ninth-grade English teacher was an older, unmarried woman whose thinning rust-colored hair was so brittle looking, I was tempted to try to snap off a piece. She dressed in flowing layers of black and ocher that hid her tiny body, with pointy-toed high-heeled boots that laced up around her skinny calves. And she had this resin bracelet with a dead beetle encased inside that she assured us was real. She was strict and tough and a little bit scary. I loved her.

On the first day of class, she handed out pastel-colored workbooks that were to serve as our journals. She told us journals were sacred, that she wouldn't judge their contents. Our first assignment was to write about our most memorable experience from the summer. Delilah looked at me and mouthed the words *Charlie shirtless*. Holding back a giggle, I opened the pale yellow book and began to describe the jumping rock.

Writing in the journal quickly became my favorite part of ninth grade—sometimes Ms. George gave us a theme to explore; other times she left it up to us. It felt good to give shape and order to my thoughts, and I liked using words to paint pictures of the lake and the bush. I wrote a full page about Sue's pierogies, but I also imagined terrifying tales of vengeful ghosts and medical experiments gone wrong.

Four weeks into the school year, Ms. George asked me to stay after class. Once the other students had filed out, she told me I had a natural talent for creative writing and encouraged me to enter a short-story competition being held across the school board. Finalists would attend a three-day writers' workshop at a local college during March break.

"Polish up one of your horror narratives, dear," she said, then shooed me out the door.

I took the journal to the cottage Thanksgiving weekend so Sam could help me decide which idea to work on. We sat on my bed with the Hudson's Bay blanket pulled over our legs, Sam flipping through the pages and my eyes stuck to him like a tongue to a metal pole in winter. Ever since Sam had told me he hadn't kissed anyone, I couldn't stop thinking about how I wanted to put my mouth on his before someone else got there.

"These are really good, Percy," he said. His face turned serious, and he gave me a *there, there* pat on my leg. "You're such a sweet, pretty girl on the outside, but really you're a total freak." I grabbed the workbook from his hands and swatted him with it, but my brain had jammed on the word *pretty*.

"I mean it as a compliment," he laughed, holding his hands up to shield himself. I raised my arm to whack him again, but he grabbed my wrist and yanked me forward so that I tumbled on top of him. We both went still. My eyes moved to the little crease in his bottom lip. But then I heard footsteps coming upstairs and I scrambled off him. Mom appeared in the doorway, frowning behind her oversized red frames.

"Everything okay up here, Persephone?"

"I think you should go with the brain blood one," Sam croaked after she left.

~~~

MOM AND DAD said we could spend March break in Barry's Bay if I didn't get into the workshop, and for a second I wondered if maybe I shouldn't bother entering. I floated the idea to Delilah as we were walking home from school, and she pinched my arm.

"You've got better things to worry about than the Summer Boys," she said.

I clutched her arm. "Who are you and what have you done with Delilah Mason?" I wailed.

She poked her tongue out. "I'm serious. Boys are for fun. Lots of fun. But don't let one stand in the way of your greatness."

It took every ounce of my self-control not to double over with laughter. But that was that.

I worked on the story throughout the fall. It was about an idyllic-seeming suburb where the smartest, most attractive teenagers were sent away to an elite academy. Except that the school was actually a nightmarish institution where their brain blood was harvested to formulate a youth-giving serum. Sam helped me work through the details over email. He poked holes in the plot and the science and then brainstormed solutions with me.

Once I finished, I mailed him a copy with a signed cover page and a dedication to him "for always knowing just the right amount of blood." I called it "Young Blood."

Five days later, he phoned the house after suppertime. "I'm going to stop thinking about what we can do over March break," he said. "There's no way you aren't going to win."

~~~~~

WE DROVE TO Barry's Bay on Boxing Day. The bush seemed like a different world than it was in summer—the birches and maples were bare and a foot of snow covered the ground, the sun bouncing off the crystals in tiny glittering specks. The pine boughs looked as if they were coated in diamond dust. One of the year-round residents had plowed our driveway and lit the fire, and the smoke billowed from the cottage's chimney. It looked like a scene on a Christmas card.

As soon as we unpacked, I bundled up in my red wool peacoat and put on my white boots with the furry pom-poms and a knit hat and matching mittens. I grabbed the parcel I'd carefully wrapped for Sam and headed out the door. My breath hit the air in silvery puffs, and the wind bit my fingers through my mittens. I was shivering when I climbed up the Floreks' porch.

Sue opened the door, surprised to see me.

"Percy! It's so good to see you, honey," she said, giving me a hug. "Come in, come in—it's freezing!" The house smelled like it did at Thanksgiving—of turkey and woodsmoke and vanilla candles.

"Merry Christmas, Mrs. Florek. I hope you don't mind me coming over without calling. I have a present for Sam and wanted to surprise him. I figured he'd be home?"

"I don't mind at all. You're welcome here anytime—you know that. He's . . ." She was interrupted by a chorus of agonized groans and then laughter. "He's in the basement playing video games with a couple of friends. Take your things off and head down." I stared at her blankly. In theory, I knew Sam had other friends. He'd begun mentioning them more than when we first met, and I'd been encouraging him to put the homework aside and hang out with them. I'd just never met them.

Do I want to meet them? Do they want to meet me? Do they even know I exist?

"Percy?" Sue gave me an encouraging smile. "Hang your coat up, okay? They're nice kids, don't worry."

I walked down the stairs in my socked feet, and when I got to the bottom, I was met with three sets of surprised eyes.

"Percy!" Sam said, standing up. "I didn't think you were here yet."

"Ta-da!" I replied, dipping into a half curtsy as the other two boys put their controllers down and got to their feet. Sam gave me a tight hug, just like he would if it were only the two of us. I closed my eyes briefly—he smelled like fabric softener and fresh air. He felt thicker, more solid.

"Oh man, you're cold," he said, pulling away. "Your nose is bright red."

"Yeah, I don't think my stuff is warm enough for up north."

"Let me grab you a blanket," he offered, then left me standing in the middle of the room while he dug around in a chest.

"Hi," I said, waving to Sam's friends. "Since Sam clearly doesn't know how to make introductions, I'm Percy."

"Oh, sorry," Sam said, handing me a multicolored patchwork afghan. "This is Finn," he said, pointing to the one with unkempt black hair and round glasses. Finn was almost as tall as Sam. "And this is Jordie." Jordie had dark skin and close-cropped hair. He was shorter than the other two but not as wiry. All three wore jeans and sweatshirts.

"The famous Percy. Nice to meet you," said Finn, smiling.

So they do know about me.

"Bracelet Girl," said Jordie with a smirk. "Now we can finally see why Sam never hangs out with us in the summer."

"Because I'm clearly more interesting?" I joked and curled up in the leather armchair while Finn and Jordie plunked back down on the couch and picked up the controllers. Sam sat down on the arm of the chair.

"Exactly," he said.

"Three updates?" I asked.

He pushed his hair back and gestured to the TV. "New video game." And his shirt. "New hoodie." He pointed to a pile of hockey skates. "We made a rink on the lake. You're going to love it." He paused and adjusted the blanket on my lap. "We've got extra winter gear you can borrow. Your turn."

"Umm," I began, like I hadn't planned what I'd tell him. "I got a laptop for Christmas. Mom brought an espresso machine up with us, so if you want to get into latte art, we've got you covered. And"—I held back a smile—"I got into the writers' workshop."

His face lit up, an explosion of blue eyes and white teeth. "That's amazing! Not that I'm surprised, but still. It's a huge deal! I bet it was really competitive." I grinned up at him.

"Hey, congratulations," Finn said from the couch, giving me a salute.

"Yeah," Jordie chimed in. "Sam told us about your story. Wouldn't shut up about it, actually."

I raised my eyebrows, feeling lighter than popcorn.

"I told you I thought it was good," Sam said. He tilted his head toward the large gift in my lap. "Is that for me?"

"No," I replied, innocently. "It's for Jordie and Finn."

"She's good," said Jordie, pointing his index finger at me before going back to the game.

"It's stupid," I added quietly, my eyes on Sam's friends. He followed my gaze.

"I got something for you, too," he said, and I saw Jordie elbow Finn.

"You did?"

"It's upstairs," he said. "Guys, we'll be back in a sec," he announced, and we padded up to the main floor. Sam pointed to the stairs leading to the second floor. "In my room."

I had been inside Sam's bedroom only a couple of times. It was a cozy space with navy-blue walls and thick carpeting. Sam kept it tidy—the bed was made with a blue plaid duvet, and there were no piles of clothes on the floor or stray papers on his desk. Next to the bed was a bookshelf filled with comics, secondhand biology textbooks, and full sets of J. R. R. Tolkien and Harry Potter. A large black-and-white poster showing a sketch of an anatomical heart, with labels pointing to the various parts, hung on the wall.

There was a new framed photo on his desk. I put the gift down and picked it up. It was a picture of Sam and me from my first summer at the lake. We were sitting at the end of his dock, towels wrapped around our shoulders, hair wet, both squinting into the sun, a barely detectable grin on Sam's face and a toothy one on mine.

"This is a good shot," I said.

"Glad you think so," he replied, opening up his top drawer and handing me a small present covered in brown paper and tied with a red ribbon.

I opened it carefully, tucking the ribbon in the pocket of my sweatpants. Inside was a pewter frame holding the same photo. "So you can take the lake home with you," he said.

"Thank you." I hugged it to my chest and then groaned. "I really don't want to give you yours. This is so thoughtful. Mine is . . . silly."

"I like silly," Sam said with a shrug and picked his present up from the desk. I bit my lip while he tore off the paper and examined the cartoon naked man on the *Operation* board game lid. His hair fell over his forehead, making it hard to read his expression, and when he looked at me it was with one of his unreadable stares.

"Because you want to be a doctor?" I explained.

"Yeah, I get that. Genius over here, remember?" He smiled. "Definitely the best gift I got this year."

I exhaled in relief. "Swear on it?" He pinched my bracelet between his thumb and forefinger.

"I swear." But then his face scrunched up. "I don't want this to sound bad, but I think that maybe sometimes you worry too much about what other people think." He rubbed the back of his neck and bent his head so that his face was level with mine.

I mumbled something incoherent. I knew he was right, but I didn't like that he saw me that way.

"What I'm trying to say is that it doesn't matter what other people think about you, because if they don't like you, they're clearly morons." He was so close I could make out the darker flecks of blue in his eyes.

"But you're not other people," I whispered. His eyes flicked down to my mouth, and I leaned a tiny bit closer. "I do care what you think."

"Sometimes I think no one gets me the way you do," he said, the pink of his cheeks deepening to scarlet. "Do you ever get that feeling?" My mouth felt dry and I ran my tongue over my top lip. His gaze followed its path, and I could hear him swallow thickly.

"Yeah," I said, putting a shaking hand on his wrist, sure that he would close the gap between us.

But then he blinked like he had remembered something important and straightened to his full height and said, "I don't ever want to mess that up."

7

Now

SAM AND I WALK TO THE TAVERN AFTER FINISHING OUR ICE creams, and when we arrive at the back door, we stand looking at each other awkwardly, unsure of how to part.

"It's been so great to see you," I tell him, tugging at the hem of my dress and hating how phony my voice sounds. Sam must hear it, too, because he raises his eyebrows and jerks his head back just slightly. "I was going to try to hit the liquor store before it closes," I say. "There's a bottle of wine with my name on it. It's kind of a lot being back here." I wince.

Why did I say that? How is it that I've seen Sam for all of an hour and the lock has come flying off my big mouth?

Sam runs his hand over his face and then through his hair. "Why don't you come in for a drink? Twelve years is a lot of time to catch up on." It doesn't escape my notice that he's already done the math.

I shift on my feet. There's nothing more I want than to spend time with Sam, to just be near Sam, but I need some time to figure out what I'm going to say to him. I want to talk about the last time we saw each other. To tell him how sorry I am. To tell him why I did what I did. To come clean. But I can't go there tonight. I'm not prepared. It would be like going into the fight of my life without any armor.

I look around the quiet side street.

"C'mon, Percy. Save your money."

"Okay," I agree. I step into the dark kitchen behind him, and when he flicks on the lights, my eyes slide down the slope of his back to the curve of his butt, which is a very big mistake because it is a stupidly great butt. It is at this precise moment that he turns around, catching me mid-ass-ogle.

"Bar?" I ask, feigning ignorance. I brush past him and through the dining room doors, turning on the lights in the main room. With my hand still on the switch, I take in the space. I have to blink a few times to process what I see because it's wild how little has changed. Pine planks cover the walls and ceiling; the floors are some kind of tougher wood, maple maybe. The effect is of being in a cozy cabin, despite the large size of the room. Historic photos of Barry's Bay hang on the walls along with antique logging axes and saws and paintings from local artists, including a few of the Tavern itself. The stone fireplace sits where it always did, and the same family photo is placed on the mantel where it always was. I make my way over to it while Sam takes a couple of glasses from the shelf behind the bar.

It's a framed shot of the Floreks in front of the Tavern, which I know was taken the day the restaurant opened. Sam's parents are wearing massive smiles. His dad, Chris, towers over Sue with one arm wrapped around her shoulder, holding her tight to his side. A toddler Charlie clutches his free hand. Sue is carrying an infant Sam; he looks about eight months old, his hair is so fair it's almost white, and his arms and legs are deliciously dimpled. I studied this photo countless times as a teen. I touch Sue's face now. She's younger than I am in this photo.

"I always loved this shot," I say, still examining the picture. I hear the gurgle of liquid being poured into glasses and turn to see Sam, *adult Sam*, watching me with a pained expression.

I walk to the bar and put my hands on the counter as I take a seat in front of him. He passes me a generous tumbler of whisky.

"You okay?" I ask.

"You were right earlier," he says, his voice rough as gravel. "It's a lot having you here. It kind of feels like I've been punched in the heart." My breath hitches. He lifts his glass to his lips and tosses his head back, downing its contents.

I am suddenly one thousand degrees hotter and hyperaware of the dampness under my armpits and how my bangs are stuck to my forehead. There's probably a cowlick up there. I try to push them off my face.

"Sam . . ." I begin, then stop, not sure what words come next.

I don't want to do this now. Not yet.

I raise my glass to my mouth and take a large sip.

Sam's gaze is relentless. His ability to maintain eye contact was something I got used to after I first met him. And as we got older, that blue stare set fire to my blood, but now its pressure is overwhelming. And I know, *I know*, that I shouldn't find him attractive right now, but his dark expression and his hard jaw are unraveling me. He is undeniably gorgeous, even when he's a little intense. Maybe especially so.

I tip back the rest of the whisky and gasp at the burn. He's waiting for me to say something, and I've never been able to evade him. I'm just not ready to open up our wounds now, not before I know whether we'll survive them a second time.

I look down at my empty glass. "I've spent twelve years thinking about what I would say if I ever saw you again." I grimace at my own honesty. I pause, counting four breaths in and out. "I've missed you so much." My voice trembles, but I keep going. "I want to make it better. I want to fix things. But I don't know what to say to do that right now. Please just give me a little more time."

I keep my attention on my empty glass. I have both hands wrapped around it so he can't see them shake. Then I hear the soft pop of the bottle's cork. I glance up, my eyes wide with fear. But his are soft now, a little sad even.

"Have another drink, Percy," he says gently, filling the glass. "We don't have to talk about it now."

I nod and take a deep breath, grateful.

"*Na zdrowie*," he says, touching his glass to mine and raising it to his lips, waiting for me to do the same. Together, we gulp down our drinks.

His phone buzzes in his pocket. It's not the first time it's gone off this evening. He checks the screen and shoves it back in his shorts.

"Do you need to get that?" I ask, thinking of Chantal and feeling a pang of guilt. "I don't mind."

"No, they can wait. I'll switch it off." He lifts the bottle of whisky. "Another?"

"Why the hell not?" I attempt a smile.

He pours more and then comes around the bar to sit on the stool beside me. "We should probably take this one slowly," he says, tilting his glass. I ruffle my bangs with my fingers, partly from nerves and partly in the hope of making them somewhat presentable.

"You once swore you'd never get bangs again," Sam says, looking at me sideways. I turn in my seat to face him.

"These," I pronounce, "are my breakup bangs!" And, *wow*, am I drunk already?

"Your what?" he asks, swinging to face me with a lopsided grin, brushing my legs with his in the process. I look down where his thighs bracket mine, then quickly back to his face.

"You know—breakup bangs," I say, trying to enunciate as clearly as possible. He looks mystified. "Women get new hairstyles when we get dumped. Or when we dump someone. Or sometimes just when we need a fresh start. Bangs are like the New Year's Eve of hair."

"I see," Sam says slowly, and it's clear what he means is *I really don't see* and also *That's crazy.* But a smile plays across his mouth. I try not to focus on the little crease in the middle of his bottom lip. Booze and Sam are a dangerous combination, I realize, because my cheeks are toasty and all I can think is how much I want to suck on that crease.

"So were you the dumper or the dumpee?" he asks.

"I got dumped. Just recently." I try to focus on his eyes.

"Ah, shit. Sorry, Percy." He moves his head down to my level so he's right in my eye line. *Oh god,* did he notice I was staring at his mouth? I force myself to meet his eyes. He's wearing an odd stern expression. My face is burning. I can feel beads of perspiration forming above my upper lip.

"No, it's okay," I say, trying to subtly dab at the sweat. "It wasn't *that* serious. We weren't together very long. I mean, it was seven months. Which is long for me—the longest for me, actually. But, like, not long for most grown-up people."

Oh, good, I'm rambling now. And maybe slurring?

"Anyway, it's fine. He wasn't the guy for me."

"Ah," he says, and when I look back to him, he seems more relaxed. "Not a horror fan?"

"You remember that, huh?" Delight tingles in my toes.

"Of course," he says with open, disarming honesty. I smile— a huge, dopey, whisky-fueled smile. "Who could forget being subjected to years of shitty scary movies?" This is classic Sam, teasing but always gentle and never unkind.

"Excuse me?! You *loved* my movies!" I give him a playful punch on the arm, and, *Jesus*, his bicep is like concrete. I shake my fist, looking at him in disbelief. He wears a small grin as if he knows *exactly* what I'm thinking. I take a sip of whisky to cut the tension that's closing in.

"Anyway, no. Sebastian definitely *did not* like horror movies," I say, and then I rethink this. "Actually, I don't know. I never asked. And we never watched one together, so who knows? Maybe he loved them." I leave out the part about how I haven't told anyone I've dated about this odd passion of mine. That I don't even watch scary movies anymore. To Sam, my love of classic horror films was probably a basic biographical Percy fact. But to me, it was far too intimate a detail to reveal to any of the men I saw. And, more to the point, after that first summer at the lake, I've associated those films with Sam. Watching them now would be too painful.

"You're joking?" Sam asks, clearly confused.

I shake my head.

"Well, you're right," he murmurs. "He's definitely not the guy for you."

"What about you?" I ask. "Still reading anatomy textbooks for kicks?"

His eyes grow wider, and I think his cheeks have gone darker under the stubble. I hadn't meant to bring up that particular memory. Of his hands and mouth on me in his bedroom.

"I didn't . . ." I start, but he interjects.

"I think my textbook-reading days are over," he says, giving me an out. But then he adds, "Calm down, Percy. You look like you've been busted watching porn."

I let out a relieved sound that is halfway between a laugh and a sigh.

We finish our drinks in a happy silence. Sam pours more. It's dark outside now, and I have no idea how long we've been here.

"We're going to regret this tomorrow," I say, but it's a lie. I would endure a two-day hangover if it meant I could have another hour with Sam.

"Do you stay in touch with Delilah?" he asks, and I almost choke on my drink. I haven't spoken to Delilah in years. We're friends on Facebook, so I know she's some kind of political PR ace in Ottawa, but I pushed her away not too long after I messed everything up with Sam. My two biggest friendships: gone within months. Both because of me.

I run my finger around the rim of my glass. "We stopped being close in university," I say. The truth of this still stings, though it's not the whole story, not even close. I look at Sam to see if he can tell.

He shifts his weight on the stool, looking uncomfortable, and takes a big drink. "I'm sorry to hear that. You two were really tight for a while there."

"We were," I agree. "Actually," I add, glancing up at him, "you probably saw her more than I did since you both went to Queen's."

He scratches the scruff on his jaw. "It's a big campus, but yeah, I ran into her once or twice." His voice is coarse.

"She'd get a kick out of seeing how you've grown up," my stupid whisky mouth blurts. I look down at my drink.

"Oh?" he asks, bumping my knee with his. "And how did I grow up?"

"Cocky, apparently," I mutter, squinting at my glass, because somehow there are two of them.

He chuckles and then leans toward me and whispers in my ear, "You grew up pretty cocky, too."

~~~

SAM SITS BACK and studies me.

"Can I tell you something?" he asks, his words running together just a little.

"Of course," I choke out.

His eyes are slightly unfocused, but he has them set on mine. "There was this incredible used book and video store in Kingston when I was premed," he begins. "They had a huge horror section—all the good stuff you loved. But other movies, too. Obscure ones that I thought maybe you hadn't seen. I spent *a lot* of time there, just browsing around. It reminded me of you." Sam shakes his head, remembering. "The owner was this grumpy guy with tattoos and a huge mustache. One day he got super pissed at me coming in all the time and never buying anything, so I grabbed a copy of *The Evil Dead* and plunked it on the counter. And then I just kept going back, but of course I had to buy something each time. I ended up with *Carrie, Psycho, The Exorcist*, and all those terrible *Halloween* movies," he says. He pauses, searching my face. "I never put them on, though. My roommates thought I was nuts to have all these movies I didn't watch. But I just couldn't bring myself to. It felt wrong without you."

This shakes me.

I've spent hours, days, entire years wondering if Sam could possibly long for me the way I did for him. In some ways, it seemed like wishful thinking. In the months following our breakup, I left countless messages on his dorm room phone, sent text after text, and wrote email after email, checking to see how he was, telling him how much I missed him, and asking if we could please talk. He didn't respond to a single one. By May, someone else answered the phone—a new student had moved into his room. I considered driving up to Barry's Bay, telling him everything, begging for forgiveness, but I thought he'd probably wiped me, my name, and all memory of us from his mind by that point.

There's always been a small, hopeful part buried inside me that felt he *must* sometimes find his mind drifting to me, to *us*. He was everything to me, but I know the same was true for him. Hearing him talk about the video store dislodges that deeply hidden sliver of hope, just a little.

"I don't watch them, either," I admit in a whisper.

"No?"

"No." I clear my throat. "Same reason."

We're looking at each other, unblinking. The tightness in my chest is almost unbearable. The temptation to lean into him, to show him what he means to me with my hands and my mouth and my tongue, is almost impossible to ignore. But I know that wouldn't be fair. My heart is a stampede of animals escaping the zoo, but I sit still, waiting for his response.

And then Sam smiles and his blue eyes glint. I can feel what's coming before he speaks, and I'm already smiling.

I know you, I think.

"You mean you finally got decent taste in films?"

His smart-ass comment chases away the heaviness looming over us, and we both fall into a fit of laughter. Clearly the whisky has taken its full effect because my cackles are broken up with hiccups, and tears are streaming down my face. I put my hand on Sam's knee to steady myself without realizing that I've touched him. We're still cracking up, and I'm taking big gasping breaths to try to calm down, when a woman's voice silences our outburst.

"Sam?"

I look up and Sam turns toward the kitchen doors, my hand falling from his knee as he shifts. In the doorway stands a tall blonde. She looks like she's around our age, but she's dressed immaculately in white sailor-style trousers and a matching sleeveless silk blouse. She's thin and crisp looking, her hair pulled back into a low bun at the nape of her long neck. I am suddenly fully aware of how crumpled my red dress is and how disheveled my hair must be.

"Sorry to interrupt," she says, walking toward us, car keys clenched in one hand. Her expression is cool, and I feel rather than see her sizing me up because I'm looking to Sam in confusion.

"I tried calling you several times," she says, her hazel eyes oscillating between us. I met some of Sam's cousins when we were kids, and I'm trying to place this woman among them.

"Shit, sorry," he says, the words of his apology blurring together. "We got a bit sidetracked."

She purses her lips. "Are you going to introduce us?" she asks, waving toward me. She has the fair Florek coloring but definitely not the warmth.

Sam turns and gives me a crooked smile that doesn't reach his eyes.

"Percy, this is Taylor," he says.

"Cousin?" I ask, but Taylor answers for him.

"Girlfriend."

~~~~

SAM IS INTRODUCING me to Taylor. His girlfriend. Not his cousin.

Sam has a girlfriend.

Of course he has a girlfriend!

How had I not considered this? He is a hot doctor. He's tall and he's got those eyes, and the messy hair is working for him. I'm pretty sure whatever hard surface he's keeping under his T-shirt would make me weep. The Sam I knew was also kind and funny and brilliant—too smart for his own good, really. And he's so much more than all that. He's Sam.

Taylor is standing in front of us, her hands on her hips, looking fresh and stylish and imposing in her all-white outfit while I am sitting with my mouth hanging open. What normal person wears all white without getting some kind of stain on the front, anyway? Come to think of it, who wears dress pants and a matching silk top on a Thursday night in Barry's Bay? On *any* night in Barry's Bay? I want to squirt her with one of the restaurant's ketchup bottles.

"Taylor, *this* is Percy," Sam says as though he's mentioned me before, but Taylor looks at him blankly. "Remember? I've told you about Percy," he prods. "She had a cottage next door. We hung out all the time when we were kids."

Hung out? Hung out?!

"How cute," Taylor says in a way that makes it sound like she doesn't think our childhood *hangouts* are very cute at all. "So you two are just catching up?" She directs the question to Sam, but her eyes flash over to me, and I can see the assessment she's making: threat or no? My dress is wrinkled and possibly sweaty. There's an ice cream stain on my boob. And there's no way I don't smell like whisky. Her shoulders relax a little—she doesn't think there's anything to worry about.

Sam is saying something in response to Taylor, but I have no idea what because I'm suddenly so nauseated that I have to hold on to the counter.

I need air.

I start taking deep breaths. *Iiiin one, two, three, four* and *ouuut one, two, three, four.* The whisky, which was warm and honey-sweet moments ago, now tastes stale and sour in my mouth. Puking is a very real possibility.

"You all right, Percy?" Sam asks, and I realize I've been counting out loud. He and Taylor are both looking at me.

"Mm-hmm," I hum tightly. "But I think the whisky is catching up to me. I should probably go. It was nice meeting you, Taylor." I get down from my spot at the bar and take a step forward, and my foot catches on the leg of Sam's stool. I stumble right in front of Taylor, who, by the way, smells like a fucking rose garden.

"Percy." Sam grabs my arm, and I close my eyes for a brief moment to steady myself. "You can't drive." I turn back to him, and he's got this look on his face like he feels sorry for me. I hate it.

"It's okay," I start. "No, I mean, I know I can't drive. But it's okay because I didn't drive. I walked here."

"Walked? Where are you staying? We'll give you a ride," Sam offers.

We.

We.

We.

I look at Taylor, who is not doing a very good job at hiding her annoyance. Then again, if I found my hot doctor boyfriend drunk with a strange, clumsy woman who thought I was his cousin, I would be annoyed, too. And if that boyfriend were Sam, annoyance wouldn't cover it. I would be murderous.

"Clearly you both need a drive," Taylor says. "Let's go. My car's out back."

I follow Taylor and Sam. I can picture them together on a date—both tall and fit and stupid good-looking. She could be a ballet dancer, with her willowy limbs and her hair pulled back in that neat bun. He's built like a swimmer—broad through the shoulders, narrow at the hips, with legs that are muscular but not bulky. His calves look cut from marble. He probably still runs. They probably run together. They probably run together and then have the kind of sweaty, post-run sex that fit, happy people have.

Taylor leads the way out the kitchen door, and Sam holds it open for me to pass through. I wait for him to lock up while Taylor slides into her white BMW. I notice that her handbag and loafers are also white. This woman probably shits white.

"You okay?" he says quietly.

I'm too drunk to think about how to answer his question with a convincing lie, so I smile at him weakly before walking to the car.

I sit in the back, feeling like a child and a third wheel and also very dizzy.

"So how did you two meet?" I ask even though I really *do not* want to know the answer.

What is wrong with me?

"At a *bar*, of all places," says Taylor, giving me a look in the rearview mirror that tells me she doesn't spend a lot of time picking up guys over a few beers. The idea of Sam just being out in

the world, out in bars, looking for women to meet, is so horrify-
ing that I need a moment to collect myself. "It was, what, two
and a half years ago, Sam?"

Two years. Two years is serious.

"Mmm," Sam offers by way of a reply.

"And what do you do, Taylor?" I ask, quickly changing
the subject. Sam looks over his shoulder, sending me a funny
look, which I take to mean, *What are you up to?* I choose to ignore it.

"I'm a lawyer. Prosecutor."

"Are you kidding me?!" I squeak. I don't know if it's Sam or
the alcohol that has so thoroughly removed my filter. "A lawyer
and doctor? That should be illegal. You two are, like, taking all
the rich, hot people away from the rest of us."

Oh, I am so very, very drunk.

Sam erupts with a big, booming laugh. But Taylor, who
clearly doesn't appreciate my inebriated sense of humor, remains
quiet, giving me a puzzled look in the mirror.

The drive is short, and we're at the motel in under five minutes. I point out room 106, and Taylor pulls up in front of it. I
thank her for the drive in a cheery (possibly demented-sounding)
voice and, with zero grace, tumble out of the car and shuffle to
the door, getting my key from my bag.

"Percy!" Sam calls from behind me, and I close my eyes
briefly before I turn around, the full weight of my humiliation
pressing down on my shoulders. I want to crawl into bed and
never wake up. He's rolled down the window and is leaning over
his muscular forearm that's resting on the edge. We look at each
other for a second.

"What?" I say, my voice flat. I'm done pretending to be perky
Percy.

"I'll see you soon, okay?"

"Sure," I reply and turn back to the door. Once I've got it unlocked, the headlights move, but I don't look back to see the car pull away. Instead, I run to the bathroom and throw my head into the toilet bowl.

~~~

I LIE IN bed blinking up at the ceiling. I know it must be well into the morning because the sun is already high. I haven't turned my head to look at the clock because I don't want to wake the beast of a headache that lurks in my temples. My mouth tastes like I spent the night licking the floor of a roadhouse pub. Yet I smile to myself.

I found Sam.

And I felt it. The pull between us. The one that had been there since we were thirteen, the one that only got stronger as we got older, the one I tried to deny twelve years ago.

I didn't break it. I broke us. I can fix it.

And then she emerges through the fog of my hangover in a white pantsuit: Taylor. *Blech.* I find a small petty pleasure in her name. Taylor is one of those used-to-be-trendy names that now sound dated and pedestrian. My mother would find it *vile.*

We met, what, two and a half years ago, Sam?

I scrunch my nose at the memory of Taylor's forced casualness. I would be shocked if she didn't know how long they've been together down to the second.

Sam has a girlfriend. A beautiful, successful, presumably intelligent girlfriend. Someone whom I'd probably like under different circumstances.

I need a distraction.

I chance tilting my head toward the clock and am relieved that the pounding doesn't get worse. I spot two purple chocolate bar wrappers on the bed beside me and remember taking them from the mini bar after I puked. It's ten twenty-three. I groan. I should get up. I booked today off, so I don't need to work, but I need to shower. Even I can smell me. Taylor probably wakes up in a pressed pantsuit. She probably keeps a bar of 75 percent fair-trade dark chocolate in her kitchen drawer and eats a single square on special occasions. As much as I can mix with pretentious interior designers and architects, or recommend a trendy new restaurant that actually has good food and service, or spend the evening in heels without showing pain on my face, I'll always be messy underneath.

Usually I do a good job of keeping that side of myself under wraps. But now and then it'll come out, like the time I called Sebastian's progressive-seeming bearded best friend "the worst kind of misogynist" over dinner after he'd repeatedly looked down our server's shirt and asked me whether I'd go to part-time or quit work entirely after I had children. Sebastian looked at me slack-jawed, having never seen me snap like that, and I apologized for my outburst, blaming it on the wine.

Still in yesterday's sundress, I ease out of bed and inch toward the bathroom. I'm stiff, but I'm not nauseated. I loosen my belt and pull the dress over my head, take off my underwear, and then step under the hot spray. As the soap and water lift the smog from my brain, I make a plan to head over to the public beach after breakfast. Sam and I never swam at the beach when we were young. Once or twice we bummed around the nearby park with his friends, but the beach was reserved for town kids who didn't live on the lake. I know there's no dock and no raft, but I am desperate for a swim.

After my shower, I towel dry my hair until it's damp and run a comb through it. I chance a look at my phone.

There's another text from Chantal: CALL ME.

Instead, I write her back: Hey! Can't talk right now. No need to come here. I'm OK. Ran into Sam yesterday.

I can picture her rolling her eyes at my response. I know I'm probably not sneaking anything by her, and I feel guilty for not calling, but being here and seeing Sam yesterday feels so surreal, I can't imagine having to put it in words.

I press send and then put on my bathing suit, a bright red two-piece that I have rare occasion to use, and a pair of denim shorts. I'm about to throw on a shirt before heading to the motel restaurant, when there's a knock at the door. I freeze. It's too early for housekeeping.

"It's me, Percy," says a deep, scratchy voice from outside.

I unlock the door. Sam is looming in the doorway with damp hair and a fresh shave. He's wearing a pair of jeans and a white T-shirt, a coffee cup and a paper bag in one hand. It's every straight hungover woman's fantasy standing at the entrance of my room. He holds them out and then looks me over, slowing down over the one-shouldered bathing suit top I'm wearing. His blue eyes are somehow brighter today.

"Want to come to the lake?"

~~~~~

"WHAT ARE YOU doing here?" I ask, grabbing the coffee and the bag. "Never mind, I don't care why. You're my hero."

Sam laughs. "I told you I'd see you soon. I figured you'd forgive me for overserving you if I came bearing food, and I know you don't like sweets at breakfast. Or at least you didn't used to."

"Nope, still don't," I confirm, sticking my nose in the bag. "Cheese and ham croissant?"

"Brie and prosciutto—from the new café in town," he replies. "And a latte. Barry's Bay is fancy now."

"I noticed a more refined air yesterday." I grin, taking a sip. "Taylor won't mind if I come to the house? She might feel uncomfortable since we *hung out* all the time when we were kids." And *this* is the problem with seeing Sam before I've had time to figure out how to talk to him or at least before I've had coffee. Words come into my head and then out of my mouth with no lag time between—it was that way when we were teenagers, and clearly that hasn't changed, no matter how much I've grown, no matter what kind of successful woman I've become. I sound petty and childish and jealous.

Sam rubs the back of his neck and looks over his shoulder, thinking. In the two seconds it takes for him to shift his gaze back to me, I've melted into a sticky pool of embarrassment and reassembled myself into what I hope is a normal-seeming human.

"The thing about Taylor and me—" I cut him off with a frantic shake of my head before he finishes the sentence. I don't want to know about the thing with him and Taylor.

"You don't need to explain," I say.

He stares at me blankly, blinking just once before pressing his lips together and nodding his head—an agreement to move on. "At any rate, something urgent came up with a case she's been working on. She had to go back to Kingston this morning."

"But the funeral is tomorrow." The words come out in a burst, thickly coated with judgment. Sam, rightfully, looks taken aback by my tone.

"Knowing Taylor, she'll find a way to come back." It's an odd response, but I let it slide.

"Shall we?" he asks, pointing his thumb over his shoulder at a red pickup truck I hadn't noticed until now. I look at him in shock. There's nothing about Sam that says red pickup truck, except for being born and raised in rural Ontario.

"I know," he says. "It's Mom's, and I started driving it when I moved up here. It's a lot more practical than my car."

"Living in Barry's Bay. Driving a truck. You've changed, Sam Florek," I say solemnly.

"You'd be surprised by how little I've changed, Persephone Fraser," he replies with a lopsided grin that sends heat where it should not.

I turn around, discombobulated, and throw my towel and a change of clothes in a beach bag. Sam takes it from me and tosses it into the back of the truck before helping me climb in. Once the doors are closed, the rich smell of coffee mixes with the clean scent of Sam's soap.

As he starts the engine, my mind begins racing. I need a strategy, ASAP. I told Sam last night I'd give him an explanation for what happened all those years ago, but that was before I met Taylor. He's moved on. He has a long-term relationship. I owe him an apology, but I don't have to unload my past mistakes on him to do it. Do I?

"You're quiet," Sam says as we head out of town toward the lake.

"I guess I'm nervous," I say honestly. "I haven't been back since we sold."

"That Thanksgiving?" He glances at me, and I nod.

Silence falls over us. I used to twist my bracelet when I was anxious. Now I bob my knee up and down.

When we turn onto Bare Rock Lane, I roll down the window and take a deep inhale.

"God, I missed this smell," I whisper. Sam puts his large hand around my knee, stopping its jitterbugging, and gives it a gentle squeeze before moving his hand back to the wheel and pulling into his driveway.

8

Summer, Fifteen Years Ago

MY FEET CRUNCHED ON THE DRIVEWAY, THE AIR HEAVY WITH
dew and the lush smell of moss, fungi, and damp earth. Sam had
taken up running in the spring, and he was determined to convert
me to his cause. He mapped out an entire beginner's program to
start today, my first morning at the cottage. I was instructed to
eat a light breakfast no later than seven a.m. and meet him at the
end of my driveway at eight a.m.

I stopped when I saw him.

He was stretching, his back turned to me with headphones in
his ears, pulling one arm over his head and leaning to the side. At
fifteen, his body was almost foreign to me. Somehow, he'd grown
at least another six inches since I'd last seen him over the Christmas break. I'd noticed it yesterday, when he and Charlie came to
help us unload. ("It's officially an annual tradition," I heard
Charlie tell Dad.) But I didn't have time to properly inspect Sam
before both he and Charlie had to leave to get ready for their
shifts at the Tavern. Sam was working in the kitchen three nights

a week this summer, and I was already dreading the time apart. Now, his black running shirt lifted to expose a slice of tanned skin. I watched, mesmerized, a flush creeping up my neck.

His hair was the same thick tangle and he still wore the friendship bracelet around his left wrist, but he must have been well over six feet tall now, his legs stretched almost endlessly past the hem of his shorts. Almost as improbable as his height was that he was somehow thicker, too. His shoulders, arms, and legs all carried more bulk, and his butt was . . . well, it could no longer be mistaken for a Frisbee.

I tapped him on the shoulder.

"Jesus, Percy," he said, spinning around and taking off his headphones.

"Good morning to you, too, stranger." I wrapped my arms around his waist. "Six months is too long," I said into his chest. He squeezed me tightly.

"You smell like summer," he said, then put his hands on my arms and stepped back. His gaze traveled over my spandex-clad form. "You look like a runner."

That was his doing. I had a drawer full of exercise gear based on the list of items he'd suggested. I had put on shorts and a tank top as well as a sports bra, which Sam had embarrassingly included on his list, and one of the cotton thongs Delilah gave me before she left for her mother-daughter European vacation, which he had not included. My hair, now well past my shoulders, was gathered into a thick ponytail high on my head.

"Fake it till you make it, right?"

He hummed and then turned serious and took me through a series of stretches. During my first squat, he stood behind me and put his hands on my hips. I almost tumbled backward with the shock of his grip.

When I was suitably limber, he ran his hand through his hair and went over the plan: "Okay, let's start with the basics. The most important part of learning to run is . . ." He drifted off, waiting for me to fill in the blank.

"Good shoes?" I guessed, looking down at my new Nikes. He shook his head, disappointed.

"Didn't you read the couch to 5K article I mailed you?" He'd clipped it from a running magazine, complete with some kind of complicated time and distance chart. I read it . . . once . . . ish.

"The most important part of learning to run is walking," he said with his hands on his hips. I smothered a giggle. This bossy thing was entirely new and sort of adorable and definitely funny. "So we'll spend the first week doing a 3K out and back, increasing the distance you spend running each day until you're running the whole 3K by the end of the week. You'll take two rest days a week, and by the end of week two, you should be running a full 5K."

I barely understood a word he'd said, but five kilometers sounded pretty far. "How far do you usually go?"

"To town and back. It's about 12K." My jaw dropped. "I worked my way up to it. You will, too."

"Nope. No way!" I cried. "There are too many hills!"

"Calm down. We'll take it day by day." He gestured down the road and started walking. "C'mon. We'll walk for the first five minutes." I looked at him dubiously, but picked up my pace to match his.

If my elementary school's annual track-and-field day of hell hadn't already made it obvious years ago, it was now: I was not a natural runner. Ten minutes in, I was brushing sweat off my face and trying to ignore the fire in my lungs and thighs.

"Three updates?" Sam asked without a hint of breathlessness.

I scowled. "No talking."

He slowed his stride after that. At the halfway point, I took my top off, wiped my face with it, and tucked it into the back of my shorts. We walked the last leg of the route, my legs as shaky as a baby deer's.

"I never knew you were such a sweater," Sam said when I toweled off with my top again.

"I never knew you were such a masochist." This running thing was not adorable anymore.

"That writers' workshop really improved your vocabulary." I could hear the smirk in his voice. I hit him across the chest.

The Floreks' drive came before ours, and I turned down it. "I need to jump in the lake, like, right now," I said, cutting around the house and heading down the hill to the water with Sam beside me, a lopsided grin on his face.

"I don't know what you find so funny," I huffed.

"I'm not laughing." He raised his hands.

I took off my shoes and socks as soon as we reached the dock, then peeled my shorts down and tossed them aside.

"Geez!" Sam cried from behind me. I spun around.

"What?" I snapped just as I realized I was wearing a pink thong and that Sam was staring at my extremely bare ass. I was too hot and pissy to care.

"Problem?" I asked, and his eyes flashed to mine, then down to my bum, and then up to my face again. He muttered a *fuck* under his breath and looked skyward. He was holding both hands over his crotch. My eyebrows shot up. Not knowing what to do, I ran down the dock and cannonballed into the water, swimming under the surface for as long as I could.

"You coming in?" I hollered back to him when I came up for

air, a cocky grin plastered on my face. "The water might cool you off."

"I'm going to need you to face the other direction before I do that," he called back, still shielding himself.

"And if I don't?" I swam closer.

"C'mon, Percy. Do me a favor." He looked truly pained, which served him right for subjecting me to his workout routine. But inside I was ecstatic. I paddled out to give him space while he jumped in. We were about six feet apart, treading water, and staring at each other.

"I'm sorry," he said, moving a bit closer. "It's just my body's reaction."

Body's reaction?

"Got it," I said, more than a little deflated. "Half-naked chick equals erection. Basic biology."

After our swim, Sam turned away when I climbed onto the dock. I lay on my back, letting the sun dry me off, my hands forming a cushion behind my head. Sam spread out beside me in the same position, his shorts sopping wet.

I slanted my head toward him, and said, "I think I should keep a bathing suit here for next time."

~~~

I LEFT ONE of my bikinis at the Floreks', along with an extra towel, so I could jump into the lake as soon as we returned from the torture Sam called running. He swore I would grow to love it, but by the end of our second week, the only thing I had grown was a sprinkling of freckles across my nose and chest.

We had just got back from a sluggish 5K, and I had grabbed my suit off the line, waved to Sue, who was weeding the garden, and popped inside to the bathroom to change while Sam did the same in his room. I tugged off my sweaty gear and tied on the string bikini Mom had finally okayed, yellow with white daisies, then headed to the kitchen to wait for Sam. I was gulping down a glass of water at the sink when someone cleared their throat behind me.

"Good morning, sunshine!" Charlie was leaning against the doorway wearing sweatpants and no shirt, his standard uniform. Not that I minded. Charlie was ripped for a seventeen-year-old.

"It's not even nine a.m.," I panted, still out of breath. "What are you doing up?"

"Good question," Sam said, coming into the kitchen. He took the glass from my hands and refilled it. While Sam drank, Charlie looked me up and down without shame, lingering on my chest. When his gaze reached my face again, his brows drew together over his green eyes.

"You look like a tomato, Pers," he said, then turned to Sam. "Why do you keep forcing your cardio on her? Bad hearts run in our family, not hers." Sam pushed his hair back.

"I'm not forcing her. Am I, Percy?" He looked at me for backup, and I cringed.

"No . . . technically, you're not *forcing* me . . ." I drifted off when Sam's expression crumpled.

"But you don't like it," Charlie finished, eyes narrowed at me.

"I like how it feels afterward, when it's over," I said, trying to find something positive to say. Charlie grabbed an apple from the fruit basket on the kitchen table and took a big bite.

"You should try swimming, Pers," he said, his mouth full.

"We swim every day," Sam said in the monotone he reserved for when his brother annoyed him.

"No, like real distance swimming. Across the lake," Charlie clarified. Sam looked over at me, and I tried not to look too excited. I couldn't count the number of times I'd stared at the far shore and wondered whether I could ever make it across. It sounded awesome.

"That sounds interesting," I said.

"I can help you train if you want," Charlie offered. But before I could respond, Sam cut in: "No, we're good."

Charlie looked me over again, slowly. "You'll need a different bathing suit."

~~~

TRAINING FOR SWIMMING was way more fun than running. It was also a lot harder than I thought it would be. Sam collected me from the cottage every morning after his run, and we'd walk back to his place together so he could change into his suit. We devised a warm-up routine, involving a series of stretches on the dock and laps to and from the raft. Sometimes Sam swam beside me, giving pointers on my form, but usually he bobbed on a pool noodle.

Charlie had been right about the bathing suit, too. During my first warm-up, I had to keep adjusting the top to keep everything from falling out. That afternoon, Sam drove us in the little boat to the town dock and we walked to Stedmans. It was half general store, half dollar store, and it had a little bit of everything, but there was no guarantee they'd have what you were looking for.

As luck would have it, there was a rack of women's suits right at the front. Some had those old-lady skirts attached to them, but there was also a handful of plain one-pieces in cherry red. Practical, cheap, and cute enough: the perfect Stedmans find. Sam found a pair of swim goggles in the sporting section, and I paid for both with one of Dad's fifties. We spent the change on ice creams at the Dairy Bar—Moose Tracks for Sam and cotton candy for me—and walked back to the dock, taking a seat on a bench by the water to finish the cones. We were looking over the lake quietly when Sam leaned over and circled his tongue around the top of my cone where it was melting in rivulets of pink and blue.

"I don't get why you like this so much—it tastes like sugar," Sam said, before he noticed the shock on my face.

"What was that?" I asked. My voice came out an octave higher than usual.

"I tried your ice cream," he said. Which, okay, I know was obvious, but the way a current buzzed across my skin, he might as well have licked my earlobe.

~~~~~

AS MY DISTANCES increased, Sam rowed beside me in case I ran into trouble and as protection from other boaters. When I suggested he turn on the motor so he could relax, he brushed me off, saying I didn't need gasoline in my lungs while I swam. I practiced daily, dead set on making it to the other side of the lake by the end of August.

The week before my big swim, I waited in the Floreks' kitchen for Sam to change into his bathing suit, helping Sue unload the dishwasher.

"Did he tell you he's lifting his dad's old weights every morning before his run?" Sue asked me as she put a pair of glasses into the cupboard. I shook my head.

"He's really into the whole fitness thing, huh?"

Sue hummed. "I think he wants to make sure he can pull you out if he needs to," she said, squeezing my shoulder.

On the morning of the swim, I made my way down to the

water, Mom and Dad following with mugs of coffee and an old-school camera. When Sam came down to the dock, I walked over in my bare feet, holding my towel and goggles.

"Today's the day. How are you feeling?" Sam asked from the boat when I padded onto the dock.

"Good, actually. I can do this." I beamed and threw my towel in with him.

"Good, good," he muttered, checking around the boat for something. He seemed . . . nervous.

"How are *you* feeling?" I asked. He looked up at me and scrunched his nose.

"I know you'll do great, but I gotta admit I'm a little worried if something goes wrong." I hadn't heard Sam sound pan-icked before. But today he was panicked. I stepped down into the boat.

"The water's calm, you know CPR, you have an extra life jacket as well as a life preserver, there's a whistle in the boat to call for help, not that you'll need it since we have an audience." I pointed up to where my parents had joined Charlie and Sue on the deck, and waved at them.

"We're rooting for you, Percy," Sue called down.

"And," I continued, "I'm an excellent swimmer. There's noth-ing to worry about." Sam took a deep breath. He looked a bit pale. I wrapped my finger around his bracelet. "I swear, okay?"

"You're right," he sighed. "Just remember to take a break if you need to—you can always float for a bit."

I patted him on the shoulder. "So, should we do this thing?"

"Let's," Sam said. "I'd wish you luck, but you don't need it."

Once I was in the water, I pulled my goggles on, gave Sam a thumbs-up, and then turned my attention to the far shore—a small, rocky beach was my target destination. I took three deep breaths, then pushed off from the lake bottom with my feet and set off in a steady front crawl, my arms and feet working in tandem to propel me forward. I didn't rush my strokes, and soon the rhythm became almost automatic, my body taking over from my mind. I could see the side of the boat when I tilted my head for air, but I didn't pay it much attention. I was doing it! I was swimming across the lake. My lake. With Sam beside me. A rush of pride ran through me, powering me on and distracting me from the burning in my legs and the ache in my neck. I kept going, slowing down when I needed to catch my breath.

I switched to breaststrokes for several minutes to relieve the tension building in my shoulders, then resumed the crawl. At times, I could hear Sam cheering me on, but I had no idea what he was saying. Every so often I'd raise a thumbs-up in his direction to let him know I was okay.

The closer I got, the stiffer my limbs began to feel. The ache in my neck and shoulders grew intensely, and I struggled to keep my focus on my breathing. I clenched my jaw against the pain, but I didn't stop. I knew I wouldn't. I was going to make it. And when I did, I pulled my body up on the sandy shore, flung my goggles aside, and lay with my head on my hands, my legs still in the water, breathing fire through my lungs. I didn't even hear Sam pull the boat up on the beach—didn't notice him until he was crouched beside me with his hand on my back.

"Percy, are you okay?" He shook me gently, but I couldn't move. It was like my body was covered by the lead blanket they make you wear for an X-ray. Sam's voice was suddenly right in my ear. "Percy? Percy? Let me know if you're okay." I turned my head to him and opened one eye. He was inches away, his face lined with worry.

"Mmmm," I groaned. "Need to lie here."

Sam let out an enormous breath, and his expression transformed to glee. "Percy, you did it! You actually did it! You were amazing!" Words kept tumbling from his mouth, but I struggled to comprehend them. I felt delirious. "I can't believe how you just kept going and going, with no breaks. You were like some kind of machine!" He was wearing the most gigantic smile. Sam only seemed to get better and better looking, like he was growing into himself, and when he smiled like that, it was completely disarming. *He is pretty.* I found myself smiling at the realization.

"Did you just say that I'm pretty?" Sam asked, laughing.

Oh god, I must have said that bit out loud.

"You must really be out of it." He took off his shirt and lay down beside me with his lower half in the water, his hand on my back. He smelled like sun and sweat. I closed my eyes and inhaled deeply.

"I like how you smell, too," I whispered, but this time he didn't respond.

After about five minutes or five hours, Sam announced that we should probably head back so no one worried. I slowly crawled to my hands and knees and, with Sam's help, made it into the boat on legs that wobbled as though they were filled with lake water Jell-O. "Drink this," he ordered, passing me a blue Gatorade and wrapping a towel around me. Once I'd had a few gulps, a smile burst across his face again. "I'm so proud of you," he said.

"Told you she was a swimmer," Charlie said to Sam as he pulled me out of the boat, giving my shoulder a squeeze.

"She really is," Sam replied. The smile seemed permanently attached to his face, so much bigger and more open than the lopsided half grin he usually wore. There was an assembly line of hugs when I got out of the boat. First Mom ("You looked great out there, honey"), then Dad ("Didn't know you had it in you, kiddo"), and finally Sue, who squeezed me tightest of all. I was an inch or so taller than her now, and she felt soft and small. She held on to my hands when we pulled away.

"You're an awesome kid, you know that?" Her pale blue eyes crinkled at the corners. "Let's get some food in you. I'm making breakfast."

To this day, I don't think I've ever eaten as much bacon as I did that morning. My parents had gone back to the cottage, but Sue made enough food to feed ten people. She cooked Canadian and regular bacon, and the boys watched with fascinated stares as I dug into piece after piece, along with scrambled eggs, toast, and fried tomato.

At the end of the meal, Sue looked each of us in the eye, and said, "I'm so impressed by each of you this summer. You're really growing up. Charlie, you've been such a help in the kitchen, and, Sam, I'm grateful that you're working with me now, too. I don't know what I'd do without my boys." She said this with total conviction, her voice steady despite the sentiment.

"You'd probably chain some other poor teenager to the dishwasher," Charlie replied.

Sue laughed. "Absolutely. Hard work is good for the soul. And, Percy," she continued, "it takes a lot of dedication to do what you did today—not to mention winning that writing prize of yours. I'm as proud as if you were my own daughter." She patted my hand, then went back to eating her breakfast, as though she hadn't just given me the greatest compliment I'd ever received from a grown-up. When I looked over at Sam, he was beaming.

It was the perfect end to summer.

~~~

Hi Percy,

I know Thanksgiving was just this weekend (still pretty grossed out by how Delilah drooled over Charlie, by the way), but guess what? Mom is going to let me take New Year's Eve off, so we can spend it hanging out.

Sam

~~~

Sam,

Delilah thinks Charlie is cute, but don't worry, she has a crush on her cousin's best friend. She's even forcing me to go on a double date with them, so she'll probably forget all about Charlie. Jealous?

Mom found an old fondue set at a yard sale, and is doing a '70s-themed New Year's dinner. I hope you like melted cheese.

Percy

~~~

Percy,

What kind of terrible person doesn't like melted cheese?

I don't like Delilah like that if that's what you mean. Have you met her cousin before?

Sam

~~~

Sam,

I haven't met Delilah's cousin yet. He's in 12th grade like Charlie, but he goes to a different school. His name is Buckley!!! But everyone calls him Mason because that's his last name, and I guess he doesn't like Buckley. Who would?

Countdown to NYE is on!

Percy

~~~

AS PROMISED, MOM went all in for her '70s New Year's Eve. She made fondue and Caesar salad, and the four of us sat on the floor near the fire dipping hunks of crusty bread into the yellow goo, listening to Joni Mitchell and Fleetwood Mac albums on the old record player of Dad's that Mom had repaired as a Christmas gift.

"This is actually a little gross, all of us putting our forks back into the cheese," I said, and Mom gave me a look.

"But it's so delicious," said Sam, waving a piece of drippy bread in my face.

"Couldn't agree with you more, Sam," Dad said, and plucked the bread from Sam's fork and then popped it into his mouth.

Mom served carrot cake for dessert, and then we played poker with wooden matchsticks until Sam bankrupted us all.

"I'm not sure whether to be disturbed or impressed that a fifteen-year-old can keep such a straight face," my dad commented when he handed over the last of his matches to Sam.

At midnight, Mom let Sam and me have a glass of champagne each, and the bubbles made my hands and face warm. Not long after, my parents made up the couch for Sam with sheets tucked around the cushions, poured the remaining champagne into our glasses, then went to bed.

Sam and I sat facing each other on opposite ends of the couch, the quilt spread over our legs. I was bummed about going back to the city in two days' time and wanted to stay up all night talking. He tapped my leg with his foot under the blanket.

"Are you going to tell me about how your date with Buckley went?" We hadn't discussed Delilah's cousin Mason since I first mentioned him in an email, hoping it would prompt Sam to confess his love. It didn't quite work out according to plan, and I figured Sam had forgotten all about it.

The truth was that Delilah and I had been on a couple of double dates with Mason and his friend, Patel. Last names as first names seemed to be a thing in their circle—they both went to a boys' private school not far from where I lived, and played on the same hockey team.

I was surprised that Delilah would date someone as quiet and soft-spoken as Patel, but he had these huge brown eyes and an even bigger smile.

"I can tell he's deep," she explained when I asked her about it. "Goalies are sexy, and I bet he's an amazing kisser."

Mason was obsessed with hockey and building muscle for hockey and growing out his dark hair so it would curl just right from under his hockey helmet. He had blue eyes like Delilah and was gorgeous like Delilah, and I think he probably knew it like Delilah did, too, but he was actually a pretty nice guy. I just didn't think of him constantly like I did Sam.

"It's Mason," I corrected Sam. "And there's not much to tell."

"Let's start with the basics: Do you like Buckley?" He smirked.

I kicked him. Then shrugged. "He's okay."

"Just okay, huh? Sounds serious." After a moment, he asked, "Don't you think he's a bit too old for you?"

"He's turning eighteen in a few weeks, and I'll be sixteen in February. Besides, we've only been on two dates."

"You didn't tell me about the second one."

Was I supposed to tell him about other boys? He didn't talk to me about girls.

"I didn't think you would care, and it's not like he's my boy-friend or anything," I said defensively.

"But he wants to be." It wasn't a question.

"I'm not sure. I don't think boys think of me like that."

"Like what, Percy?" Was he teasing me? Or did he not know what I meant? My head was fuzzy with confusion and champagne.

"They're not interested in kissing me," I said, looking down at our legs.

He tapped me with his foot again. "That's not true. And for the record, I do care."

~~~

SAM WAS RIGHT: Mason was interested. Delilah and I went to two of his and Patel's hockey games in January. We sat in the stands clutching foam cups of bad hot chocolate to keep our hands warm in the frigid arena. At each game, Mason waved to me from the ice before taking his position at right wing for the puck drop.

I could see why he loved hockey: He was the best player on the team by far. Each time he scored, he'd look up to me in the stands with a big smile on his face. After the second game, Deli-lah and I waited for the guys outside the locker room so we could all go for a pizza. Mason came out, hair damp and smelling of shampoo, with a huge gym bag slung over his shoulder. He wore jeans and a tight long-sleeved crewneck that stretched over his chest and arms. He was even more muscular than Charlie, and I had to admit that he looked pretty hot. When Patel and Delilah walked ahead, Mason pulled me into a doorway, told me he thought I was pretty, and gave me a soft peck on the lips. I said,

"Thank you," and smiled at him a little dazed, unsure of what came next or what he expected of me.

"I like how fresh you are," he laughed.

Both Delilah and I were invited to Mason's eighteenth birth-day party, which was being held at a swanky hotel in Yorkville at the end of the month, complete with a DJ, sushi bar, and a 120-person-long guest list. Delilah had made sure that practically all the girls in our grade knew we were going, and we had been given the appropriate level of awed respect.

The night of the party, we got ready at Delilah's—curling our hair with hot rollers and dabbing on mascara and lip gloss—but when I put on my dress, a slinky red floor-length gown Deli-lah said showed off my "killer body," she let out a horrified, "No way! You cannot wear those!"

"What are you talking about?" I looked down at my gold bal-let flats, confused.

"Those granny panties! Have I taught you nothing? Don't you have a thong?"

I looked at her incredulously. "Not on me!"

"You're hopeless," she sighed, and flung the skimpiest pair of red underwear I had ever seen at me.

"I don't think my mom would be happy about these," I said, holding them up.

"Well, she wouldn't be happy about that panty line, either, believe me," said Delilah.

I shimmied out of my underwear and slipped on the thong.

"Much better!" Delilah said and gave my butt a squeeze. "Mason won't be able to keep his hands off this." The thought made me jittery.

Delilah's parents drove us to the hotel, slipped Delilah a fifty for a cab ride home, and left us at the coat check to mingle.

"I didn't think there'd be so many grown-ups here," I whispered to Delilah, looking around the ballroom—more than half the guests were middle-aged or older.

"My uncle is kind of a big deal on Bay Street. Something to do with the stock market," she hissed back.

We danced together with some of the older girls while the boys watched from slipcovered chairs. At eight p.m., Mason's dad, a tall, soft-looking white-haired man, who Delilah said was "almost done with wife number two," gave a toast to his son, and then, to gasps from the crowd, threw him a set of keys. We all shuffled outside, huddling against the cold, where Mason's new Audi was parked at the entrance. "I'll take it home for you tonight," his dad told him with a wink and slipped him a flask. In less than twenty minutes, the remaining adults had all snuck away.

When the telltale pan flute of a Celine Dion ballad warbled over the speakers, Mason pointed at me, then himself with a smile. I walked over and he put his hands around my waist while I rested mine on the shoulders of his black suit jacket. We swayed back and forth, shuffling around in a circle, and Mason leaned down, pressing his mouth up to my ear.

"You look beautiful tonight, Percy." I looked up at his eyes, which were blue but a darker, muddier blue than Sam's, and he pulled me flush against his body so that my cheek rested at the top of his chest. "I can't stop thinking of you," he whispered.

After the song finished, he pulled me out to the hallway, where Delilah, Patel, three other boys, and an older girl joined us. One of the guys, who introduced himself as Daniels, flashed us a bottle of what he said was vodka from under his suit jacket.

"Shall we relocate the festivities?" he said, wiggling his eyebrows and putting his arm around the girl, who was called Ashleigh.

The boys all had rooms upstairs, and we congregated in the living area of Mason and Patel's suite. Daniels sat in an armchair with Ashleigh on his lap, Delilah and Patel took the sofa, and the two guys sat on the floor, leaving a chair for Mason and me. I perched on the side, but Mason pulled me onto his lap and put an arm around me, resting it on my hip. Daniels passed each of us a glass of vodka and ice. It smelled like nail polish remover and burned my lips even before I took a tiny sip.

"Don't drink it if you don't like it," Mason whispered in my ear so no one could hear, and I smiled gratefully at him, then poured mine into his glass. "Works for me." He smiled back. His thumb moved back and forth on my hip while the group talked about his new car and hockey season. It was pretty tame, considering we were a group of unsupervised teens with a bottle of alcohol, and I noticed that, other than Daniels, who was kneading Ashleigh's butt like pizza dough, no one had a refill. By eleven, the others left for their rooms, and Delilah and I stood to get our coats on.

"Before you leave, Percy, there's something I want to show you," Mason said, running his hands through his hair and sounding a little nervous.

"Yeah, I bet," Patel muttered, and Delilah whacked him in the arm.

Mason led me down a short hall to a sleek-looking bedroom, all taupes and browns, with a king-sized bed and suede headboard. He closed the door behind us and slid the closet open, knelt down, and punched a number into a small safe. When he stood, he was holding a little turquoise box.

"What's this?" I asked. "It's not *my* birthday."

"I know," he said, moving closer. "I was going to save it for your sixteenth, but I couldn't wait. Open it." His eyes moved expectantly over my face. I lifted off the lid to find a turquoise velvet pouch. Inside was a silver bracelet with a chunky, modern clasp.

"I was thinking you might want to be my girlfriend," he said and smiled, "and that maybe you needed something a little more special than this." He held up the arm that wore my friendship bracelet. I had not seen this coming.

"It's gorgeous . . . um . . . wow! I'm not sure what to say!" I stammered. Mason fastened the bracelet around my wrist.

"You can think about it, but I want you to know that I really like you." He put his hands on my hips and pulled me toward him, then brought his lips down onto mine. They were soft as he moved them gently over my mouth. He pulled back enough to look into my eyes and said, "You're so smart and funny and so beautiful and you don't even know it." He kissed me again, harder this time, and I closed my eyes. Images of Sam flashed through my mind, and when Mason ran his tongue over the seam of my lips, my knees felt as though they might buckle, and I grasped his biceps. He placed a string of light kisses on the corner of my mouth, then my nose, and then back on my mouth, and ran his tongue over my lips again. This time I opened to him, and I imagined it was Sam's tongue swirling with my own. Mason groaned and moved his hands down to my backside, pressing himself against my hip. I pulled away.

"I should go; we'll be late back to Delilah's."

Mason didn't protest, just ran his hands up my back and gave me another quick kiss, then took my hand in his.

Next to my embroidered bracelet, the silver one looked garish, and I took it off before Mom picked me up the next morning so she wouldn't ask questions. Delilah was surprised by the gift, which she called "excessive," but she didn't think it meant that Mason wanted to make things more official.

"Of course he likes you, Percy. You're a catch. And your tits have *really* come in this year," she said in a stage whisper. "Keep things light with Mason. I can tell you don't like him the way you like your Summer Boy, but maybe you can just think of it as practice if Sam ever comes around."

I emailed Sam as soon I got home.

Hi Sam,

I've been thinking about my new story more. What do you think about a lake that's haunted by a young girl who fell through the ice in the winter, leaving her twin sister behind? When the sister is a teenager, she comes back to the lake on a camping trip and she sees a strange figure in the woods, which will turn out to be her dead twin who's trying to kill her so she won't be alone. It could be scary and maybe a little sad. Thoughts?

Also: Delilah and I went to Mason's birthday party last night, and he asked me to be his girlfriend. I know you won't be surprised since you guessed that at New Year's, but I was. What do you think I should do?

Percy

~~~~

Percy,

I still think a lake full of zombie fish is the way to go. Just kidding. Creepy dead girl is definitely the best idea yet. Are you going to give the sisters obnoxious twin names, like Lilah and Layla, or Jessica and Bessica?

I asked you this before, but I think it's time to ask again: Do you like Buckley?

Sam

~~~~

Sam,

Why hadn't I thought of Jessica and Bessica before? Genius!!!
Mason's actually a nice guy, but I like someone else more.

<div align="right">Percy</div>

~~~~

Percy,

I think you have your answer.

Sam

9

Now

WE SIT IN THE TRUCK STARING AT THE FLOREKS' HOUSE. OR at least I stare at the house. Sam is watching me.

"It looks amazing," I say. And it does. The lawns are green and mowed, the flower beds are blooming and tidy, and the siding and trim on the house are freshly painted. The basketball net still hangs on the garage. There are terra-cotta pots of happy red geraniums on the porch—Sam probably planted them himself. The thought makes me squishy.

"Thanks," Sam says. "I've been trying to keep it up. Mom would hate to see her gardens taken over by weeds." He pauses, then adds, "But it's also been a good distraction from everything."

"How have you been managing all this on top of the restaurant and work?" I ask, turning to face him and waving my hand at the house. "It's a huge property for one person to maintain." God, how did Sue do it? And raise two kids *and* run the Tavern?

Sam runs a hand over his smooth cheek. Shaving only made

his cheekbones more prominent, his jaw more angled. "I guess I don't sleep much," he says. "Don't look so horrified. I got used to staying up for long stretches when I was a resident. Anyway, I'm grateful I've had something to do. I would have gone crazy sitting around the past year."

Guilt curls around my heart. I hate that he did this alone. Without me.

"Does Charlie help much?"

"Nah. He offered to come back, but he's busy in Toronto." I cock my head, not following. "He works in finance, on Bay Street," Sam explains. "He was up for a big promotion—I told him to stay in the city."

"I had no idea," I murmur. "I guess his boss has better luck getting him to wear a shirt than your mom did."

Sam chuckles. "Pretty sure he wears a suit and everything."

I clear my throat and ask the question I've been wondering all morning, "And Taylor? She lives in Kingston?"

"Yeah, her firm is there. She's not exactly a Barry's Bay girl."

"Didn't notice," I mutter, looking out the window. I can see Sam smile from the corner of my eye before he gets out of the truck and walks around to my side. Opening the door, he offers me a hand to hop down.

"I know how to get out of a truck, you know?" I say, taking his hand anyway.

"Well, you've been gone a long time, city slicker." He grins while I get out. He's got one arm on the door of the truck and the other on the side, caging me with his body. His face turns serious. "Charlie should be home later," he says, eyeing me closely. "He went into the restaurant this morning to help Julien with a few last-minute things for tomorrow."

"It'll be great to see him again," I say with a smile, but my

mouth has gone dry. "And Julien. He's still there, huh?" Julien
Chen was the long-suffering chef at the Tavern. He was terse and
funny and kind of like a big brother to Sam and Charlie.

"Julien's still there. He's been a big help to me and Mom. He
took her to chemo when I had shifts at the hospital, and when
she was in there for the last few months, he stayed with her almost as much as I did. He's taking it pretty hard."

"I can imagine," I say. "Do you ever think he and your
mom . . . you know?" The idea hadn't crossed my mind as a teen,
but as I got older, I thought it might explain why a young, single
man whose cooking skills far surpassed boiling pierogies and
cooking sausages would live in a small town for so long.

"I don't know." He runs his hand through his hair. "I always
wondered why he stuck around for so long. He didn't plan on
spending his life up here—it was just a summer job for him. I
think he had big dreams of opening his own place in the city.
Mom said he stayed for me and Charlie. The last couple of years,
though, I wondered if it was for her."

He looks back down to me with a sad smile, and without saying a word, we both walk around the side of the house and head to
the water. It feels instinctive, like I had walked down this hill only
days ago rather than more than a decade earlier. The old rowboat
is tied to one side of the dock, a new motor attached to the stern,
and the raft floats out from the dock just as it used to. My throat is
thick, but my whole body relaxes at the view. I close my eyes when
we get to the dock and breathe.

"We haven't put the Banana Boat in this year," Sam says, and
my eyes pop open.

"You still have it?" I marvel.

"In the garage." Sam smiles, a flash of white teeth and soft
lips. We walk out to the end of the dock and I steady myself be-

fore looking down the shore. There's a white speedboat attached to a new, larger dock where ours used to be.

"Your cottage looks pretty much the same from the water," Sam says. "But they've put another room on the back. It's a family of four—the kids are probably eight and ten by now. We let them swim over and use the raft."

I have an odd sensation looking out over the water and the raft and the far shore—it's all so familiar, like I'm watching an old family video except the people have been scrubbed out so I can only make out faint silhouettes where they once were. I long for those people—and the girl I used to be.

"Percy?" I don't hear Sam until he puts a hand on my shoulder. He's looking at me funny, and I realize a few tears have managed to sneak out of their holding cells. I wipe them away and try to smile.

"Sorry . . . I feel like I was just transported back in time for a second."

"I get that." Sam is quiet and then crosses his arms across his chest. "Speaking of going back in time . . . think you could still do it?" He nods to the other side of the lake.

"Swim across?" I scoff.

"That's what I thought. Too old and out of shape for it now," he says with a tut.

"Are you screwing with me?" Sam's mouth ticks up on one side. "You brought me here to insult my age and my body? That's low, even for you, Dr. Florek." The other side of his mouth moves upward.

"Your body looks good from where I'm standing," Sam says, looking me up and down.

"Perv." I unsuccessfully fight back a grin. "You sound like your brother." My eyes go wide at what I've just said, but he doesn't seem to notice.

"It's been a long time," he continues. "I'm just saying we aren't as spry as we used to be."

"Spry? Who says 'spry'? What are you, seventy-five years old?" I tease. "And speak for yourself, old man. I am plenty spry. Not all of us have gone soft." I poke his stomach, which is so hard it's like negative percent body fat. He smirks at me. I narrow my eyes, then study the far shore.

"Let's say I do it: swim across the lake. What's in it for me?"

"Other than bragging rights? Hmm . . ." He rubs his chin, and I stare at the tendons snaking along in his forearm. "I'll give you a present."

"A present?"

"A good one. You know I'm an excellent present giver." It's true: Sam used to give the best gifts. Once, he mailed me a worn copy of Stephen King's memoir, *On Writing*. It wasn't a special occasion, but he'd wrapped it up and left a note on the inside cover: *Found this at the secondhand store. I think it was waiting for you.*

"Humble as always, Sam. Any idea what this excellent gift will be?"

"None whatsoever." I can't help the laugh that bubbles out of me or the big grin across my face.

"Well, in that case," I say, unbuttoning my shorts, "how could I refuse?" Sam gapes at me. He didn't think I'd do it. "You better still know how to row."

~~~~~

I LIFT MY shirt over my head and stand with my hands on my hips. Sam's mouth is still hanging open, and while my two-piece is hardly skimpy, I suddenly feel extremely exposed. I have no issues with my body. Okay, yes, I have plenty of issues, but I recognize them as insecurities and don't tend to worry too much about my soft belly or bumpy thighs. My relationship with my body is one of the few healthy ones I have. I go to a regular spin class and do a weight circuit a couple of times a week, but it's mostly because I can manage my stress better when I exercise. I'm by no means as toned as the insufferable women who do spinning in short shorts and sports bras, but that's not the goal. I'm fitish—there are just some jiggles in places I like to think are fine to be a bit jiggly. Sam's gaze runs down to my chest and back to my face.

"I can row," he says, a suspicious glimmer in his eye. He pulls his T-shirt over his head and drops it on the dock. Now I'm the one gaping.

"Are you serious?" I squawk, flailing at his torso, my verbal filter completely removed. Eighteen-year-old Sam was in great shape, but adult Sam has a freaking six-pack. His skin is golden and so is the hair that dusts his broad chest. It gets darker as it forms a line from his belly button to below his jeans. His shoulders and arms are muscular but not in a weirdly thick way.

Sam bends over to take off his socks and sneakers, then rolls up his jeans so his ankles and the bottoms of his calves are bare.

"I know, I've gone soft," he says, his blue eyes glittering like sun on water.

I give him my most unimpressed look. "I'm not sure the shirtlessness is necessary."

"It's sunny out. It's going to be hot in the boat." He shrugs.

"You're trouble." I scowl. "I'm going to assume those aren't just decorative"—I motion at his arms—"and that you'll be able to keep up with me."

"I'll do my best," he says and steps into the boat.

I roll my shoulders and then circle my arms to loosen them up. *What the hell am I doing?* It's not like I've kept up with swimming. Sam pushes off from the dock, turns the boat with the oars so the bow is facing the far shore, and waits for me to dive in. I stand at the edge of the dock watching him, his bare feet propped on the bench in front of him. I look at the water in front of me, then back at him. I'm not sure if it's déjà vu that hits me or the weight of standing in this very spot while Sam drifts in that very boat, but my hands are shaking.

"How old are we?" I call out. It takes him a moment to respond.

"Fifteen?"

I study the rocky beach at the other side of the lake. Adrenaline surges under my skin. I take a deep breath through my nose, then dive in. A sob vibrates through me as I swim under the cool water. If I'm crying when I surface, I have no idea, and I start swimming slowly.

I can see the edge of the boat when I tilt my head for air, and I try to concentrate on how Sam is back beside me and not all the years he wasn't. It doesn't take long before my shoulders are tight with knots and my legs begin to burn, but I keep kicking and slicing my arms through the water.

I'm in a mindless rhythm when a cramp seizes my big toe. I slow down and try curling it up to ease the muscle, but an agonizing pain shoots up my calf. I try to keep kicking but the spasm gets worse, and I have to stop swimming. I grit my teeth trying to tread water and yelp when the cramp doesn't release. I can barely hear Sam shouting until I see the side of the boat right next to me.

"Are you okay?" He looks panicked. I shake my head, and then I feel his hands under my armpits, hauling me out of the water. My stomach scrapes on the side of the boat as he pulls me in, hands at my waist and then under my butt. I fall on top of him in a sopping pile of limbs.

I'm lying with my head on his bare chest, trying to catch my breath. The pain subsides if I stay still, but when I wiggle my toe, it shoots through my leg again, and I hiss.

Only then am I aware of Sam's hands, which tighten on my hips. I'm fully pressed to him, my forehead, my nose, my chest, my stomach—all I want to do is run my tongue across his warm chest and roll my hips against his jeans to relieve what's happening between my thighs. It's totally inappropriate, considering the amount of pain I'm in.

"You okay, Percy?" His voice is strained.

"Cramp," I breathe into his chest. "In my toe and calf. Hurts to move."

"Which leg?"

"Left." I feel Sam's hand move down my thigh to my calf to the muscle. Goose bumps radiate from under his fingers, and a shudder runs through me. He pauses for a second, and I lift my head to look at him. His eyes are dark and unblinking.

"Sorry," I whisper. He shakes his head so slightly it's almost imperceptible.

"It helps to relax the muscle," he says and wraps his whole hand over my calf, applying pressure, then moving in slow circles, kneading gently. My heart is beating so fiercely I wonder if he can feel it, too. I shut my eyes and involuntarily squeeze my thighs together. He must feel the movement because his left hand increases its grip on my hip. I can feel his breath on my forehead.

"Better?" The question comes out in a rasp. I shift my leg slightly, and it does feel better.

"Yeah." I push myself up, but now I'm straddling him awkwardly on the floor of the boat. His chest is slick with the water. I start brushing it off, but he puts his hand around my wrist. He's looking up at me, eyelids heavy.

"You're trouble," he says, echoing my words from earlier. The air between us pulls tight like a rubber band. I take a deep breath, and Sam's gaze follows the rise of my chest, and yep, my nipples are obscene under my top. To be fair, I'm cold and wet.

Sam swallows and meets my eyes again. I've seen this look from him before, stormy and focused and completely consuming, like I could fall into his eyes and never get out. His fingers move slightly at the back of my hip, just under the edge of my bathing suit. His other hand runs up and down the back of my thigh. *What is happening?*

Taylor, I think. *Sam has Taylor*. Sam's hand leaves my thigh and he rubs his thumb over the creases between my eyes, smoothing out the frown lines, then runs it down over my cheek, cupping my face.

"You're still the most beautiful woman I've ever known," he says, and it sounds like coarse sandpaper. I blink at him. His words are confusing and wonderful, and I feel a little high and a lot turned on. But I know we shouldn't be doing this. I shouldn't want this. He traces my lips with his thumb, and the fingers of his other hand dig more deeply into the flesh at the back of my hip.

"This is a bad idea." I choke the words out.

His eyes move rapidly across my face, and he sits up beneath me so that I'm on his lap. He rests his forehead on mine and closes his eyes, taking shallow breaths. *Is he shaking?* I think he's shaking. I move my hands to his shoulders and rub them up and down his arms.

"Hey, it's okay. Old habits, right?" I say, trying to lighten the mood, but my heart is screaming at me. "Why don't we head back and have a swim to cool off," I say, looking around, seeing now that I hadn't even made it halfway across the lake.

When I look back to Sam, his jaw is clenched as though he's trying to decide something, but he only says, "Yeah, okay."

~~~~

SAM HEADS UP to the house to change when we get back from our very short, very quiet boat ride. I had gotten a quick glimpse of my cottage from the water, a flashback of my parents sitting on the deck with cold glasses of wine. Now I sit at the edge of the dock waiting for Sam with my feet in the water, replaying what just happened, lingering on the moment when his fingers slipped under my suit. My hips still tingle where his hands gripped them. I once wanted Sam in every way I could have him—that hasn't changed. And if he had kept going, I would have, too. I'm ashamed by that truth, but it is the truth. I know myself. My self-control is on ice when I'm around him. I wonder if that would be a good premise for a book, a woman with no self-control. I smile to myself—I haven't daydreamed about stories in a long time.

I hear Sam's footsteps behind me, and I look over my shoulder. He's wearing a pair of coral-colored swim trunks that look amazing against his tanned skin and holding a pair of towels and a water bottle.

"What are you thinking about?" He puts the towels down and sits beside me, his shoulder touching mine, and passes me the bottle.

"Just an idea for a story."

"You still write like that?"

"No," I admit. "I don't really write at all."

"You should," he says gently, after a moment. "You were really good. I'm pretty sure I still have an autographed copy of 'Young Blood' in the desk drawer of my old bedroom."

I look at him wide-eyed. "You don't."

"Yeah. Actually, I know I do. It holds up." He must see the question written on my face, because he answers it without me asking. "I've been staying in my old room for a year—I went through my things a while back."

"I can't believe you still have it. I don't think I even have a copy anymore," I say with disbelief.

"Well, you can't have mine." He grins. "It's dedicated to me, if you'll remember."

"Of course," I murmur as my mind drifts into nostalgia. I wish Sue were here. She would have got a kick out of watching thirty-year-old me attempt to swim across the lake without any training.

The question leaves my throat as soon as it enters my head: "Did your mom hate me?" I turn to Sam and watch him puzzle out how to answer. He's silent for a long moment.

"No, she didn't hate you, Percy," he says finally. "She was concerned that we stopped speaking so suddenly. She asked a lot of questions—some of them I had answers for, and others I didn't. And, I don't know, I think she was hurt, too." His blue eyes fix on me. "She loved you. You were family." I press my lips together, hard, and tilt my face skyward.

This is the moment, I think. *This is the moment where I tell him.*

But then Sam speaks again. "I don't, either, by the way."

"You don't what?" I ask, looking at him.

"I don't hate you," he says simply. I hadn't known how badly I needed to hear those words until they left his lips. My bottom lip begins to tremble and I bite down on it, concentrating on the sharpness of my teeth. My courage has vanished. I'm as brittle as dry straw.

"Thanks," I say when I'm certain my voice won't break. Sam bumps me gently with his shoulder. "Shall we?" He slants his head toward the raft. "Maybe we can get some more freckles on that nose of yours." I exhale a nervous laugh. He stands up first, then holds out a hand, pulling me up.

"I would apologize in advance, Percy, but I know I won't be sorry," he says with a smirk, and before I can ask what the hell he means, he picks me up like a sack of flour, and tosses me into the water.

10

Summer, Fourteen Years Ago

IT WAS EASY TO PERSUADE SUE TO LET ME WORK AT THE Tavern. But my parents needed more convincing. They didn't understand why I'd want to spend evenings at the restaurant when finances weren't an issue. I told them that I wanted to earn my own money and, rookie mistake, that I wanted to hang out with Sam. Considering how much time we already spent together, they found this information disturbing and, being a cunning pair of PhDs, took advantage of the drive to Barry's Bay at the beginning of the summer to stage an intervention.

I should have known something was up when Dad came back from our bathroom break holding a twenty-pack of Timbits (a rare treat) that was heavy on the chocolate glazed (my favorite) and then passed the entire box to me to hold on to. (Red flag! Red flag!)

My parents lectured me so rarely, they muddled through it awkwardly. This one was classic:

Dad: "Persephone, you know how much we like Sam. He's . . ."

Mom: "He's a lovely boy. I can't imagine what it's been like for Sue to raise those two boys on her own, but she's done an impressive job."

Dad: "Right. Well, yes. He's a great kid. And we're happy you have a friend at the cottage, kiddo. It's important to expand your social circles beyond Toronto's upper-middle class."

Mom: "Not that there's anything wrong with our circle. You know, Delilah's parents say that Buckley Mason is a very promising young man."

Dad: "Though I don't know about hockey players."

Mom: "The point is that we're concerned you're spending too much time with Sam. You're practically joined at the hip, and now with the restaurant . . . We don't want you to . . ."

Dad: "To get too attached at such a young age."

I told my parents that Sam was my best friend, that he understood me like nobody else did, and that he was always going to be in my life, so they better get used to it. I said having a job would teach me to be more responsible. I left out the unrequited crush part.

Working at the restaurant felt like being a part of a highly choreographed dance, all the performers working together to execute a near-flawless routine that looked a whole lot easier than it was. Sue was a great boss. She was direct but not condescending or short-tempered. She laughed easily and knew at least half of the guests by name, and she managed the crowds with ease.

Julien controlled the back of the house with unspoken power and a glare that could turn your skin icy even in the kitchen's inferno. He was younger than Sue, maybe in his early thirties, but his back was shot from years of lugging sides of pigs and kegs of Polish pilsner. I was terrified of him until I overheard him teasing Charlie on his after-dinner-rush cigarette break: "Good thing you're going to university soon because you're about three girls away from running through the whole town." Anyone who poked fun at Charlie was okay in my book.

Charlie and Julien manned the stoves, grill, and deep fryer together. They had a silent way of communicating, working off the order sheets in a system Julien first learned from Charlie's dad. It was unsettling at first, seeing Charlie like he was at the restaurant, sweaty and serious, his forehead tight with concentration. Every once in a while I'd catch his eye, and he'd toss me a quick smile, but just as fast, he was back to focusing on the food.

Sam, being the younger of the boys, was relegated to the dishwasher and to breaking out each order. He'd pass the sheets to Julien, who'd shout out the series of dishes, and Sam would gather the necessary supplies, running up and down to the basement walk-ins when needed.

The best part of all of it was that Sue put Sam and me on the same schedule: Thursday, Friday, and Saturday nights. I liked catching his eye when I brought back the dirty dishes and how the kitchen steam turned his waves into curls. And I liked cleaning up at the end of the night with him, even though Sam's dishwashing skills often meant running a rack of cutlery through the machine twice. But I liked that, too: Sam was perfect at almost everything but washing up.

~~~

IT WAS A dry summer with fire bans across the county, and I was a tightly wound ball of frustrated teenage sexual energy. Sam picked me up on the way back from his morning runs to swim just like the year before, and on the walk over to his place, I couldn't stop staring at the way his shirt clung to his stomach or the drops of sweat running down his forehead and neck.

Now that he was sixteen, Sam was allowed to drive the Banana

Boat, and we took it to the town dock for a couple of ice creams early one evening in July. We sat on a bench by the water, finishing our cones, debating the merits of animal dissection in biology class, when Sam leaned over and ran his tongue around the rim of my cone, catching the drips of pink and blue. He'd done the same thing last summer, but this was the sexiest thing I'd ever seen.

"You've got the taste buds of a five-year-old," he said as I stared at him with wide eyes.

"You *licked* my ice cream."

"Yeah . . . what's the big deal?" He frowned.

"Like, with your tongue. You've got to stop doing that."

"Why? Are you worried your boyfriend will be mad or something?" He sounded a little angry. Delilah had been the one to convince me to keep seeing Mason, saying there was no point waiting around for my Summer Boy to get a clue. But I had explained to Sam on multiple occasions that Mason was not my boyfriend, that we were dating but that it wasn't serious. Neither Sam nor Mason seemed to understand the distinction.

"For the millionth time, Mason is not my boyfriend."

"But you kiss him," Sam said.

"Yeah, sure. It's no big deal," I replied, not sure where he was going.

He took a bite out of his cone, then squinted at me. "Would you think it was a big deal if I told you I kissed someone?"

My heart exploded into tiny particles. "You kissed someone?" I whispered.

I could tell Sam was nervous because he broke eye contact and looked out at the bay. "Yeah, Maeve O'Conor at the end-of-year dance," he said.

I hated Maeve O'Conor. I wanted to murder Maeve O'Conor.

"Maeve is a pretty name," I choked out.

His blue eyes met mine again, and he pushed his hair off his face. "It was no big deal."

~~~

THE CIVIC HOLIDAY loomed large that summer. For the first time, Mom and Dad were leaving me alone at the cottage. It was also the weekend I'd chosen to swim across the lake again. My parents didn't want to miss my now-annual feat of athleticism, but they were headed to a party in Prince Edward County, where a dean at the university had purchased a farm to turn it into a small winery. It was a must-attend event and almost all they could talk about until they waved goodbye early Saturday morning.

The air was sticky, promising a rain that probably wouldn't fall if the first half of summer was any indication. The grass around the Floreks' house had long ago turned brown, but Sue was determined to keep the flower beds in shape. She went into the restaurant earlier than usual to make extra batches of pierogies for the long weekend crowds, and Sam, Charlie, and I were tasked with watering all the gardens in the baking heat before we left for our shifts.

Like most evenings, we took the Banana Boat to the town dock and walked to the restaurant. I wore my usual—a dark denim skirt and a sleeveless blouse—and I was slick with sweat by the time we got there. I splashed my face with cold water in the bathroom and redid my ponytail, smoothing down the strands that had frizzed in the humidity, then applied a little mascara and pink lip gloss, the sum total of my makeup routine.

The tables were full from the moment we opened the doors, and by the time the last customers had been served, Sue was exhausted. Julien told her she looked like shit and forced her out the door while the rest of us closed up.

"I feel like I've been boiling in pierogi water all night," I told Charlie and Sam when I was done, joining them outside the back door, where they always waited for me, sitting with their backs against the wall, once they had finished in the kitchen. I handed them their tip-outs.

"I've been standing over pierogi water all night," Charlie said, standing to tuck the money in his pocket and pulling on his shirt to show me how damp it was. "You've got nothing to complain about. I'm jumping in the lake when we get home."

He wasn't joking. As soon as we tied up the boat, he jumped onto the dock, unbuttoned his shorts, and peeled off his shirt. Sue had left the porch light on, but it was dark at the water, the moon casting enough of a pale glow that I could just make out Charlie's bare ass when he pulled down his briefs and jumped into the lake.

"Shit, Charlie," Sam said when his head bobbed back up. "Give us some warning."

"Just doing Percy a favor," he laughed. "You kids coming in?" I'd skinny-dipped on hot-hot nights when I couldn't fall asleep but never when anyone else was around. I smelled like cabbage and sausage, and my clothes were plastered to my body. A swim sounded amazing.

"I am," I said, unbuttoning my blouse, ignoring the knots in my stomach. "Turn around while I get undressed." I dropped my shirt on the dock. Charlie swam out farther, and I checked behind me, finding Sam staring at me in my white cotton bra.

"Sorry," he mumbled, then turned away, pulling off his own T-shirt.

I stepped out of my skirt, slid off my underwear, unfastened my bra, and then dove into the water. Sam jumped in seconds later, a flash of white limbs. We kept our distance from each other, but I paddled away further still and turned onto my back, spreading my arms and legs, floating under the open sky. My feet tingled with relief. The water swirled around me, and my eyes grew heavy. Eventually someone splashed me, and Charlie said, "I think it's time to get Percy to bed."

He ran up to the house in his underwear and came back with towels, and Sam walked me home through the path.

"Ready for the swim tomorrow?" he asked when we got to the bottom of the steps.

I hummed in response. "You might have to give me a wake-up call." I said good night, climbed the stairs up to the cottage, and sprawled out naked on my bed.

~~~~~

THE SOUND OF knocking woke me suddenly. I glanced at the clock: 8:01 a.m.

"A phone call would have been fine," I grumbled after I threw on a cotton robe and trudged downstairs to open the door. Sam gave me a guilty half grin, and I motioned for him to come in.

"Thought an in-person alarm would be more effective. You seemed really tired last night." He shrugged. He was wearing a bathing suit and a hoodie. His light brown hair fell over his face in a tumble.

"You know, for such an anal guy, your hair is extremely messy." I glowered.

"Someone's grumpy this morning," he said, slipping off his sneakers.

"I just woke up, and I've really got to pee." I walked to the bathroom. "There are Cheerios in the cupboard and bagels in the bread drawer if you haven't eaten yet."

The phone started ringing mid-pee. "You mind getting that?" I yelled to Sam. "It's probably Mom or Dad."

When I came out, he held the receiver in my direction.

"Hello?"

"Percy, it's Mason." My eyes skipped to Sam's.

"Hey. I didn't think you woke up this early," I replied as Sam turned and busied himself with the toaster. There was no privacy on the main floor of the cottage, and Sam was going to hear every word.

"It's your swim today, right? I wanted to wish you good luck." Mason called the cottage to talk about once a week. If he hadn't, I think I would have forgotten about him almost entirely, the same way I forgot about nearly everything to do with my life back in the city when I was at the lake.

"It is, thanks. It's looking a little gray outside," I said, peering out the window, "but it doesn't seem like there's wind, so I should be good."

"Who was that who answered the phone?"

"Oh, that's Sam." Sam glanced over his shoulder. I'd mentioned him to Mason before, and he knew that we were friends— I just hadn't told him Sam and I were *best* friends or that I was harboring a not-insignificant crush on him. "He's spotting me while I swim, remember?" Sam pointed to himself like, *Who me?* and I bit back a laugh.

"He's there early." It wasn't an accusation. Mason was too sure of himself for jealousy.

"Yeah." I laughed nervously. "He wanted to make sure I got out of bed. Busy night last night."

"Well, I won't keep you. I just wanted to check in before your swim. And"—he cleared his throat—"to tell you that I miss you. I can't wait to see you when you come back. I want to hold you,

Percy." I watched Sam smear cream cheese on a bagel. His forearms were thick and covered in fine, fair hair that glowed in the sun. He looked big in our small kitchen. There wasn't a hint left of the gawky thirteen-year-old boy I met three years ago.

"Me too," I replied, feeling guilty for the lie as it left my mouth. I hadn't really missed Mason at all.

When I hung up, Sam handed me the bagel on a plate.

I thanked him and sat on a stool chewing while he prepared one for himself. When he was done, he stood on the other side of the counter and took a bite out of his breakfast, watching me while he ate.

"Was that the famous Buckley?" he asked, his mouth full. I gave him a flat look.

"Mason."

"Does he call a lot?"

I took a big bite of my bagel to stall. "Every week," I said after a minute. "It's probably good he does, otherwise I might forget he exists."

Sam stopped midchew, his eyebrows lifted in surprise.

"What's with the face?" I asked.

He swallowed and then cleared his throat before answering. "Nothing. It just doesn't sound like you're that into him."

"It's not that I don't like him—he's been sweet."

"Good, Percy. He should be," he said with a hint of exasperation.

"I know. That's not the issue." I looked down at my half-eaten bagel. "I told you before—I like someone else more."

"The same guy you emailed about?" Sam asked quietly as I moved sesame seeds scattered on my plate with my finger. "Percy?"

"Yep, same one," I replied without looking up.

"Does he know?" I looked up at Sam. I couldn't tell if he knew we were talking about him. His expression was impassive.

"I'm not sure," I said. "He can be hard to read."

We finished breakfast in silence, and then I changed into a racer-back swimsuit Mom had bought. She had decided swimming was the perfect hobby and wanted me to try out for the swim team in the fall. I was considering it.

You couldn't call it a nice day—it was muggy and overcast, but at least the lake was flat.

"You seem a lot less antsy today than you did last year," I said as we stepped onto the Floreks' dock.

"I actually had nightmares about it for a full week before you did that swim," he said. "I thought you were going to drown and that I wouldn't be able to save you. Now I know you can do it without breaking a sweat." He kicked off his shoes and pulled his shirt over his head, leaving both on the dock. He rolled his shoulders in backward circles a few times.

"And now you've got all that," I said, motioning at his bare torso, the shadows playing off the ridges of his chest and stomach. He chuckled.

"I'll do a couple of warm-up laps with you, and then we'll head out?"

"Whatever you say, Coach."

Sometime while we were at the water, Sue and Charlie had come out onto the deck with coffees. I waved at them from the water while Sam got the boat ready. And then, giving each other a thumbs-up, we set off.

It wasn't easy, but it wasn't as hard as last summer, either. I didn't need to switch strokes or slow down—I kept a steady, rhythmic pace. My legs were tired but didn't feel as though they were going to drag me to the bottom of the lake with their weight, and my shoulders ached but the pain didn't consume me. When I reached the shore, I sat in the shallow water catching my breath while Sam pulled the boat up on the beach.

"Seven minutes faster than last year!" he announced, hopping out of the boat, dropping a cooler bag on the sand, and sitting in the water beside me, his skin slick with sweat. "I think your mom's right; you should join the swim team. You didn't even stop to catch your breath!"

"Says the guy who practically runs a marathon every morning," I panted.

"Exactly." Sam grinned. "I should know." He passed me a cold bottle of water, and I chugged half, handing the rest to him to finish off. The wind was starting to pick up and the air smelled thick.

"Looks like it could finally rain," I said, watching the breeze dance through the leaves of a poplar.

"That's the rumor. Mom says a big storm is supposed to hit," Sam said, wrapping his arms around his knees. "Too bad she needs me to work an extra shift, otherwise we could do a scary movie night."

"*Blair Witch!*" I suggested.

"Totally. How have we not done that one yet?"

"Well, I have, many times," I said.

"Obviously."

"But never with you," I added.

"A huge oversight," Sam replied.

"The hugest." We grinned.

I was almost catatonic by the time I got back to the cottage, my belly bloated from one of Sue's epic breakfasts and my body completely drained. I passed out on the couch and didn't wake up until well after five, which meant Sam would already be at the

Tavern, whereas I had the night off. My parents left me home alone all the time in the city, but they were always around when we were at the lake. I had fallen asleep so quickly the night before that it had barely registered that they were gone. Now I wasn't quite sure what to do with myself.

Groggy, I shuffled into the bathroom and splashed water on my face, then slurped the cold liquid from my hands. I headed down to the lake with a notebook and sat on one of the Muskoka chairs at the foot of the dock. The wind had picked up since morning and was throwing whitecaps over the gray water. I jotted down a few ideas for my next story, but soon raindrops began to fall on the pages, and I was chased inside.

I boiled a hot dog for dinner and ate it with some of the rice and bean salad Mom had left. Bored, I riffled through our DVD collection until I found *The Blair Witch Project*.

It was a terrible choice. It scared me every single time I'd seen it, and I had never watched it alone. In a cabin. In the woods. On a dark and stormy night. Halfway through, I paused the movie, locked the doors, and did a sweep of the cottage, checking the closets, beneath the beds, and behind the shower curtain. Just as I pressed play again, a loud crack of thunder shook the cottage, and lightning quickly followed. With every flash, I expected to see a gruesome face pressed up against the back door window. By the time the movie ended, the storm had passed, but it was dark and rainy, and I was totally freaking out.

I made myself popcorn and put on *Uncle Buck*, hoping for a comedic distraction, but not even John Candy and Macaulay Culkin could calm me down. The wind wasn't helping things, sending bits of bark and small branches flying onto the roof in a symphony of scratches and *thunk*s. And, *wow*, I had never noticed how much the cottage creaked. It was just after eleven when I broke down and called the Floreks' number.

The phone had barely rung when Sam picked up.

"Hey, sorry to call so late, but I'm kind of losing it here—the wind is making weird noises, and I just watched *Blair Witch*, which I guess was pretty stupid. There's like no way I can sleep here by myself tonight. Can I stay over there?"

"You can stay over me. You can stay under me," the voice on the other end drawled. "Any way you want, Pers."

"Charlie?" I asked.

"The one and only," he replied. "Disappointed?"

"Not at all. I've never been more turned on," I deadpanned.

"You're a cruel woman, Percy Fraser. Let me hang up on the other line, and I'll get Sam for you."

Sam was at the door in less than five minutes, standing under an umbrella. I thanked him for walking over and apologized for being so childish.

"I don't mind, Percy," he said, then took the tote I'd thrown my toothbrush and pj's into.

He rolled his eyes when I asked if he'd brought a flashlight, because when had he ever needed a flashlight, and as we set out, I linked my arm through his, staying as close to him as possible. I almost screamed when I heard rustling in the bush and then the snap of a twig, and I wrapped my free arm around Sam's waist, gluing myself to his side.

"It's probably a raccoon or a porcupine," he said, laughing, but I kept a tight grip on him until we stepped onto the porch.

"We'll have to be quiet," he whispered as we crept inside. "Mom's already asleep. Busy night."

"You're not going to lock that?" I pointed to the door behind us as Sam moved toward the kitchen.

"We never lock it. Not even when we go out," he said, then seeing the sheer terror in my eyes, walked back over and turned the dead bolt.

The main floor was in darkness, and the faint sound of Charlie watching TV in the basement drifted up the stairs. Sam poured two glasses of water, and I studied the shadows that filled the hollows beneath his cheekbones. I couldn't remember when they had gotten so prominent.

"I'll take the couch down here, and you can sleep in my bed," he said, handing me a glass.

"I really don't want to sleep alone," I whispered. "Can't we both just sleep in your room?"

Sam ran his hand through his hair, thinking. "Yeah. We have an air mattress somewhere in the basement. Takes a while to inflate, but I'll go get it." It was late, and I didn't want to put Sam out more than I already had, but when I suggested we share his bed, he sputtered.

"I swear I don't kick in my sleep," I promised. His jaw twitched and he ruffled his hair again.

"Yeah, okay," he said uneasily. "But I need to shower. I smell like onions and deep fryer grease."

~~~~~

I BRUSHED MY teeth in the main floor bathroom and changed into the cotton shorts and tank top I usually slept in, arranged my hair in a thick braid, and then waited for Sam in his bedroom, which was neat and orderly even though he hadn't planned on having a guest over. The photo of us sat on his desk, and *Operation* stood upright on the top of his bookshelf next to a photo of him with his dad. I had knelt down to get a better look at his set of Tolkiens when he came in, softly closing the door.

"I've never read these," I said without looking up. He crouched down beside me and took out *The Hobbit*. His hair was damp and neatly combed off his face. He smelled soapy.

"I'm pretty sure you'd hate it, but you're welcome to borrow it." He handed me the book. "There's a lot of singing."

"Huh . . . I'll give it a try, thanks." We stood at the same time, and Sam loomed over me. When I looked up at him, he was turning a very pink shade of pink.

"That's the shirt you wear to bed?" he asked. I looked down, confused. "It's a little low from up here," he croaked. The tank top was white with thin straps and, come to think of it, was kind of on the revealing side. A prickly heat climbed up my chest and neck.

"You could solve that problem by not looking down it," I muttered, though a part of me—a big, hungry part—was thrilled. He ran his hand through his hair, messing it up.

"Yeah, sorry. They were just . . . there."

I eyed his cozy pants and T-shirt. It seemed like a lot of clothes for such a warm night. "Is that what *you* usually wear to bed?"

"Yeah . . . in the winter it is."

"You do know it's the middle of summer, right?" He shifted on his feet. It hit me then that Sam was nervous. Sam was almost never nervous.

"I'm aware. When it's hot, I, uh"—he rubbed his neck—"I usually, you know, sleep in my boxers."

"Okaaaay," I murmured. "Sweats it is."

We both looked over at the single bed. "This isn't going to be weird, right?" I asked.

"Nope," he said without confidence.

Sam folded back the navy-blue top sheet, and I climbed in. I wasn't sure what the protocol was here. Should I face the wall? Or was that rude? Maybe I should lie on my back? I hadn't made a decision when Sam sat down beside me, our bodies touching from shoulder to hip. I could smell his peppermint toothpaste.

"Do you want the light on to read?" He eyed the book I was still holding.

"I'm still pretty tired from the swim today, actually." I passed him the paperback, and he placed it on the nightstand and shut off the lamp.

I decided lying on my back was best, and shuffled down the bed so my head was on the pillow. Sam followed suit. We were squished up against each other. I lay there with my eyes open for a good ten minutes, my heart racing and my skin sizzling everywhere it touched his.

"I'm really hot," he whispered. Apparently neither one of us was sleeping.

"Just take off your sweats and the shirt," I hissed. "It's fine. I've seen you in your bathing suit. Boxers aren't too different." He hesitated for a few seconds, then wiggled his pants off and pulled his T-shirt over his head. I couldn't tell, but I think he folded them before putting them on the floor. We were still both awake when Sam turned his head toward me, his breath hitting my cheek.

"I'm glad this isn't weird," he said. I burst out laughing. He tried to shush me through his own laughter, but that just set me off even more. He rolled over to face me, putting his hand over my mouth. Every cell in my body came to a halt.

"You'll wake Mom, and, believe me, you don't want to do that," he whispered. "She was so tired she took her wineglass to bed with her." He slowly took his hand away, and I fought the urge to put it back on my face. We lay there silently, him turned toward me, until he spoke.

"Percy?" he asked, and I rolled onto my side. I could barely make out the shape of his body—the nights up north gave new meaning to the word *dark*. "Do you remember when I told you about kissing Maeve?"

My heart picked up a pair of drumsticks.

"Yeah," I murmured, not sure I wanted to hear what came next.

"It didn't mean anything. I mean, I don't like her like that."

The question flew out like a reflex: "Why did you kiss her then?"

"We went to the end-of-year dance together, and the last slow song of the night was playing . . . and, I don't know, it just seemed like the obvious move."

"You asked her to the dance?" He had told me he went, but he didn't say he had gone with a date.

"She asked me," he clarified. "I know I didn't tell you, but I figured we don't really talk about this stuff. I wasn't sure."

I chewed on this for a second, then asked, "Was that your first kiss?" Sam was quiet. "You're not going to tell me? You were there for mine."

"No," he replied.

"No, it wasn't your first kiss, or no, you aren't going to tell me?"

"It wasn't my first kiss. I'm sixteen, Percy."

"When?" My voice was hoarse.

"You sure you want to know?" he asked. "Because you sound a little weird."

"Yes," I hissed. I wanted to scream. "Just tell me."

"It was last year—a girl from school. She asked me to go skating, and she pushed me in the penalty box and then kissed me. It was kind of crazy."

"She sounds psycho."

"Yeah, we didn't go out again." He paused. "But I went out a couple times with Jordie's sister's friend, Olivia." *Jordie's sister is a year older than us.*

"And you kissed her?" My voice was strangled. My head was

spinning. Three girls. Sam had kissed three girls. Sam had kissed an eleventh-grade girl. It shouldn't have surprised me. He was cute and sweet and smart, but he was also mine, mine, all mine. The thought of another girl spending time with him, let alone kissing him, made me nauseated.

"Um, yeah. We kissed." He hesitated. "And we fooled around a bit."

"You *fooled around* with an eleventh-grade girl?" I squeaked.

"Yeah, Percy. Is that so surprising?" He sounded offended. "You don't make out with your boyfriend?" I took a deep breath.

"He. Is. Not. My. Boyfriend." I was whisper-yelling. I shoved Sam's shoulder once, then again, and he grabbed my wrist, holding it against his bare chest.

"And you don't make out with your non-boyfriend?" he asked.

"I'd rather make out with someone else," I blurted, immediately wanting to suck the words back into my throat.

"Who?" Sam asked. My skin went tight with adrenaline, but I kept my mouth shut. He squeezed my wrist slightly, and I wondered if he could feel how quickly my pulse raced. "Who, Percy?" he asked again. I groaned.

"Don't make me tell you," I said so quietly I wasn't sure if I'd said it out loud, but then I felt Sam's hot breath on my face and the press of his nose and forehead against mine.

"Please tell me," he pleaded softly. I was overwhelmed by him—this smell of his shampoo, his damp hair, the heat coming from his body.

I swallowed thickly, then whispered, "I think you know."

Sam stayed silent, his mouth inches from my own, but his thumb began to move in back-and-forth strokes across my wrist.

"I want to be sure," he murmured.

I closed my eyes, took a deep breath, and let the words fall from me.

"I'd rather kiss you."

As soon as the admission left my mouth, Sam's lips were on my lips, pressing and urgent. It felt like jumping off a cliff into warm honey. Just as quickly, he pulled back and rested his forehead against mine, taking quick, shallow breaths.

"Okay?" he whispered.

I shook my head. "More."

He closed the gap between us, peppering kisses on my lips, sweet and soft, but not nearly enough, and when he let go of my wrist, I put my hand in his hair, holding him closer. I ran my tongue over the crease of his bottom lip, then pulled it into my mouth. He moaned and suddenly his hands were everywhere all at once, on my back, over my hips, across my stomach. And then his tongue met mine, minty and teasing. I wrapped a leg around his and pulled our hips together. A pained, desperate noise vibrated from the back of Sam's throat, and he gripped my side, putting a sliver of space between us.

"You all right?" I asked. He didn't respond. "Sam?"

"I'm nodding," he said.

"Sorry," I whispered. "I got a little carried away."

"Don't be sorry. I liked it." He took a deep breath, then paused before adding, "But I think we should probably try to sleep. Otherwise *I'll* get carried away."

I nodded.

"Percy?" he asked.

"I'm nodding."

And then he kissed me again. At first it was slow, all hot tongue and gentle sucking. I whimpered, wanting more, more, more, and moved my hands down his back and into the waistband of his boxers. In reply, he grabbed my butt and pulled me against him. I could feel his excitement, and I pressed into him. He sucked in his breath and froze.

"We need to stop, Percy." Before I could ask if I'd done something wrong, he rasped, "I'm like really close."

I exhaled in relief. "Okay."

He brushed my face with his fingertips. "So . . . sleep?"

"Or something like that," I laughed quietly. Eventually, I turned to face the wall, a smile on my face. Somehow I did fall asleep, and just before I drifted off, I heard Sam whisper, "I'd rather kiss you, too."

~~~

SOMETHING WOKE ME suddenly. I opened my eyes, not sure where I was, feeling a weight across my middle. I blinked at the wall a few times before remembering.

I was in Sam's bed.

With Sam.

Who had kissed me.

Who had his arm wrapped around me.

Two hard knocks sounded on the door. I gasped. Sam's hand moved over my mouth.

"Sam, it's nine o'clock," Sue called. "I just wanted to make sure you didn't want to get out for a run."

"Thanks, Mom. Be down in a bit," he called back. We lay still as her footsteps moved away from the door, then Sam took his hand from my mouth, keeping his arm snug around me. I wiggled back into him, and I felt him hard against my backside.

"Sorry," he whispered. "It just happens when I wake up."

"So I have nothing to do with it? My ego might take offense at that."

"Sorry," he said again.

"Stop apologizing," I hissed.

"Right, sor . . ." He leaned his head on my back and shook it back and forth. "I'm nervous." The words were muffled against my skin.

"Me, too," I admitted. "But I don't mind. It's kind of nice."

"Yeah?"

"Yeah." I pressed back into him again. He swore under his breath.

"Percy." He held my hip away from him. "We have to go have breakfast with my mom, and I'm going to need a minute."

I smiled to myself, then turned over to face him. His hair was more rumpled than usual, and his blue eyes were hooded with sleep. He looked cute. Sam was doing a similar inspection of me, his eyes moving back and forth over my face and quickly down to my top.

"Good morning," I said.

"I like this shirt." He grinned lazily and ran his finger over the strap.

"Perv," I laughed, and he kissed me, hard and deep and long, so that I was out of breath when he pulled away.

"One for the road," he said, then added, "I'm getting you a sweatshirt. Charlie doesn't need to enjoy your pj's."

I followed Sam downstairs, wearing one of his hoodies, which came down to my thighs. Sue was sitting in her spot at the kitchen table in a floral robe, drinking a coffee, her hair pulled into a haphazard bun atop her head, reading a romance novel. There was a faint smile across her lips. It disappeared as soon as she saw us hovering at the doorway.

"Percy slept over last night," Sam explained. "She called after you went to sleep—freaked herself out watching horror movies."

"I hope that's okay, Sue. I didn't want to be alone."

Sue looked between us. "And where did she sleep?"

"In my bed," Sam replied. I would have lied to my parents before admitting a boy slept in my bed. But Sam wasn't much for lying.

"Sam, fix two bowls of cereal," Sue ordered. He did as he was told, and I sat across from her, making uncomfortable small talk about my parents' trip. Once Sam came to the table, she cleared her throat.

"Percy, you know you're always welcome here. And, Sam, you know I trust you. However, given how much time you two spend together and now that you're getting older, I think it's time we had a serious talk." I glanced at Sam; his jaw hung open. I twisted my bracelet underneath the table.

"Mom, that's really not necess—" Sue cut him off.

"You are far too young for any of it," she began, looking at each of us. "But I want to make sure if anything ever happens between the two of you—or with anyone else," she added with her hands raised when Sam tried to interrupt, "that you are being safe and that you are being respectful toward one another."

I looked down at my cereal. There was nothing to disagree with.

"Percy, Sam told me you're seeing an older boy in Toronto." I lifted my eyes to meet hers.

"Yeah, sort of," I murmured.

She pinched her lips together, disappointment flickered in her eyes. "Do you like this boy?"

"Mom!" Sam was red with embarrassment. Sue leveled him with a look, then turned back to me. I could feel Sam's eyes on me, too.

"He's nice," I offered, but Sue waited for more. "I'm pretty sure he likes me more than I like him."

Sue reached over and put her hand on mine, fixing me with her eyes. I knew where Sam got that from. "I'm not surprised. You're a kind, smart girl." She squeezed my hand and then leaned back. She went on in a sterner voice, "I don't want you to ever feel like you have to do anything you don't want to with any boy, no matter how nice he is. There's no rush. And anyone who wants to rush isn't worth rushing for. Does that make sense?"

I told her it did.

"Don't take any crap from any boy—not even my own sons, okay?"

"Okay," I whispered.

"And you," she said, looking to Sam. "The best girls are worth waiting for. Trust and friendship come first, then the other stuff. You're only sixteen, just about to start eleventh grade. And life, hopefully, is long." She smiled sadly. "Okay, that's enough mom talk," she said, putting both hands on the table and pushing herself out of the chair.

"Oh! One more thing: If Percy wants to sleep over again, you, my dear son, will be on the couch."

~~~~

MY PARENTS RETURNED and so did the hot, dry days, turning the air thin and dusty. A small brush fire started on the rocky point across from the cottage. We saw smoke billowing from the scrub and then watched boaters pull up to help put it out. Sam, Charlie, and I took the Banana Boat over and anchored it just out from shore. I waited while the boys joined the water-bucket chain. The flames were only ankle height, but when Sam and Charlie climbed back into the boat after it had been put out, they were so chuffed with themselves you'd have thought they had rescued a baby from a burning building.

Sam and I swam and worked and talked about pretty much everything—how tired he was of small-town life and small-town thinking, how I was considering trying out for the swim team, the finer points of the *Saw* movies—but we never talked about the night we kissed. I wasn't sure how to bring it up. I was waiting for the perfect moment.

Mason phoned the cottage landline now and then, but we only talked for a few minutes until the conversation fizzled out. After one of our calls, Dad looked at me over the top of his glasses and said, "Every time you talk to that kid, you look like you're trying to go to the bathroom after eating too much cheese." *Gross.* But he had a point. I just didn't want to break things off with Mason on the phone. I was waiting until I got back to the city.

The weather changed the third week of August. A thick cover of dark clouds settled over the province, their overstuffed bellies drenching everything from Algonquin Park to Ottawa. Cottagers packed up early and left for the city. A light mist moved in over the lake, making everything look black and white. Even the green hills on the far shore looked gray, as though they had been shrouded in gauze. Dad wasn't much of an outdoorsman and was happy to have us all inside, keeping the fire fed to ward off the damp. Mom and I snuggled up on the couch. I worked on my story while she made her way through a half-dozen books she was considering adding to her gender-relations course syllabus. Sam sat at the table working on a one-thousand-piece puzzle of fishing lures with Dad, who talked animatedly to him about Hippocrates and ancient Greek medicine. I tuned it out, but Sam was captivated. Just like working at the restaurant gave me a taste of freedom in the form of a paycheck, I got the sense that talking with my dad gave Sam a window into a larger world of possibilities. I think I gave him that, too, in a way. He loved it when I talked about the city and the different places I'd visited—the museums, the huge movie theaters and concert halls.

After six straight days of heavy rain, I woke up to the sun beaming in through the triangles of glass in my bedroom, the reflection off the lake dappling the walls and ceiling. Sam took me on a hike through the bush, following a streambed that had been dry all season but was now bubbling over the rocks and branches in its way. The weather had turned cool after the rain, and I wore blue jeans and my old U of T sweatshirt; Sam had thrown on a plaid flannel button-up, rolling the sleeves past his forearms. It was damp underfoot and mushrooms had sprouted up all over the forest floor, some with jolly yellow-and-white domed caps and others with flat pancake tops.

"Here we are," Sam announced after we'd walked through dense bush for about fifteen minutes. I peered around his shoulder and saw that the gentle slope we'd been climbing had flattened, making a small pool of water. A fallen tree, covered in emerald moss and pale lichen, lay across its middle.

"I like to come here in the spring when the snow has just melted," he said. "You wouldn't believe how loudly the water in this stream rushes." He climbed onto the tree and scooted down, patting the spot beside him. I shimmied over till we were both sitting with our legs dangling above the pond.

"It's beautiful," I said. "I'm kind of waiting for a gnome or fairy to appear from over there." I pointed to a thick, rotting tree stump with brown mushrooms growing at its base. Sam chuckled.

"I can't believe we're going back to the city next weekend," I murmured. "I don't want to leave."

"I don't want you to, either." We listened to the gurgle of the stream, swatting away mosquitoes, until Sam spoke again.

"I've been thinking," he began, his voice quiet and shaky but his eyes direct.

I knew what was coming. Maybe I'd been waiting for it. I tilted my head down so my dark hair fell around my face, and studied our feet.

"About us. I've been thinking about us," he said, then nudged my foot with his. I peered over at him—the humidity had made his hair curl at the ends—and smiled weakly.

"I can't tell you how many times I've thought about kissing you that night in my room." He gave me a shy grin, and I looked toward the ground again.

"You think it was a mistake, don't you?"

"No! That's not it at all," he said quickly and put his hand over mine, lacing our fingers together. "It was incredible. I know it sounds corny, but it was the best night of my life. I think about it all the time."

"Me too," I whispered, looking at our reflections in the pool below.

"You and me are special," he started. "There's no one else I'd rather spend time with than you. There's no one else I'd rather talk to than you. And there's no one else I'd rather kiss than you." He paused, and my stomach swooped. "But you're more important to me than kissing. And I'm worried that if we rush that side of things we'll fuck up everything else."

"So what are you saying?" I asked, looking at him. "You just want to be friends?"

He took a deep breath.

"I don't think I'm saying this right." He sounded frustrated with himself. "What I mean is that you're not just any friend to me . . . you're my best friend. But we go for months without seeing each other, and we're really young, and I've never had a girlfriend before. I don't know how to do relationships, and I don't want to screw it up with you. I want to be everything, Percy. When we're ready."

I fought the stinging in my eyes. I was ready. I wanted everything now. At sixteen, Sam was it for me. I knew it then, and I think I knew it that night three years ago when Sam and I sat on my bedroom floor eating Oreos and he asked me to make him a bracelet. I moved my eyes to his wrist.

He pulled my hair back from the side of my face, and I squeezed my eyes shut. "Can you look at me, please?"

I shook my head.

"Percy," he pleaded while I wiped a tear with my sleeve. "I don't want to put pressure on you and me that we can't handle. We've both got big plans—eleventh and twelfth grade will decide what schools we can get into and whether I can get a scholarship." I knew how important grades were to Sam, how expensive his schooling would be, and how he was counting on an academic prize to help with tuition.

"So we just go back to being friends like nothing happened, and then what? We find other boyfriends and girlfriends?" I glanced at him. I could see the agony and worry on his face, but I was angry and embarrassed, even though, somewhere deep, I knew what he was saying made sense. I didn't want to screw things up, either. I just figured we could handle it. Sam was the most mature boy I knew. He was perfect.

"I'm not looking for another girlfriend," he said, which made me feel a teeny-tiny bit better. "But I realize I'd be a huge jerk if I told you I don't think we should be together right now and then asked you not to see anyone."

"You're a huge jerk either way," I said. I meant it as a joke, but it tasted like burned coffee on my tongue.

"Do you really mean that?"

I shook my head, attempting a smile. "I think you're pretty great," I said, my voice breaking. Sam's arm encircled my shoulders, and he squeezed tight. He smelled like fabric softener and damp soil and rain.

"Swear on it?" he said, his words muffled by hair. I felt for his bracelet blindly and tugged.

"I think you're pretty great, too," he whispered. "You have no idea how much."

11

Now

SAM AND I ARE LYING ON THE RAFT, EYES SHUT TO THE SUN.
I'm drifting in a haze—of his hands on my hips and his fingers
on my calf and *You're still the most beautiful woman I've ever known*—
when a shout comes from the shore.

"This is a sight for sore eyes." I sit up, shielding my face.
Charlie is standing on the hill. I can see his dimples from the
water, and I can't help but grin back. I wave. "You kids hungry?"
he calls down. "I was thinking of turning on the barbecue." I
look at Sam, who's now sitting up beside me.

"I don't need to stay," I offer. Sam scans my face briefly.

"Don't be weird," he says. "Food sounds great," he yells back
to Charlie. "We'll be up in a sec."

Charlie is on the front deck lighting the barbecue when we join
him. I'm wearing a towel wrapped around my shoulders and Sam is
rubbing his hair dry. I sneak a peek at the muscles that run up the
side of his torso before Charlie turns to face us. When he does, his
eyes light up like fireflies. His hair is cropped so close to his head it's

only a little longer than a buzz cut. His square jaw looks like it's made from steel. It's in direct contrast to the sweetness of his dimples and his pretty plush lips. He's barefoot and wearing a pair of olive-colored shorts and a white linen shirt, the sleeves rolled up and the top three buttons undone. He's not as tall as Sam, and he's built like a firefighter, not a banker. He's still movie-star good-looking.

Those Summer Boys did an exceptional job of growing up. Delilah Mason's squeal rings in my ears, and her absence gnaws at my gut.

Charlie glances at Sam before embracing me tightly, apparently not worried about my wet bathing suit. "Persephone Fraser," he says when he pulls away, shaking his head. "It's about fucking time."

Charlie makes sausages he grabbed from the Tavern with grilled peppers, sauerkraut, and mustard, and a Greek-style salad that looks like it could be photographed for a food magazine. There's something different about Charlie. He's paying closer attention to Sam than he ever did when we were kids. Every so often, he sneaks a long look at Sam as if he's checking on him, and he's been ping-ponging between us like we're some kind of riddle he's trying to unravel. His eyes still dance like spring leaves in the sunlight, and he wears his smile easily, but he's lost the lightness he had when we were younger. He seems sad and maybe a bit on edge, which I guess makes sense given the circumstances.

"So, Charlie," I say with a grin as we eat, "I've met Taylor already. Tell me about the woman you're seeing this month." It sounded funny enough in my head, but Charlie is giving Sam a tense glare. I see Sam shake his head ever so slightly, and Charlie's jaw flexes.

"You've got to be kidding me," Charlie mumbles.

They eye each other silently, then Charlie turns to me. "No girlfriend right now, Pers. You interested?" He winks, but his voice is flat. My face flushes hot.

"Sure. Just let me drink about fifty more of these," I say, picking up my empty beer bottle. Charlie's face splits into a smile, a real one.

"You haven't changed a bit, you know that? It's kind of freaking me out."

"I'll take that as a compliment." I hold up my beer. "Who wants another?"

"Sure," Sam says, but he's still shooting daggers at Charlie.

I gather up the dirty plates, rinse them off, and stack them in the washer. The house is pretty much the same as when I was a teenager—the walls have been painted and there are a few new pieces of furniture, but that's about it. It still feels like Sue. It still *smells* like Sue. I grab three more beers, and just as I'm about to head back out, I hear Charlie's raised voice.

"You never learn, Sam! It's the same shit all over again."

Sam murmurs something harshly, and when Charlie speaks again, he's quieter. I can't make out what he says, but he's obviously upset. I leave the beers on the counter and slip away to the bathroom. Whatever's going on, I know I'm not supposed to hear it. I splash water on my face, count to thirty, then head back to the kitchen. Charlie is grabbing his wallet off the top of the fridge.

"You're leaving already?" I ask. "Did I say something wrong?" Charlie walks around the counter to me.

"No, you're perfect, Pers." His pale green eyes move across my face, and I feel a little light-headed. He tucks a strand of hair behind my ear. "I made plans to catch up with some old friends. I don't get back here as much as I'd like."

"Sam said you live in Toronto. You never looked me up."

He shakes his head. "Didn't think that would be a good idea." He looks over his shoulder at the sliding door that leads to the deck. "I know he seems like he's got it all together, but don't let that big brain of his fool you—he's a moron a lot of the time."

"Spoken like a true brother," I say, not sure what he's getting at. "Listen, before you head out, I just wanted to say thank you for calling me."

"Like I said, I thought you should be here. It feels right." He steps toward the doorway, then turns around. "I'll see you tomorrow, okay? I'll save you a seat."

"Oh," I say, taken aback. "You don't have to do that." I shouldn't sit with the Florek family. I'm not family. Maybe I was once but not now.

"Don't be silly. Besides, I could use a friend. Sam will have Taylor."

I blink at how sharply that sentence hits me, then nod.

"Sure. Of course."

After Charlie closes the front door behind him, I head out to the deck with a couple of beers. It's early evening now and the sun is starting its slow descent into the western sky. Sam is standing, his forearms on the railing, staring out over the water.

"You okay?" I ask, moving beside him and handing him a beer.

"Yeah. Believe it or not," he says, looking at me from the corner of his eye, "Charlie and I get along way better than we used to. But he still knows how to push my buttons."

We finish our beers in silence. The sun is hitting the hills on the far side of the lake with a magical golden light. I let out a sigh—this was always my favorite time of day at the cottage. A boat full of cheering teens roars past, pulling a young woman on water skis. A few seconds later, waves from the lake crash against the shore.

"I haven't been sleeping," Sam says, still staring ahead.

"You mentioned that," I reply. "It makes sense—you're going through a lot right now."

"I'm used to functioning with hardly any sleep because of

work, but I could always crash when I had the chance. Now I just lie there, wide awake, even though I'm exhausted. Do you ever have that?" I think about all the nights I used to lie in my bed, thinking about Sam for hours on end. Wondering where he was. Wondering who he was with. Counting the years and days since I'd seen him last.

"Yeah, I've had that," I say, glancing at him. The setting sun is kissing the high points of his cheekbones and the tips of his eyelashes.

"I'd blame it on my old bed, but I've been using it for the past year."

"Wait a sec. The same bed you used to have? It must be half your size!"

He laughs softly. "It's not that bad. I thought about moving into Mom's room a few months ago, when it was clear she wasn't coming back from the hospital, but the thought just depressed me."

"And what about Charlie's room?" Charlie had a double bed growing up.

"Are you kidding? I'm fully aware of how many girls he had in that room. I *definitely* wouldn't have got any sleep."

"Well, presumably the sheets have been washed at least once in the last decade," I say, laughing and watching the skier take another lap around the lake. I can feel Sam looking at me.

"Whatcha thinking about?" I say, not moving my gaze from the water.

"I have an idea," Sam says. "Come with me." His voice is soft, a low nuzzle.

I follow him through the sliding door, into the kitchen, and then he opens the door to the basement, flicking on the light in the stairwell. He holds his arm out for me to descend first. I walk down the creaky stairs and stop suddenly when I get to the bottom landing.

Other than a new flat-screen, it's exactly the same. Same red plaid couch, same brown leather armchair, same coffee table, all in the exact same spot. The patchwork afghan hangs over the back of the couch, and the floor is still covered with scratchy sisal carpeting. The same family photos hang on the wall. Sue and Chris on their wedding day. Baby Charlie. Baby Sam with toddler Charlie. The boys sitting in a gigantic snowbank, their cheeks and noses pink from the cold. Awkward school pictures.

Sam stands behind me on the landing, and his closeness makes the back of my neck prick.

"Is this a time machine?"

"Something like that." He moves around me and crouches beside a large cardboard box in the corner of the room. "I'm not sure if you'll think this is awesome or if you'll think I'm nuts."

"Can't it be both?" I ask and kneel down beside him.

"It's definitely both," he agrees. He lifts the corner of the lid and then pauses, his eyes meeting mine. "I think I bought these for you." He untucks the four flaps over the top of the box and holds them open so I can see inside. I look back up at Sam.

"Are these all . . ."

"Yep," he says before I finish my question.

"There must be dozens."

"Ninety-three, to be precise." I begin pulling out the DVDs. There's *Carrie* and *The Shining* and *Aliens*. The Japanese and American versions of *The Ring*. *The Evil Dead*. *Misery*. *Poltergeist*. *Scream*. *Creature from the Black Lagoon*. *The Silence of the Lambs*. *A Nightmare on Elm Street*. *Leprechaun*. *Alien*. *Land of the Dead*. *It*. *The Changeling*.

"And you've never watched them?"

"Told you you'd think I was crazy." That's not what I'm thinking. I'm thinking that maybe Sam missed me as much as I missed him.

"I think I rubbed off on you, Sam Florek."

"You have no idea," he replies.

"I think I do." I hold up the first and second *Halloween* movies and smile. He chuckles and rubs his forehead.

"It's your turn to pick," he announces.

"You want to watch one?" Somehow I didn't see that coming.

"Yeah, I thought we could." Sam narrows his eyes.

"Like right now?" This almost feels more intimate than what happened in the boat earlier.

"That's the idea," he says, then adds, "I wouldn't mind the distraction."

"Do you even have something to watch these things on?" He points at the PlayStation. I screw my mouth up. Looks like we're watching a movie.

"Do you have popcorn?"

Sam smiles. "Of course."

"Okay. You go make some, and I'll choose a movie." I give the order with confidence, but really I just need a minute alone, away from Sam. Because I feel like I've been scraped over a cheese grater.

Once Sam heads upstairs, I take my phone out of my back pocket. There's a missed call from Chantal and several texts wanting to know how my run-in with Sam went. I cringe and shove the phone back in my pocket and then riffle through the DVD box.

I can do this, I think. I can be friends with Sam. I don't know how to do that anymore, but I am determined not to leave here on Monday and never see him again. Even if it means dealing with him being in a relationship with someone else. Even if it means planning his fucking wedding.

I'm standing in front of the TV holding the movie behind my

back when Sam returns to the basement, a large bowl of popcorn in one hand and two more beers in the other.

"Want to guess which one I picked?" Sam puts the bowl and drinks on the coffee table and faces me with his hands on his hips. His eyes scan my face and then a grin touches his mouth.

"Nuh-uh," I say before he speaks.

"*The Evil Dead.*"

"Are you kidding me?" I wave the DVD in the air. "How did you do that?"

Sam stalks around the coffee table to me, and I hold the movie above my head, like I'm playing keep-away. He reaches around me to take the movie from my hand, brushing his chest against mine in the process. He pulls the DVD, and my arm along with it, down to our sides, his fingers overlapping mine. We are a few inches apart. Everything goes blurry except for the details of Sam's face. I can see the darker specks of blue that encircle his irises and the purplish rings under his eyes. I glance down at his mouth and stop on the crease that parts his bottom lip. *Friends. Friends. Friends.*

"Old habits, right?" Sam asks, and it sounds like velvet.

"Huh?" I blink up at him.

"The movie—you want to watch it for old times' sake."

"Right," I say and let go of the DVD.

"Did you mean what you said earlier?" he asks. "That you don't want to know about Taylor and me? I can respect that, if it's not something you want to talk about. Charlie has other opinions, but . . ." He drifts off. "Percy?" I have my eyes closed, bracing myself for impact. I can hear him announcing that they're getting engaged so clearly in my mind, it seems like a foregone conclusion.

"You can tell me," I say, looking up at him. "We can talk about it . . . about her." His shoulders seem to relax a little, and he motions for me to go sit on the couch. He pops the DVD in, lowers the light, and sits down on the couch, placing the popcorn between us. We're in our old positions, curled up at either end of the couch.

"So we've been seeing each other for a little over two years," he says.

"Two and a half years," I correct for some goddamn unknown reason, and even in the dim light I can see the corner of his mouth flit upward a little.

"Right. But the thing is we haven't been together that whole time. We were actually broken up for, like, six months of it. And I felt like it was done. I knew that it was done, but Taylor has this way of talking you into something. It's probably why she's a great lawyer. Anyway, we got back together about a month ago, but it wasn't working. It hasn't been working." He pauses, running his hand through his hair. "I don't want you to think what happened earlier in the boat . . ." He stops himself and starts again. "What I'm trying to say is that we're not together."

"Does she know that?" I ask. "She introduced herself as your girlfriend last night," I remind him.

"Yeah, she was then," he says. "But she's not now. We broke up. I ended things. After we dropped you off."

"Oh." It's all I can manage to get out of the noise that's whirling around my head.

Is this because of me? It can't be because of me.

As much as I would like to insinuate myself into Sam's life like the past twelve years haven't happened, like I didn't completely betray him, I know I don't deserve that. I stare into the bowl of popcorn. He's waiting for me to say more, but I can't grasp any of the words floating around in my head and smoosh them into a sentence.

"She's going to be there tomorrow," he says. The funeral, he means. "I didn't want you to get the wrong idea. I just wanted to be honest with you."

I hold my face still so he can't tell that he's delivered a direct blow, slamming into my weakest spot with precision. He keeps talking. "I also wanted to make sure you knew I wasn't being totally inappropriate earlier." I venture a peek up at him. "Maybe just a little out of line." His mouth moves into a one-sided smirk, but his eyes are wide, waiting for reassurance. And at the very least I owe him that, so I reach for a joke.

"I get it. You're obsessed with me." Except it doesn't sound funny when it leaves my mouth, doesn't drip with the sarcasm I'd intended.

He blinks at me. If the TV wasn't casting a blue light over his face, I feel certain I'd see a flush moving across it.

I open my mouth to apologize, but he picks up the remote.

"Shall we?" he asks.

Throughout the movie, I keep sneaking glimpses of Sam instead of watching. About an hour in, he starts yawning. A lot. I move the popcorn bowl onto the coffee table and pull out the throw pillow from behind me.

"Hey." I nudge Sam's foot with mine. "Why don't you stretch out and shut your eyes for a bit?" He looks over at me with heavy lids. "Take this." I pass him the pillow.

"All right," he says. "Just for a bit." He tucks his arm under the pillow and lies on his side, his legs extending well onto my side of the couch and his feet bumping up against mine.

"This okay?" he whispers.

"Of course," I say and pull the afghan over our legs and up to his waist. I snuggle down into the couch.

"Good night, Sam," I whisper.

"Just a few minutes," he murmurs.

And then he falls asleep.

~~~

SAM AND I are a tangle of limbs when I wake up. We're still on either end of the couch, but my leg is across his leg, and his hand is wrapped around one of my ankles. My neck aches, but I don't want to move. I want to stay here all day, with Sam sleeping soundly, a hint of a smile across his lips. But the funeral starts at eleven this morning, and light is streaming in from the small basement windows. It's time to wake up.

I unfurl myself from Sam and gently shake his shoulders. He groans at the disruption, and I whisper his name. He blinks up at me in confusion and then a crooked grin slowly spreads across his mouth.

"Hey," he croaks.

"Hey." I grin back. "You slept."

"I slept," he says, rubbing his face.

"I didn't want to wake you, but I figured I should so you weren't rushing around before the funeral."

Sam's grin fades, and he sits up and leans forward, his elbows on his knees and his head resting in his hands.

"Is there anything I can do to help? I can go to the Tavern to set up or . . . I don't know . . ." Sam straightens, and then rests his head on the back of the couch. I sit facing him, my legs crossed beneath me.

"It's all taken care of. Julien will be at the Tavern this morning finishing up. He told us to stay away till after the service." He pinches the bridge of his nose. "But thank you. I should probably just get you back to the motel."

Sam brews a pot of coffee and pours us each a traveler's mug.

I try to make small talk, but he gives one-word answers, so after we climb into the truck, I decide I should just keep my mouth shut. We don't speak during the short drive to the motel, but I can see the tension in Sam's jaw. It's almost eight when we pull into the parking lot, and aside from a few cars, it's deserted. I unbuckle my seat belt but don't move. I know something is wrong.

"You okay?" I ask.

"Believe it or not," he says, looking out the front window, "I was kind of hoping today would somehow never come." I reach out and put my hand over his, rubbing my thumb back and forth. Slowly, he turns his hand over, and I watch as he curls his fingers through mine.

We sit there, saying nothing, and when I look up at Sam, he's staring out the windshield, tears streaming down his face. I move over on the seat and lean against him, placing our clasped hands onto my lap and wrapping my free hand around them both. His body is shaking with silent sobs. I place a kiss on his shoulder and squeeze his hand tighter.

My instinct is to tell him it's going to be okay, to soothe him, but I let the grief wash over him instead. Waiting it out with him. Once his body is still and his breaths are steady, I pull my head back and brush away some of his lingering tears.

"Sorry." He mouths the word, barely a thread of a whisper. I hold on to his eyes with my own.

"You have nothing to be sorry for."

"I keep thinking about how I'm almost the same age as Dad was when he died. I always hoped I had Mom's genes, that I wasn't cursed with his bad heart and his short life. But Mom wasn't even fifty when she got sick." His voice breaks and he swallows. "I can't believe how selfish I am for thinking about this when her funeral is today. But I don't want that. I feel like I haven't even started to live yet. I don't want to die young."

"You won't." I cut him off, but he keeps going.

"I might. You don't . . ."

I put my hand over his mouth. "You won't." I say it again, hard. "Not allowed." I shake my head, feeling my eyes go watery.

He blinks once, looks down at where my hand is pressed against his mouth, and then back to my eyes. He stares at me for several long seconds, and then his eyes darken, black pupils engulfing the blue. I can't move. Or I won't move. I'm not sure which it is. Both my hands, the one clutching Sam's and the one over his lips, feel like they've been dipped in gasoline and lit on fire. His chest rises and falls in fast breaths. I'm not sure I'm breathing at all.

Sam grips my wrist, and I think he's going to pull my hand away from his mouth, but he doesn't. He closes his eyes. And then he plants a kiss in the center of my palm. Once. And then again.

He opens his eyes and keeps them on mine as he kisses my palm once more and then slowly runs the tip of his tongue up the middle of my hand, sending a molten wave through my body and between my legs. The sound of my gasp fills the silence of the truck, and suddenly Sam is lifting me on top of his lap so my thighs straddle his, and I clutch his shoulders for balance. His hands skim up and down the backs of my legs, his fingers brushing under the hem of my shorts. He's looking at me with an open kind of awe.

I don't notice that I'm biting my lip until he uses his thumb to release it from my teeth. He places his hand on my cheek and I turn into it, kissing his palm. His other hand moves further up the back of my shorts, sliding under the edge of my panties. I whimper into his hand.

"I missed you," he rasps. A wounded kind of sob spills out from me, and then his mouth is on mine, taking the sound into him, swirling his tongue around mine. He tastes like coffee and comfort and warm maple syrup. He moves to my neck, leaving a trail of hot kisses up to my jaw. I tilt my head back to give him full access, arching toward him, but the kisses stop. And his mouth is on my nipple, sucking the peaked flesh through my tank top, gently biting down before sucking again. The noise that escapes me is unlike any I've heard myself make before, and he looks up at me with a cocky half grin on his face.

Something in me snaps, and I pull up his T-shirt, tracing my hands over the hard curves of his stomach and chest. He shifts toward the center of the seat and then spreads my knees wider so that I'm sitting flush against him. I roll my hips against the hardness beneath me, and he hisses and then grips onto my sides, holding me still. My eyes flash up to his.

"I won't last," he whispers.

"I don't want you to," I say back. He's breathing heavily. His cheeks are damp from tears, and I kiss each one. His hands come to both sides of my face and he brings my forehead to his, his nose moving along the side of mine. I can feel each of his exhalations on my mouth. He traces his thumb across my lip again and then softly presses his mouth against mine. I push my hands underneath his shirt and up his back, trying to pull him closer, but he holds my head and plants gentle kisses against my mouth, watching my reaction to each one. A frustrated hum sounds in the back of my throat because it's not nearly enough. He laughs gently, sending goose bumps down my arms. I try to sit up taller on my knees so I can take more control of the kiss, but Sam's hands come back to my hips and keep me pushed against him. His hands are under the back of my shorts, his fingers digging into my ass, and then he thrusts up against me, and I moan. An "oh god" escapes me, and my thighs shake when he brings his lips lightly against my ear and whispers, "Maybe I don't want you to last, either."

His mouth covers mine, and his teeth pull at my bottom lip and then he laps his tongue over the same spot. When his tongue moves inside my mouth, I feel the vibration of his groan and roll my hips over him again. One of his hands leaves my ass and cups my breast, then pulls the tank top down, hooking it underneath. His fingers pinch my nipple, and I feel it between my legs.

"Fuck, Percy," he gasps. "You feel so amazing. You have no idea how often I've thought about this." His words wrap around my heart, sending melted butter down my limbs.

"I do," I whisper. His mouth moves to my neck and he lightly presses his tongue along my collarbone up to my ear, and I rub against him, trying to find the top of my delight.

"I do," I say again. "I think about you, too." The confession slips from my mouth, and Sam growls and moves me against him, one hand under my shorts, freeing my breast from my bra with the other. When he takes my nipple hungrily into his mouth and looks up into my eyes, the orgasm begins to rise quickly. I'm murmuring incoherently, an inarticulate jumble of "Sam" and "keep going" and "almost." He moves me faster and harder over him and sucks me deeper into the wet heat of his mouth, and when his teeth press into my flesh, a zipper pulls up my spine, and I shudder violently. His mouth is back on mine, swallowing my moans, his tongue eagerly moving against mine, until my body goes liquid, and I lean against him, little quakes still rippling through me.

"I want you. I've always wanted you," he murmurs as I pant. I lean back, my bare breast cool from the dampness of his mouth.

"You're so fucking gorgeous," he says. I move my hand up his thigh, over the thin material of his sweatpants, until I find the hard ridge of his erection.

I kiss the crease on his bottom lip, then cover it with my mouth, sucking and biting while I move my hand under his waistband and around the warm length of him, moving my hand back and forth. When I run my tongue flat up his neck to his ear, pulling the lobe with my teeth, and whisper, "You're the most beautiful man I've ever known," he grabs my hand and pulls it out of his pants, then squeezes my hips and brings me down against him, and his pelvis bucks underneath me. A loud, strangled cry leaves his mouth. His orgasm rips through him in three waves, and I leave kisses on his neck until it ebbs and then I curl against his chest and listen to the sound of his heavy breathing. His arms fold around me, and we stay like that for several quiet minutes.

But when I sit back to look up at him, his brows are furrowed.

"I loved you," he whispers.

"I know," I say.

Hurt eyes move across my face. "You broke my heart."

"I know that, too."

12

Summer, Thirteen Years Ago

"SAM FLOREK IS A FUCKING LUNATIC, AND DON'T YOU forget it." Delilah was sitting on my bed, her pale legs folded underneath her, delivering a pep talk as I packed for the cottage. "You are a smart, sexy, seventeen-year-old woman with a ridiculously hot boyfriend, and you don't need some small-town loser who doesn't appreciate how incredible you are bringing you down!"

Delilah was on an anti-man kick. She broke up with Patel when he went away to McGill, and threw everything she had at school. She had gotten it in her head that she was destined to change the world, and she wasn't going to let any guy stand in her way. Her grades were better than mine. Though she and Patel were now "on again" for the summer.

"You know it's weird to call your cousin ridiculously hot, right?" I said, cramming bathing suits into my overstuffed suitcase.

"It's not weird if I'm just stating a fact," she replied. "But you're missing my main point, which is that I don't want you to get hurt again. You're too good for Sam."

"That's not true." I may have spent the past ten months convincing myself that I was over him and that he was right to want to keep our relationship purely platonic, but I didn't believe for a second that I was too good for him. "And he's not a loser," I added.

Sometimes I wondered if Sam called things off last summer because he didn't want to attach himself to me when he had all these big plans to go away to school and become a doctor and never look back. He didn't want to get stuck in Barry's Bay, but at my most anxious I thought that maybe he didn't want to get stuck with me, either.

I had joined the swim team, to my mother's delight, and had distracted myself with practice, writing, and Mason's hockey games, while Sam had spent the year studying or working to save for university. He barely took a break. I had to convince him to go to parties or spend a night playing video games with Finn and Jordie. He never mentioned girls, but I knew he wouldn't waste time dating—not that I cared. Okay, I cared. He was still my best friend. But that was it. Best friend. Nothing more.

"I'll be the judge of that once and for all when we come up to visit," Delilah said, reaching into the suitcase and pulling out my team suit. "I get that you actually swim when you're up there, but please tell me you're packing something a little more exciting than this," she said, holding up the navy one-piece. I smiled: Delilah was nothing if not predictable. I grabbed a gold string bikini and threw it at her.

"Happy?"

"Thank god. What's the point of all that time you spend pickling yourself in chlorine if you aren't going to show off the results?"

"Some people call it exercise," I laughed. "You know, for health?"

"Pfff . . . as if you and Mason don't lie around naked talking about how hot your hot athletic bodies are," she scoffed.

"Again, he's your cousin."

Delilah and Patel started having sex a while ago and she assumed the same was true of Mason and me. To correct her would mean having a detailed conversation about exactly what was happening between us, which I preferred to keep to myself.

"I can't help it if the Mason family gene pool is prone to extreme good looks." Delilah tossed her hair over her shoulder. She wasn't wrong. Even with her red hair and explosive personality, she looked softer than me, with roller-coaster curves that were irresistible to the boys in our high school, who constantly stopped by our lunch table to flirt. She dismissed them all with a flick of her wrist.

I gathered up a couple of notebooks and paperbacks and placed them on top of the piles of clothing.

"I'll never get this zipped up," I said, trying to shove everything down in my suitcase.

"Good, then you'll have to stay!"

"I'll see you in a month, D. It'll fly by. Give me a hand here?" Delilah pushed down on the bulging case while I zipped it up.

"Is Charlie still as hot as I remember?" She wiggled her eyebrows. Delilah's version of man hating was admittedly pretty thirsty. Charlie had started school at Western in the fall, and I hadn't seen him since the Christmas break.

"He's not ugly," I told her. "But you can be the judge of that, too." My parents had agreed to let me have Mason, Delilah, and Patel up for the Civic Holiday, which they would be spending in Prince Edward County for a second year.

Mason had stayed in Toronto for university, and we had made it official in the fall. I'd been holding out hope that Sam would change his mind about us, but when I saw him over Thanksgiving, it was like the night we spent in his bed had never happened. The next weekend, I let Mason feel me up under my skirt at the movie theater. "I hope you start calling me your boyfriend now," he had whispered in my ear, and I agreed that I would, reveling in the feeling of being wanted.

Sam had spotted the silver bracelet around my wrist as soon as he walked through the door to the cottage on Christmas Eve. My parents had invited the Floreks for holiday cocktails, and he pulled me aside and held up my wrist that wore the friendship bracelet as well as the one Mason had given me.

"Have any updates for me, Percy?" he asked, his eyes narrowed. It wasn't exactly how I planned to tell him about our relationship, with our parents standing nearby and Charlie within earshot, but I didn't want to lie to him, either.

"The silver doesn't really go with ours," was his only response.

~~~~

THAT SUMMER, THE tension between Sam and Charlie was obvious almost as soon as I got out of the car. The Florek brothers stood towering by the back door of the cottage a full meter apart.

"You're looking more gorgeous than ever, Pers," Charlie told me, his eyes on Sam, before pulling me into a long hug.

"Subtle," Sam mumbled.

Charlie helped unload but had to leave early to get ready for his shift, giving me another lingering embrace before he departed.

"For the record," he whispered in my ear so no one else could hear, "my brother is a fucking idiot."

"What's going on with Charlie?" I asked Sam when we were lying on the raft later that afternoon.

"We're not exactly seeing eye to eye on a couple of things," he said vaguely. I rolled onto my stomach and rested my face on my hands.

"Care to elaborate, Dr. Florek?"

"Nah," said Sam. "It's nothing."

That night, Sam invited me to come over after dinner. I showed up in my sweats with a copy of my latest story for him.

"I brought homework," I said when he opened the door, holding up the pages.

"I've got something for you, too." He smiled. I followed him to his room, trying not to think about what happened the last time we were in there.

He pulled out a stack of three somewhat worn books, tied up with white ribbon, from the top shelf of his closet: *Rosemary's Baby*, *Misery*, and *The Handmaid's Tale*. "I spent months tracking these down at yard sales and the secondhand store," he said, sounding a bit nervous. "The Atwood isn't really horror, it's dystopian, but we read it in English and I think you'll love it. And I got the other two because I thought you might want to see the words that created some of your favorite movies."

"Wow," I said. "Sam, these are so amazing."

"Yeah?" He seemed unsure. "Not as fancy as a silver bracelet, though."

I wasn't even wearing the bracelet. Was it jealousy? I hadn't known Sam to be insecure about money before, but maybe that was it.

"Not as fancy, but way better," I said, and he looked relieved. I passed him the revised version of the ghost story I'd long been tinkering with.

"Reading time?" he asked, flopping onto the end of his bed. He patted the spot beside him.

"You're going to read it in front of me?"

"Uh-huh," he said, not looking up from the page and holding his index finger over his mouth to shush me. I settled onto the bed beside him and dug into *The Handmaid's Tale*. About half an hour later, Sam put the pages down and ran his hand through his hair. He'd cut it a little shorter since I'd seen him last. He looked older.

"This is really great, Percy," he said.

"Swear on it?" I asked, putting my book down.

"Of course." He sounded surprised I'd asked and pulled on my bracelet absentmindedly. "I'm not sure if I'm terrified of the dead sister or if I feel sorry for her—or both."

"Really? That's exactly what I was going for!"

"Really. I'm going to read it again and make notes, okay?" It was more than okay. Sam was my best reader. He always had ideas to make the characters stronger or questions that pointed out a hole in the story's logic.

"Yes, please. Delilah's critique was very Delilah and totally useless, as always."

"More sex?"

"Exactly," I laughed. An awkward silence fell upon us, and I racked my brain for something not sex related to say, but Sam spoke up.

"So when did you and Buckley get serious?" he asked, squinting at me.

"Are you ever going to call him Mason?"

"Probably not," Sam deadpanned.

"Well, I'm not sure if I'd say we're *serious*," I said.

"But he's your boyfriend now."

"Yeah, he is." I played with the frayed hole in the knee of my jeans.

"So I think I know the basics: He's Delilah's cousin, plays hockey, went to a—*shudder*—private school for boys and is now at U of T, buys his girlfriend expensive-looking jewelry, has a terrible name." I was surprised by how much he'd remembered from our emails. "But you haven't really told me what he's like."

"He's nice." I shrugged, and studied the woman in a red robe on the cover of the book. What was *she* hiding?

"You've mentioned that." Sam bopped my knee with his. "What does he think about your writing?" He tapped the sheets of paper on the bed.

"I don't know, really," I said. "I haven't given him any of it to read. It's kind of personal, you know?"

"Too personal for your boyfriend?" Sam asked, smirking.

"You know what I mean." I kicked him. "I'll share one with him at some point, but it's scary to have other people read your work."

"But it's not scary when I read them?" He looked up at me from under his lashes.

"Well, when you read them in front of me, it is," I evaded. "But no, I trust you." Sam seemed satisfied with that answer.

"So other than the fact that he's nice, what do you like about him?" It wasn't a snarky question. He seemed genuinely curious. I twisted the embroidered bracelet around my wrist.

"He likes me back," I said truthfully, and Sam didn't ask any more questions after that.

~~~~

EVERY NOW AND then I'd learn something about Charlie that threw my entire perception of him into question. He was driving around in a trusty old blue pickup truck that his grandfather had handed down to him "on account of my excellent grades," he explained. I'd laughed, when he'd told me, assuming he was joking, but his dimples vanished. I frowned. "Full academic scholarship and everything," he said. "Don't look so shocked."

He still preferred to take the Banana Boat in to work. "I like feeling the wind on me after spending the night in that hellhole," he explained. "Besides," he continued with a wink, "the boat is more convenient for post-shift skinny-dipping." And *that* was the Charlie I knew.

Jumping in the lake butt naked after our shifts had become a ritual. I assumed Sue knew what was going on—we weren't exactly quiet—and my parents had seen me walk into the cottage with a towel wrapped around me and my work clothes in my fist, but no one seemed to care too much. I caught bits and pieces of body parts, and that wasn't *always* by accident, but mostly it was an innocent way to blow off steam.

Charlie's latest fling, Anita, joined us on occasion. She was a bit older and had a cottage further down on the lake, but her presence did nothing to stop Charlie from crossing any and every line he could.

We were swimming after a Thursday shift. Charlie and Anita drank beers standing in the water by the end of the dock, whispering and laughing and kissing, while Sam and I floated on pool noodles further out.

"Don't you think Percy's a knockout?" Charlie asked loud enough for us to hear.

"I already told you that I do," Anita giggled. I could see the tops of her small breasts peeking out from the water and felt my face heat.

"Right, I must have forgotten," Charlie said to her with a kiss on her cheek.

"I'll bet," Sam laughed, but I felt uneasy. It seemed like Charlie was working up to something. I inched toward Sam and my foot kicked his leg, startling him. We were close enough now that I could see the way his chest glowed milky white under the water.

"You know, Pers," Charlie drawled, "Anita and I both think you're hot. Maybe you should join us sometime."

My mouth dropped open, and I felt Sam's foot wrap around my ankle.

"Leave her alone, Charlie," Anita scolded. "You're freaking her out."

"I have a boyfriend," I replied, trying to sound bored but bracing myself. It didn't seem like Charlie had hit the punch line yet.

"Oh, that's right," Charlie replied. "Some rich guy. Sam told me. It's too bad, though I'm not surprised. A beautiful, smart, funny girl like yourself, who not to mention grew *quite* the rack last year."

"Charlie," Sam warned.

"What? It's true. Don't tell me you haven't noticed, Samuel," he went on. "Seriously, Pers, I can't imagine that any guy wouldn't be falling over himself to be with you." Bull's-eye.

"Fuck you, Charlie," Sam said, but his brother was whispering something to Anita, who was looking in my direction and making a sad *awww* noise.

"*Oh my god.*" I hadn't realized the words had left my mouth until I noticed Sam staring at me.

"You okay?" he whispered, but I didn't reply. Charlie and Anita were climbing out of the water, neither of them in any hurry to cover themselves with a towel.

"We'll be in the basement," Charlie called out as they headed up. "Offer still stands, Pers."

"Percy?" Sam prodded me with his foot. "I'm sorry. That was far, even for Charlie."

"You told him?" I whispered. "About last summer?" I swallowed back the lump in my throat and faced Sam, not caring about how much of me he could or couldn't see.

"Yeah, not about all of it. But he sort of cornered me after Christmas Eve at your place, after he heard you talking about Mason and the bracelet."

"Great. It wasn't enough to be rejected the first time around, now your brother and Anita know, too." I sucked in my breath, feeling the nettle sting of tears.

"I'm sorry, Percy. I didn't think he'd ever bring it up. You don't need to be embarrassed—my brother thinks I'm the idiot in this scenario." I looked up at the stars, and he wrapped both his legs around mine, drawing me closer.

"Hey," he whispered, putting one of his hands on my waist. I went stiff.

"What are you doing?" I asked.

"I just really want to hold you," he said, his voice strained. "I hate that he upset you." We floated there for a moment before he spoke again. "Can I?" There were a million reasons I should say no, or at least two good ones: I had a boyfriend, and that boyfriend was not Sam.

"Okay," I whispered.

"Come here," he said. We swam closer to shore to a spot hidden from the view of his house, standing where the water came up to the middle of his chest and my shoulders. We faced each other, maybe a foot apart until Sam stepped closer and wrapped his arms around me. He was warm and slippery, and I could feel his heart beat in impatient thumps against my chest.

"Charlie's right, you know," he said. "You are beautiful and smart and funny." I curled myself against him more tightly. His hands slid up and down my back, and he whispered, "And any guy would fall over himself to have you."

"Not you," I said.

"That's not true," he rasped. He bent down and leaned his forehead against mine, cupping my face with his hands.

"You're driving me crazy," he said. I closed my eyes. Ice dripped down my spine as a fire blazed in my middle. I loved Sam, but this wasn't fair. Maybe he didn't know what he wanted, didn't know how cruel he was being, but I couldn't let myself be played with while he figured it out.

"You're confusing me," I said and pushed him away. "I should go home."

~~~

I BARELY SLEPT. Sam let me go home without a word of protest—without any words, actually. Shortly after two a.m., I pulled out the notebook he'd given me for my fifteenth birthday, with the inscription *For your next brilliant story*, turned to one of the empty pages and wrote, *Sam Florek is a fucking lunatic*, before I started to cry hot, angry tears. I had spent the past year trying to move on, and I thought I *had* moved on. Was I kidding myself?

Sam didn't say anything when he came by after his run. We barely said more than a word to each other that morning. It wasn't until I cut my swim short and climbed up on the raft to maybe take a nap that he spoke up.

"I'm sorry about last night." He was sitting next to me, his feet in the water. *What part of it was he sorry for, exactly? Was he sorry for almost kissing me? Sorry for jerking me around?*

"Okay," I said, keeping my eyes closed and my cheek pressed to the warm wood, rage coiling up from my toes.

"I know you have a boyfriend, and it was a dick move," he continued. He didn't get it. I pushed myself up to sit beside him. His face was full of apology.

"Whether I have a boyfriend or not is for me to worry about, not you," I sneered. "What you need to think about, Sam, is how your actions are in complete contrast to your words."

He took a deep breath. "You're right, Percy." He lowered his face so that our eyes were level. "You said I was confusing you, and I'm sorry for that. Can we just go back to how things were?"

"I don't know? Can *you*?" My voice went up an octave. "Because I've spent the past year acting like things are normal between us. You didn't want me, and that's fine. I'm seeing someone. I've pretended that nothing happened between us, because that's what *you* wanted. And I think I've done a pretty great job." I stood up before he could respond. "I'm going to go home. I didn't get much sleep last night, and I need to take a nap before work tonight. I'll see you then, okay?" I dove off the raft and swam toward shore without waiting for a goodbye.

There were ominous-looking clouds in the sky by late afternoon, so Charlie and Sam picked me up in the truck. I squeezed into my usual spot between them, in no mood to make small talk with either one.

"Think any more about that offer, Pers?" Charlie asked with a dimpled smile, his vision locked on Sam.

"You know what, Charlie?" I said, narrowing my eyes. "Screw you. You want to piss off Sam, that's fine. But leave me the hell out of it. You're too old for this shit!" Charlie blinked at me.

"I was just joking around," he mumbled.

"I *know*!" I cried, hitting my hands against my thighs. "And I'm sick of it."

"Okay, okay. I hear you," he said. "I'll be good." He pulled the truck out of the driveway, and none of us spoke the rest of the ride.

~~~

IT WAS RAINING the next morning when Sam showed up at the cottage dressed in his running gear and dripping wet.

"Sam, you look like you've been drowned," my dad bellowed when he opened the door for him. Sam's shirt was plastered to his body, emphasizing the muscles in his chest and stomach. He looked good for a drowning victim. It pissed me off. "Wait here, I'll get you a towel," Dad said.

"You better get him a change of clothes, too," Mom called from the couch. Dad tossed him a bath sheet and headed upstairs to find something dry for Sam to wear.

"What are you doing here?" I asked while he rubbed the towel over his head.

"I always come after my run. Also," he added in a lower voice, "I want to talk to you. Can we go upstairs?"

I didn't see any way to disagree in front of my parents without causing a scene, and I'd had my fill of Sam-related drama this week. Dad handed Sam a stack of clothes as we passed him on the steps, and he changed in my parents' room while I waited in mine, sitting cross-legged on my bed, listening to the patter of rain on the roof.

As mad as I was at him, when Sam entered the room wearing a pair of my dad's track pants that were several inches too big in the waist and a green fleece pullover that was several inches too short in the arms, I burst out laughing.

"I hope you don't plan on having a serious conversation while wearing that."

"I don't know what you're talking about," he said with a grin, his eyes sparkling.

I miss this, I thought, and felt the smile vanish from my face. Sam closed the door and sat across from me on the bed.

"I was wrong," he began. "So wrong." My eyes collided with his. "And you were wrong, too. Yesterday, when you said I didn't want you." He spoke softly, his blue eyes fixed on mine. "I did want you. I do want you. I've always wanted you." I felt a sharp pressure in my lungs, like his words had sucked all the oxygen out of them. "I'm sorry for making you think otherwise, for confusing you. I thought we should focus on school for now. What my mom said last summer—that we had plenty of time to be in a relationship—made sense to me. And I thought we would mess things up if we tried to be something more, but I messed things up trying not to be."

"You really did," I said, a poor attempt at humor. He smiled anyway.

"I told you last summer that I don't know how to do this." He motioned between us. "I said we should wait until we're ready." He took a deep breath. "I don't know if we're ready, but I don't want to wait anymore." He put his hands over mine and squeezed.

I wanted to jump onto his lap and throw my arms around his neck and kiss the crease on his lip. I also wanted to pummel him. Because what if he changed his mind again? I didn't think I could survive that.

"Sam, I have a boyfriend," I told him, forcing the words to sound strong. "A boyfriend, who, by the way, is going to be here in just over a week. I just need you to respect that right now."

"Of course," he said, though his voice was ragged. "I can do that."

~~~

"SO, THAT'S HIM." Sam peered through the kitchen window into the dining room, where Mason, Delilah, and Patel were sitting at a four-top while my former favorite server, Joan, handed out menus. They didn't arrive at the cottage until midafternoon, just a couple of hours before my Saturday shift, so they decided to show up for dinner to spend more time with me. Mason said they wanted to surprise me. It worked. I wasn't going to mention their presence to Sam, but Joan had burst into the kitchen after seating them to tell me I was "one lucky bitch" for having "such a hot boyfriend." I used to like Joan.

Mason did look good, though. Now that hockey season was over, he'd cut his dark hair shorter, which had the effect of drawing attention to his jawline. He was wearing a tight black tee that made all the hours he spent at the gym abundantly clear, a pair of aviators tucked into the neck of his shirt.

"Yep," I said, feeling the heat from another body behind us. Charlie leaned over me, taking a quick look through the window.

"I'm better looking," he declared, then went back to his station.

Things got more awkward when Delilah insisted on Sam coming out to say hello. I apologized as he made his way to the table, wiping his hands on his jeans and pushing his hair off his face. He shook hands with Mason and Patel, but Delilah threw her arms around him, mouthing "holy shit" to me from over his shoulder.

"Come over after your shift tonight, Sam," Delilah told him. "And bring that handsome brother of yours." Sam raised his eyebrows and looked to Patel, who just grinned and shook his head in amusement.

"I think Charlie has plans with his . . . Anita later, but yeah, I'll come over. After washing off the sausage and sauerkraut," he added, "unless you like that sort of thing." He grinned at Delilah, who beamed back. Mason watched the exchange with a smile on his lips that didn't quite reach his eyes.

The three of them were already drunk by the time I got home. I could hear Mason and Patel arguing in slurred voices about whether beards or mustaches were the superior form of facial hair before I got inside. Delilah was sprawled over Patel's lap on the couch reading a Joan Didion memoir, her tank top riding up her stomach. She was very clearly not wearing a bra. She lifted her head when I walked in, her eyes slow to focus on my face.

"Persephone!" she called, holding her arms outspread and waving me in for a hug. "We *missssed* you!" I bent over to give her a squeeze.

"Looks like you survived without me." Empty beer bottles were lined up in a row on the kitchen counter. A few of Dad's records were scattered on the floor, but someone had managed to put on *Revolver.* There was a melting bowl of ice and a bottle of tequila open on the coffee table, and the guys each held glasses of the clear liquid.

"Come sit, babe," Mason said, pulling me down onto him and planting a kiss below my jaw. "No offense, but you kind of smell." I elbowed him in the stomach.

"I'll go shower." I moved to stand, but Mason held me tight, running his tongue up my neck.

"Mmm . . ." he murmured with a chuckle. "Tastes like pierogies."

"Very funny. Now if you'll allow me to excuse myself, I'll go clean up."

I lingered longer in the shower than I needed to. I knew that Sam would be arriving any minute, and I was half dreading it and half excited. It felt like this huge part of my life was closed off to him, and now I could introduce him to the people I spent time with when he and I weren't together. I wanted Delilah to see him. I wasn't worried about Sam and Mason. Mason wasn't the jealous type, and Sam wasn't the confrontational type. And I thought maybe if I saw them in the same room together, I would be reminded that Sam was just a regular guy. That maybe I had built him up as this mythical creature, a perfect friend and potential boyfriend who wouldn't seem so precious and rare out in the real world.

When I came out of the bathroom, Sam was sitting at a dining chair he'd pulled up beside the couch, his still-wet hair combed neatly off his face. He was wearing the dark denim jeans that I knew were his nice jeans and a white button-up, the sleeves rolled past his tanned forearms. His feet were bare. He looked good. He looked grown-up. I, on the other hand, was wearing a pair of terry cloth shorts and a pink Barry's Bay pullover. Mason passed him a full tumbler of tequila, and they clinked their glasses together before tossing back a gulp. I could see Sam struggling to keep a straight face; he wasn't a drinker.

"Don't you usually drink that stuff with limes and salt or something?" I asked, joining them.

"We neglected to bring limes," Mason explained. "But this is really good shit, so it's wasted on shots anyway." He filled another tumbler and passed it to me. I took a small sip and coughed at the burn.

"Yeah, really good shit," I rasped, still coughing. Mason pulled me toward him, and I froze, realizing he wanted me to sit on his lap.

"Come keep me company, babe," he said, tugging harder. I perched awkwardly on the end of his knee. Delilah, who had made it to an upright position, threw me a questioning look. I moved my eyes toward Sam, who was watching Mason's hands trace curlicues on my bare thigh. His brows drew together, then he downed the rest of his drink. Delilah's gaze swung between the two of us, her eyes widening with understanding, a drunken smile forming on her lips.

"Thatta boy," Patel said to Sam, reaching for the bottle to pour him more.

"So, Sam," Delilah purred, leaning toward him with her elbows on her knees and her face propped on her hands, "it's been so long since I last saw you. You're like a big, juicy piece of man now. Tell me all about this girlfriend of yours." Sam looked at me in confusion, but I had no idea where she was going with this.

"No girlfriend," he said, tipping back more of his drink.

"That's hard to believe," Delilah went on. "You know," she said, looking at Patel and Mason, "Sam can be a real heartbreaker. He can play *very* hard to get." I gave her a warning look, but she just smiled and shook her head slightly. "He once flat-out refused to kiss Percy in a game of truth or dare." *Thank god.*

"That's harsh, man," Patel said while Mason pulled me back against his chest.

"Poor baby." He wrapped his arms around my waist and pressed his lips to the side of my neck. "I'll make it up to you tonight." I automatically looked to Sam, who was staring at us with a clenched jaw and dark eyes. He was bouncing his knee.

"Anyone want a snack?" I jumped off Mason's lap and headed to the kitchen.

"I'll help," Sam offered and followed me while Patel and Mason reminisced over a particularly memorable childhood game of seven minutes in heaven.

I was on my tiptoes reaching for a serving bowl when Sam came up behind me.

"I can get that," he said, grazing his fingers over mine.

"You smell nice," he whispered as he brought the bowl down to the counter. A chill ran through me at the feel of his breath on my ear, and I shivered.

"The wonders of soap," I replied. "I almost didn't recognize you in this snazzy ensemble."

"Snazzy?" His eyes glinted.

"*Very* snazzy." I grinned.

"You two coming back with the snacks already?" Delilah hollered from the couch. I dumped a bag of chips into the bowl and placed it on the coffee table, perching on the arm of Mason's chair. He and Patel had moved on to an impassioned hockey-related argument.

"Don't mind them," Delilah told Sam. "They're slightly obsessed. But we've got better things to discuss, like our dear Persephone." She poked him on the leg. "I hear that you are her very favorite reader. She won't shut up about how great your feedback is."

Sam's face cracked into a wide grin. "Is that so?" he said, looking at me.

I rolled my eyes. "His ego is healthy enough as it is, D."

"I disagree," said Sam. "Tell me more about how smart I am, Delilah."

"I'd find you a lot more intelligent if you told her to up the sex and romance content," she said, laughing.

"What are you all giggling about?" Mason piped up.

"Percy's stories. What do you think of them?" Sam asked, and my stomach dropped. I still hadn't shown Mason my writing.

"She's never let me read one," he said, eyes narrowing at Sam.

"No? She's incredibly talented," Sam told him, eyes sparkling. "She asks me for feedback on them *all the time,* but she really doesn't need it. She's a natural writer."

"Is she?"

Sam went on like he hadn't heard him. "You should read 'Young Blood.' She wrote it a couple of years ago, but it's still my favorite. God, remember how late we'd stay up talking about character names, Percy?"

Sam was marking his territory, and all I could do was murmur in agreement.

"I didn't realize how close you two were," Mason said, eyeing me now. "It's so nice Percy has a friend up here to keep her company."

He pulled me down onto his lap, turning me at the same time, so that I was straddling him.

"What are you doing?" I whispered.

"You don't mind, do you, guys?" He tilted his head to look around me. "I haven't seen my girl in ages." He took my face in his hands and brought my mouth down to his, kissing me sloppily. When he let me come up for air, Sam was already halfway to the door.

"I should head out if I want to run tomorrow," he said, not looking at me. And then he was gone.

Sam kept his distance for the the rest of the weekend, and I was itchy for everyone to leave so I could see him. The summer was already half gone, and I was resentful that Mason's behavior meant I lost time with Sam. He had been particularly handsy the entire visit, like he was trying to lay claim to my body. It made me anxious. Even his goodbye kiss was a groping, tongue-filled affair.

Sam was different after Mason's visit. Reserved. Sometimes our eyes would meet across the kitchen or when we were hanging out in the basement, and the air would crackle. But otherwise, it was like he had put a lid on his feelings for me, which was exactly what I'd asked for. But as it got closer to the end of summer, I realized it wasn't what I wanted. I wanted to crack the lid open.

I broke up with Mason the last week of summer break in an

awkward *You're a great guy!* phone call. He was surprised but took it better than Delilah, who pouted about the end of our double dates before I reminded her she was planning to pause things with Patel for the school year.

Sam and I were sitting on his bed reading in our damp bathing suits the last day before I'd be heading back to the city with my parents. It was hot, and Charlie and Anita had annexed our usual basement hideaway. Sue had refused to put on the AC, so Sam closed his bedroom blinds and set up a fan to oscillate between us, he at the end of the bed, his back pressed to the wall, and me at the head facing him, knees drawn up toward my chest. He was studying a diagram in one of his anatomy textbooks while I was reading *The Stand*. Or I was trying to. I hadn't managed to make it through a page in the past ten minutes. I couldn't stop looking at Sam: the tan line around his ankles, the muscles of his calves, the bracelet around his wrist. I stretched my leg out to rest it on his thigh, and as soon as my foot made contact, he jolted.

"You okay, weirdo?" I asked. He eyed me and then sprung off the bed and dug through his dresser drawer.

"Do me a favor," he said, throwing me his old Weezer T-shirt. I pulled it over my head while he sat down, his nose back in the textbook.

I prodded his leg with my toe and noticed an apple blush creeping into his cheeks. Getting a rise out of Sam was one of my top three favorite things to do, and it was a rare thrill these days. But something had punctured a hole in his calm reserve, and I wanted to rip it wide open with my teeth.

"And you're kicking me because . . ." he said in a deep monotone, not looking up from the page, brows knit. I put both feet on his lap, feeling his whole body stiffen.

"That must be a fascinating book—you've been reading it all summer."

"Mmm."

"Really good plotline?"

"Riveting," he deadpanned. "You know, I can usually count on you not to give me shit about studying."

"No shit-giving here," I swore, then dug my heel into his thigh. "Lots of sexy parts, huh?" He finally looked at me from the corner of his eye, shook his head, and then returned to the book.

"Actually," I said, moving my feet off his lap and sitting up with my knees bent out in front of me, pressing my toes into his thigh, "the human body is pretty sexy. I mean, not the picture of that skinless man you're looking at . . ."

"It's a diagram of the muscular system, Percy," he said, turning his face to me. "This"—he put one hand around the back of my leg—"is a calf muscle." His voice was sarcastic, but it felt like someone had replaced the blood in my veins with caffeine. I wanted his hand on me. I wanted his *hands* on me.

He looked down at where he gripped my leg and back to me. His eyes were a question mark.

"Calf muscle?" I said. "Good to know . . . I'll be sure to try to use it one day. I've heard of this thing called running." I laughed, and he moved his hand away.

We sat with our books open for several minutes, neither of us turning a page. I felt the promise of something more between us slipping, to be tucked away like the old box of embroidery floss in my desk drawer. So I tried to hold on.

I pushed my toes under his thigh.

"Learn anything else from that book of yours?" I asked. His eyes snapped to mine. He nodded slowly.

"Want to enlighten me, genius?" I made my best attempt to sound playful, but my voice was shaky.

"Percy . . ." It took every ounce of confidence I had to not break eye contact.

"I guess I'll just have to get some other future doctor to educate me," I teased, and he blinked rapidly. And then I knew. I knew that this was his weak spot. He hated the idea of someone else touching me. When he moved his hand back to my calf, I wanted to scream in triumph.

He didn't grip it this time. Instead, he ran his fingers back and forth over the muscle, shooting electricity through my body, every nerve ending sparking to life. Sam's lips were set in a serious, straight line, his face a mask of concentration. We both watched his hand moving over my calf and then slowly down my leg. He grasped it at the bottom. He looked up at me with a grin.

"Ankle," he said.

I let out a sound that was somewhere between a laugh and a gasp. He shifted so that he knelt at my feet and took my other ankle in his right hand so that he was holding on to both my legs. He looked into my eyes for one, two, three seconds. I swallowed. And then, watching my reaction, he skimmed a finger slowly up my leg.

"Shin."

I had plotted, dreamed, obsessed about Sam touching me. I had lain on my bed with my hand between my legs fantasizing about his hands and his shoulders and the crease in his bottom lip. I wanted so badly to touch him, to move my fingers along the faint line of hair that led from his belly button and into his bathing suit. And now I was frozen. I was terrified of ruining the moment, of shaking Sam out of whatever magic had come over him.

He cupped his palm around my knee following with his

other hand on the opposite knee. He pushed them apart and crept slightly up the bed so he was between them, then grabbed my ankles and pulled my legs flat against the bed. He leaned over me, and my arms shook from holding myself upright. I could feel his breath on my face. Without moving his eyes from mine, he whispered, "Lie back, Percy."

I did what he told me to, my heart pounding in my chest, and he knelt between my legs, looking down at me, his eyes dark. His long torso blocked the breeze from the fan, and suddenly I was overheating. I could feel sweat forming on my upper lip. Not taking his eyes off mine, he put his hand back on my knee.

"Knee," he whispered. I blinked up at him. The air felt heavy.

"Knee, huh? What grade level is that book at?" I teased.

A small smile played at his lips. "*Vastus medialis, vastus lateralis, tensor fasciae latae,*" he said softly, moving his fingers higher. It felt like all my nerve endings concentrated underneath his fingers. He grazed the soft flesh on the inside of my thigh. "*Adductor longus,*" he murmured, and I sucked in a breath. He trailed his index finger from the sensitive part of my inner thigh, following the crease between the top of my leg and my pelvis, under the hem of the T-shirt. He flattened his hand over the protrusion of my hip bone, then wrapped it around my hip, over the ties of my bikini. He held it there, watching me, the smile gone from his face. I wanted to pull him down on top of me and feel his weight pressing me into the bed. I wanted to tug at the waves in his hair and put my mouth on his warm neck, but I kept still, my chest rising and falling.

He pushed the shirt up over my stomach, and slowly he untied the bow at one side of my bathing suit. When he had it loosened, he pulled the strings apart and ran his hand up and down the curve of my waist and hip. "*Gluteus medius.*" He moved his hand around to the back. "*Gluteus maximus.*" I let out a nervous laugh.

"Done with anatomy lessons for today?" he asked, his voice hoarse and deep. I swallowed and shook my head. His eyes flashed with victory, and he shimmied the shirt up higher. I lifted my upper back off the bed and he pulled the T-shirt off over my head. I lay back and the sudden exposure of air on my damp suit made me shiver. His eyes dropped to the pieces of triangular fabric that covered my chest, where my breasts spilled from the sides, my nipples tight peaks against the cool material. His gaze lingered, and when he looked back at me, his eyes were the deepest shade of blue I'd ever seen them.

He moved his body down the bed slightly, then leaned down, pressing his mouth to the skin below my belly button, whispering the names of muscles as he moved his mouth across my stomach, leaving a trail of kisses on my body. He ran his tongue over the crevice of my belly button and then moved it in a hot, wet line up the middle of my stomach, pausing to deliver kisses to different parts of my abdominals. My hips jerked, and I gripped the sheets in my fists. He passed the space between my breasts, and when he pressed his tongue to the hollow between my collarbones, a guttural moan sounded in my throat. I flattened my hands against his back, where his skin was hot and smooth, and he sucked on my neck just below my jaw, then ran his tongue to my ear, nipping at it slightly.

"*Auricular lobule,*" he whispered, his lips moving against my earlobe. Then he hovered over me, his face directly above mine. He held himself up with one arm while his hand moved to my waist, down over my bare hip.

I moved my arms around his neck, and he brought his lips to mine softly. I kissed him back, harder, parting his lips with my tongue. His mouth was a warm cave that I wanted to explore. It tasted like salt and oranges. I dug one hand into his hair and bit his lower lip. When we pulled away, he moved his hand to my inner thigh.

"I want to touch you, Percy," he whispered roughly. "Can I?"

I let out a strangled-sounding yes. He shifted his weight onto his side, and we both watched as his fingers crept under the gold fabric. He traced the damp cleft between my legs, my bathing suit falling to the side with the movement. He pressed his finger gently inside, and then looked up at me, his face filled with amazement.

"Are we doing this?" he said quietly, and I didn't know if he meant what was happening right now or some bigger question about us, but either way my answer was the same.

"Yeah, we're doing this."

13

Now

CHANTAL IS DEEPLY COMMITTED TO SUNDAY BRUNCH. RIGHT now she will almost certainly be in her favorite booth at her favorite restaurant, splitting the paper with her fiancé. She will take Arts first and he will have Opinions, and then they'll switch. They will have their coffees, and her eggs Benny will be on its way. I would be disturbing her ritual. She's barely verbal, let alone ready to deal with my crisis, until she's had at least two cups of caffeine. At least that's what I tell myself as I quickly write a message to her, delete it, and then put the phone on the bed beside me. Again. I shake my head at myself. Fifth time's the charm, right? I pick up the stupid thing and type out another text, punch send, and then throw the phone down. I sit and wait—for one minute, then five—and when no reply comes, curse myself for sending it in the first place and shuffle off to the bathroom.

I run the shower until it steams up the mirror, then step under the hot spray and put my head against the tile, letting the anxious stream of thoughts billow around me like mustard gas. *What the fuck is wrong with me? What kind of a person takes advantage of their former (newly single!) boyfriend on the day of his mother's funeral? Sam is never going to let me stay in his life. And why should he? I'm a shitty, selfish person who is clearly incapable of being his friend.*

I don't register that I'm crying until I feel my shoulders shaking. Disgusted with my own self-pity, I push off the wall, scrub myself roughly with soap, wash my hair, and dry off.

I arrive at the church ten minutes early, and the lot is already full with dusty pickup trucks and well-used sedans. A young man is directing cars to park in the adjoining field. I leave the car at the end of a haphazard row, and walk toward the church, the heels of my black pumps digging into the grass, making me look as off-kilter as I feel.

Sam is standing in a small cluster of people in front of the church steps. I stop short at the sight of Taylor beside him, legs as long as a giraffe's, hair as golden as a sunbeam. Even though Sam and Charlie had mentioned she was coming, I somehow didn't expect to see her. I feel like the wind has been knocked out of me. I squeeze my eyes shut, trying to steady myself. When I open them, Charlie is looking at me from across the parking lot. He raises his hand, and the whole group turns my way.

As I move closer, I immediately recognize the thin, middle-aged man as Julien. There's an elderly couple who must be Charlie and Sam's grandparents on their dad's side. Sue's parents aren't around anymore. There's another couple, who I think are Sue's brother and sister-in-law from Ottawa. I take a deep breath and paste a warm smile on my face, though my stomach is roiling.

"Everyone, this is Percy Fraser," says Charlie as I join them. "You probably remember her. She and her parents had the cottage next door when we were kids." I greet the family with hugs and condolences, pretending that this is a funeral like any other and that I don't feel Sam watching me intensely.

"You look well, Percy," Julien says, giving me a loose hug. I rub his upper arms with both hands as he pulls away. His eyes are red and he smells like stale cigarette smoke.

I turn to Sam and Taylor last. He shut down so quickly this morning after what happened, because of course he did. Who wants to open up the *you left me brokenhearted* conversation the morning of their mother's funeral? I'm afraid to meet his eyes now, afraid of what I'll find there. Regret? Anger? Hurt?

So I fix my gaze on Taylor instead. Her hand is resting on Sam's shoulder, in a way that screams *mine*. Sam may have ended things with her, but she is clearly not done with him. In reply, I glue on a serene smile that says, *I didn't just make your ex-boyfriend come in his pants*, and keep it there, though bile is rising up my throat. She's stunning in a tailored black jumpsuit, her hair in a glossy low ponytail. My black sheath dress feels drab in comparison. She's wearing very little makeup and no jewelry and somehow manages to look intentionally minimal. If I walked around wearing only mascara and lip gloss, I'd just look tired. As it is, I spent five minutes alone applying several layers of concealer around my puffy eyes and red nose.

When I finally look at Sam, it's like seeing him for the first time. He's standing as straight as a red pine, wearing a crisp white shirt and an expensive-looking black suit that's cut close to his body. He's freshly shaven and his hair is combed and held in place with some kind of styling product. He looks like an actor who plays a doctor on TV rather than an actual doctor.

Sam and I were always bumming around in bathing suits or work clothes, and I've only seen him in a suit once before. Now he looks like such an adult, such a man. A man who *should* have a gorgeous lawyer on his arm instead of a basket case around his neck. He and Taylor make a striking couple, and it's hard not to feel that they're designed to have smart, successful, impossibly gorgeous babies together.

I lean in to give him a hug, and it feels like coming home and saying goodbye and four thousand days of longing.

"We should probably head in," Taylor says, and I realize I've been pressed to Sam's chest for a second too long for polite company, but just as I pull back, he squeezes his arms around me a little tighter, just for a second, before releasing me with an unreadable look on his face.

This is the biggest church in town, but it's still not large enough to seat everyone who's shown up this morning. People are standing in rows behind the back pews, crowding around the doorways, and spilling outside. It's an incredible show of love and support. But it also means the church is hot and stuffy. By the time we get to the front pew, my neck and thighs are already damp. I should have worn my hair up. I sit between Charlie and Sam, where a large photo of a smiling Sue stares out at us, surrounded by arrangements of lilies, orchids, and roses. I wipe at the sweat on my upper lip then rub my hands on my dress.

"You okay, Pers?" Charlie whispers. "You seem twitchy."

"Just hot," I tell him. "How about you?"

"Nervous," he says, holding up a folded piece of paper that I assume contains his eulogy. "I want to do her proud."

When it's time for Charlie to speak, he grips the edge of the podium with white knuckles. He opens his mouth, then closes it again, looking out into the crowd for several long seconds until he starts to speak, his voice audibly shaking. He stops, takes a deep breath, and then begins again, steadier now. He talks about how Sue held the family and the business together after his dad died, and though he has to pause a couple of times to collect himself, he makes it through, no tears shed, an obvious look of relief in his green eyes.

To my surprise, as Charlie returns to the pew, Sam rises. I hadn't realized he was speaking today. I watch him as he strides confidently to the front of the church.

"Many of you will find this scandalous, but Mom didn't really like pierogies," he begins with a small smile across his lips, and the room rumbles with low laughter. "What she did love, however, was watching all of us eat them." He keeps his eyes mostly on his page, but he's a beautiful speaker; while Charlie's eulogy was earnest and reverent, Sam's is gently teasing, breaking the sadness in the room with lighthearted stories about Sue's struggles and triumphs in raising two boys. Then he looks up and scans the crowd until he settles on me briefly before looking down again. I can see Taylor observing me from the corner of my eye, and my heart laces up its running shoes and takes off in a sprint.

"Mom lived without my dad for twenty years," he says. "They had been friends since kindergarten, started dating in ninth grade, and got married after high school. My grandfather will tell you that there was no way to convince either one of them to wait just a little bit longer. They knew. Some people are lucky like that. They meet their best friend, the love of their life, and are wise enough to never let go. Unfortunately, my parents' love story got cut far too short. Just before she died, Mom told me she was ready. She said she was tired of fighting and tired of missing Dad. She thought of death as a new beginning—said she was going to go spend the rest of her next life with Dad, and I'd like to think that's exactly what they're doing now. Best friends together again."

I'm mesmerized by him. Every word is an arrow to my soul. I'm about to throw my arms around him when he sits, but then Taylor pulls his hand onto her lap and holds it between hers. The sight of their intertwined hands slaps me with reality. They make sense together. They are a carefully wrapped gift with crisply folded edges and a satin bow. Sam and I are a trash fire with more than a decade of time and a big fat secret between us. Tomorrow I'll head back to Toronto, away from this town, away from Sam. It was crazy to come back, to expect I could make things better. Instead, I threw myself at him at his most vulnerable. And as right and perfect and good as it felt with his lips against mine again, I shouldn't have let this morning happen without being honest with him first. Despite everything I've done to move on, I'm right back where I was at eighteen.

Charlie offers me his arm as we amble out of the church, and then I walk slowly back to the car with a heaviness pressed against my chest. I rest my head on the steering wheel.

I shouldn't be here. I shouldn't have come.

But I can't leave now, not when there's a wake to get through, so I wait for the heavy feeling to lift a little and then I drive to the Tavern.

~~~

THE RESTAURANT IS more boisterous family reunion than post-funeral gathering. I watch the smiling relatives and friends mingle with plates of Sue's pierogies. The tables have been cleared out of the way to make room for the crowd, and someone has made a mix of Sue's favorite country songs. It doesn't take long before a group of children forms a dance circle, hopping and flailing to Shania Twain and Dolly Parton. The scene is so sweetly wholesome, and I am an impostor standing within it.

I ignore the phone vibrating in my purse and take a glass of wine from the young server behind the bar, trying to find a friendly face to pass an acceptable amount of time chatting with before I can skulk back to the motel. Charlie is holding court with the smokers who congregate outside on the patio. Sam and Taylor are nowhere to be seen, and Julien has been either hiding in the kitchen or refilling the chafing dishes on the buffet table. I head back to help him, but the space is empty, the back door propped open. I step toward it to see if he's out back smoking but hesitate when I hear voices.

"You're nuts, man," says a deep voice. "Are you sure you want to go down this road again?"

"No," I hear Sam reply. "I don't know." He sounds confused, frustrated. "Maybe I do."

"Do you need us to remind you what a mess you were last time?" a third voice asks. I know I should leave. But I don't. My feet are stuck to the floor while my phone starts buzzing again.

"No, of course not. I was there. But we were just kids." And now I know it's me they're talking about. I stand there in my dress, damp with perspiration, holding still for the firing squad.

"Don't give me that bullshit. I was there, too," the first guy spits. "Just kids? You were pretty fucked up for just being a kid." I don't want to hear the rest. I don't want to hear about how badly I broke Sam.

"Sam," the other voice says more gently, "it took years, remember?"

I am going to be sick.

I turn and dart through the swinging doors into the dining room and run right into Charlie.

"Whoa! Got somewhere better to be?"

Charlie's dimples fade once his eyes focus on my face. "You look pale and kind of sticky, Pers. Is everything okay?"

I can't seem to find enough air to reply, and my heart is beating so rapidly I can feel it pulse against every inch of skin. Maybe this time it actually is a heart attack. I might die. Right now. I try to breathe, but the edges of the room are going fuzzy. Charlie leads me back into the kitchen before I can tell him not to. I hear an awful wheezing gasp and realize it's coming from me. I bend over, trying to catch my breath, then crumple onto my hands and knees. I hear muffled voices, but they sound far away, like I'm swimming beneath mud and they're up on the shore. I squeeze my eyes shut.

There's a featherlight pressure on my shoulders. Through the mud, I can hear a voice counting slowly. *Seven. Eight. Nine. Ten. One. Two. Three* . . . It keeps going, and after a little while, I start to adjust my breathing to its pace. *Four. Five. Six. Seven* . . .

"What's happening?" someone asks.

"Panic attack," the voice replies, then it continues counting. *Eight. Nine. Ten.*

"Good, Percy," it says. "Keep breathing." I do. I keep breathing. My heart starts to slow down. I take a deep, long breath and open my eyes. Sam is crouched in front of me, his hand on my shoulder.

"Do you want to stand up?"

"Not yet," I say, embarrassment replacing the impending-death feeling. I take a few more breaths, then open my eyes again, and Sam is still there. I slowly kneel upright and Sam helps me off the floor, his hands clutching my elbows and his forehead wrinkled with concern. Behind him stand two men, an extremely handsome Black man, and a stretched-out pale guy with inky hair and glasses.

"Percy, do you remember my friends, Jordie and Finn?" Sam asks.

I start to apologize to them, but then I notice Charlie off to the side. He's looking at me closely like he's worked something out, connected dots that didn't quite fit together before.

"It was a panic attack?" he asks, and I know he doesn't mean what's just happened.

I reply with a slight nod.

"Do you get them a lot?" Sam asks, brows pulled together.

"Not in a long time," I tell him.

"When did they start, Percy?"

I blink at him. "Um . . ." My eyes flash to Charlie for a split second. "About twelve years ago."

14

Fall, Thirteen Years Ago

DELILAH AND I WERE SITTING IN THE CAFETERIA THE FIRST week of our senior year, and I was smiling so hard a snow plow couldn't have scraped the grin off my face. I had just bought a used Toyota that weekend, and freedom was pulling up the corners of my lips like marionette strings. Dad had agreed to split the cost of a secondhand car with me, stunned I had managed to save $4,000 in tips alone.

"Don't be one of *those* girls," Delilah said, waving a french fry in my face. I had just mentioned the idea of quitting the swim team. Practice was during the week but races were mostly on weekends, and I had big plans to spend every weekend in Barry's Bay with Sam.

"What girls?" I asked, my mouth half-full with a bite of tuna sandwich, as a cute red-haired boy sat down across from Delilah, holding out his hand.

"Seriously?" she asked, pointing another fry in his direction, before he could get a word out.

"I'm new here," he stammered and pulled his hand away. "I thought I'd say hi."

Delilah gave me a look that said, *Can you even imagine?* and glared at him.

"What, you think because we're both gingers we should get together and have little carrot-topped brats together? Not gonna happen." She shooed at him. "Buh-bye."

He looked at me to check whether she was serious or not.

"She looks a lot sweeter than she is." I shrugged.

After he left, Delilah turned back to me. "As I was saying, you don't want to be one of those girls who has nothing interesting to say because all she thinks about is her boyfriend, and all she does is darn his socks or whatever. *Those girls* are boring. Don't get boring on me, Persephone Fraser. I'll be required to break up with you."

I laughed, and she narrowed her eyes. She wasn't joking.

"Okay," I said, holding up my hands. "I won't quit. But Sam's not my boyfriend. We haven't, you know, put a label on it yet. It's new."

"It's not new. It's, like, one hundred years old," she said with a shake of her head. "It doesn't matter whether you label it or not, you two are together," she said, watching me. "And stop smiling so much. You're making me nauseous."

~~~

ON THE WEEKENDS when I didn't have swimming, I would pack the car on Thursday nights and drive north straight from school on Friday afternoon. This did not sit well with Mom and Dad at first, but I won them over with the *I'm going to be eighteen soon* and *What's the point of having a cottage if we don't use it?* arguments and assured them I would study while I was gone. What I didn't tell them was that I was also planning to shove my tongue down Sam's throat as soon as I got him alone. They found out anyway.

The day after Sam had put his hands over every square inch of my body in August, Sue had spotted a hickey on his neck. True to Sam's unwavering brand of honesty, he told her precisely who'd given it to him. Sue called my mom just before my first solo trip to the cottage to make sure she and Dad were aware of what was going on. Mom never said anything to me about it, but, according to Sam, Sue told Mom that Sam and I had started a "physical relationship" and then put him on the phone with my mother so he could promise her he'd treat me with respect and care.

My parents *never* talked to me about sex, and it blew my mind that this conversation took place. But when I unpacked my weekend bag, there was a box of condoms inside with a Post-it note stuck to it, the words *Just in case* written in Mom's handwriting.

Sam worked Fridays, and I usually drove right to the Tavern to wait until he finished for the night. He was cooking with Julien in the kitchen since Charlie was away at school. If the restaurant was still busy by the time I got there, I'd tie on an apron and bus tables or help out Glen, the pimple-faced boy who'd replaced Sam at the dishwasher. If it was quiet, I'd take my homework to the bar and study until Julien let Sam go.

Sam insisted on showering after his shift, so we always went back to his place. On the drive, we filled each other in on our weeks—the swim practices, bio exams, Delilah dramas—and then we raced upstairs. We had approximately thirty minutes after Sam's shower to feel each other up before Sue got home after closing. We kept the light off, a frantic clash of tongues and teeth and hands, and when Sue's headlights shone through Sam's bedroom window, we'd pull our tops back on and run downstairs to the kitchen, throwing the plates of food Julien had sent home with us in the microwave. We'd eat at the kitchen table, sneaking glances and nudging each other's feet under the table while Sue fixed her own dinner.

"You two are as subtle as elephants," she told us once.

By late September, the leaves were changing and the water was already too cold for swimming, so we created a new morning routine. It involved me sleeping late until Sam knocked on the back door after his run. He'd make weak lattes while I fixed bagels or cereal and we'd eat at the counter talking about the story I was working on or Finn's new girlfriend, whom neither Sam nor Jordie could stand, or university applications, which were due in January.

Delilah, Sam, and Jordie all had their hearts set on Queen's in Kingston—the university had a beautiful, historic campus and was considered one of the top schools in the country. Delilah wanted in for poli-sci, Sam for premed, and Jordie for business (Queen's was renowned for all three programs). Sam was still gunning for a scholarship; as hard as Sue worked, there wasn't enough to put a dent in the hefty tuition and residence fees. Unless my grades took a sudden nosedive, I would be heading to the University of Toronto, as per my parents' dream, fueled partly by their allegiance to the school and partly because half of my tuition would be covered by their faculty discount. I was applying to the English program and wanted to take as many creative writing courses as possible if I got in. U of T was a great school, but needless to say, I would have preferred if Sam and I were planning to go to university together. Toronto was almost three hours away from Kingston by car, two and a half if I drove fast and traffic was good. A small, parasitic worm of worry was burrowing inside my brain—telling me that this wouldn't last once Sam went away to school.

My parents came up for Thanksgiving, and our families spent the holiday meal together, with the addition of Julien, whom Sue had finally persuaded to join us. With Charlie back for the long weekend, there were seven of us around the Floreks' dining room table, and between Charlie and Julien, Sam and I were subjected to relentless jokes about our relationship. Not that we minded. We held hands under the table and laughed at my parents' initial shock over Julien's sharp tongue and Charlie's innuendos about teen pregnancy.

We were all together again at Christmas, but my parents returned to the city for New Year's while I stayed and worked at the Tavern. At midnight, Sam dragged me downstairs to the walk-in refrigerator and kissed me against the boxes of citrus.

"I'm so in love with you," he said when we pulled apart, his breaths escaping in cold puffs of air.

"Swear on it?" I whispered, and he smiled and kissed the inside of my wrist over the top of my bracelet.

With my parents' blessing, Sue agreed to let me stay the night at their place, and after we all showered and changed into our pj's, she popped a bottle of prosecco, poured herself a fishbowl-sized glass, and headed to her room, leaving Sam and me with the rest. We put something in the DVD player, then cuddled up under a blanket on the basement couch.

I waited ten minutes to make sure Sue wasn't going to check on us and then crawled onto his lap, my knees on either side of his thighs. I was wired from work and my insides fizzed with his *I love you* and also with prosecco. I pulled his T-shirt over his head and then kissed my way up his chest, his neck, and then to his mouth, where our tongues found each other. He began to unbutton my pink flannel top, his fingers shaking with excitement, and then stopped when he saw there was nothing underneath. He looked up at me, his pupils swallowing the blues into a midnight ocean. With the exception of what had happened in his room in August, we hadn't gone further than making out with shirts off, bra on. I opened the remaining buttons.

"I'm so in love with you, too," I whispered and shrugged out of the shirt. His eyes dropped to my chest and he grew harder beneath me.

"You're perfect," he rasped when his eyes found mine again, and I smiled brightly then moved against him. His hands grabbed my waist, then roamed over my breasts, and he groaned.

I leaned close to his ear so our skin was pressed together, and said softly, "I want to show you how much I love you." I moved my hand between us and put my fingers around the shape of him. He bit down on his lip and waited, his chest moving with his deep inhalations.

"Okay," he breathed, and we both worked his pants off his legs. "I'm not going to last long," he said, his voice deep and gravelly. He moved his hand across my breast, pinching the stiff pink peak. "I could come like this just looking at your hard nipples." My eyes flashed to his. I'd never heard him talk like that, and it sent a hot current through me. I pulled at the waistband of his boxers and then shifted so he could slide them all the way off, watching wide-eyed. I put my hand around him, tentative and unsure. I had no idea what I was doing.

"Show me how," I said, and he wrapped his hand over mine.

～～～

SAM, JORDIE, AND Delilah all got acceptance letters to Queen's that spring, and I was thrilled for them and especially for Sam, who won one of a handful of academic scholarships that would cover the bulk of his tuition. My acceptance to U of T was met with great fanfare from my parents and Sam, but I couldn't help feeling like I was standing on the ground while everyone else boarded a rocket ship.

Not that Sam gave me any reason to feel that way. We emailed constantly when we were apart, already making plans for when we could see each other when we both started university. He sent me the schedule for the train that ran between Kingston and Toronto—the trip was under three hours—and the sweetest, nerdiest list of bookstores and hospitals he thought we should visit in both cities.

By April, Toronto was in bloom with tulips and daffodils, and the buds on the magnolia and cherry blossom trees were getting fat. But up north, clumps of icy snow still hung around the edges of Bare Rock Lane and throughout the bush. Sam and I trudged up along the streambed, our boots sinking in where the snow was still surprisingly deep, and slipping on the damp ground where the sun had managed to break through the boughs. It smelled both fresh and fungal, like one of Mom's expensive mud masks, and there was so much rushing water, we had to raise our voices over the roar.

The stream was quieter by the swirling pool where the old fallen tree lay across its belly. It was a bright day, but chilly in the shade of the pines, and the bark was soggy even through my jeans. I was glad for the quilted jacket Sam convinced me to wear.

"So there's this big party at the end of the year," he said once we settled, handing me one of Sue's oatmeal-raisin cookies from the pocket of his fleece. "It's right after graduation, and, uh, everyone gets dressed up . . ." He pushed his hair out of his eye— he hadn't cut it in months and it tumbled over his forehead in a waterfall of swooshes and swoops.

"You mean prom?" I asked, grinning.

"There is a prom, but it's nothing special. This is like a grad party except it's in a big field in the middle of the bush." He raised his eyebrows as if to ask, *So what do you think?*

"Sounds fun, which you have time for now," I said, taking a bite of the cookie.

He cleared his throat. "So I was wondering, if it doesn't conflict with your grad, if you wanted to go with me." He winced slightly and clarified, "You know, as my date."

"Will you be wearing a suit?" I smiled, picturing it already.

"Some people wear jackets," he said slowly. "Is that a yes?"

"If you wear a suit, then I'm in," I elbowed him in the ribs. "Our first date."

"The first of many," he elbowed me back. And my smile fell.

"There'll be other dates, Percy," he promised, reading my mind and lowering his face to mine. "I'll come see you in Toronto, and you'll come to Kingston—whenever we can." There was a stinging in my nose, like I had eaten a spoonful of wasabi.

"Four years apart is a long time," I whispered, playing with my bracelet.

"For you and me? It'll be nothing," he said softly, and before I could ask, he hooked his index finger around my bracelet and gave it a gentle tug. "I swear," he said. "And besides, we've got time. We've got all summer."

But he was wrong. We didn't have all summer at all.

~~~~~

SAM READ SCHOOL textbooks—*for fun!*—in his downtime and landed a full academic scholarship to one of the most competitive programs in the country, so obviously I knew he was smart.

But finding out that he had the highest GPA in his class rocked me.

"So you're, like, smart-smart," I said when he called to tell me the news. "Why didn't you tell me?"

"I study and school comes pretty easy to me," he replied. I could almost hear him shrug. "It's not that big of a deal, really."

But it was that big of a deal. Having the top marks in his graduating class meant Sam was its valedictorian and therefore required to give a speech at his graduation.

I drove to Barry's Bay the day of his grad ceremony, which was also the night of the big after-party, the strapless white dress Delilah and I picked out at the mall hanging from a hook in the back of the car. My graduation—a sweltering uneventful affair held late afternoon on the school's soccer field—had been a few days earlier. When I got to the cottage, I had just enough time to shower, change, put on a little makeup, and fix my hair in a side braid that hung down over one shoulder. I had made Sam find out what kind of footwear the girls wore to a fancy bush party, so I headed to the Floreks' in a pair of silver flip-flops with rhinestones on the straps.

Charlie was already home from his second year at Western, and Sue and the boys were sitting on the porch with sweaty glasses of iced tea when I walked down the driveway. The three of them together at home early on a Friday evening in summer was a rare sight. Sam rose from his wicker chair and walked across the porch to greet me, wearing a black suit, a white shirt, and a black tie. He'd cut his hair, and he looked like a teenage James Bond.

I can't believe he's mine, I thought as I ran my hands along his shoulders and down his arms, but what I told him was, "I guess this will do." He gave me a smile that said he was probably aware of how well he cleaned up and a chaste kiss on my cheek before Sue had us pose for photos.

From the moment we stepped inside his school, it was clear Sam wasn't just a brain, he was well-liked. It wasn't a surprise, exactly. I knew Sam was awesome—I just didn't know everyone else did, too. Guys threw him high fives and handshake/back-pat combos, and several girls threw their arms around his neck with sighs of *I can't believe it's all over*, not bothering to look in my direction. I knew Jordie and Finn a little, but this whole other world he was a part of, maybe was at the center of, was totally foreign to me.

In some ways, Sam had remained in my mind the scraggy boy I first met, a kid who had trouble relating to his classmates after his dad's death and then a teenager too busy to party unless I pushed him. But watching him stride onto the stage in his cap and gown to the cheers of his classmates was like seeing his metamorphosis happen in an instant. He delivered his speech in a deep, clear voice—he was self-deprecating and funny and hopeful; he was completely charming. I was transfixed and proud, and as I stood with the rest of the audience applauding him, a seed of dread sprouted inside me. Sam had been tucked away safe for me in Barry's Bay, but in September, he would be part of a much bigger world—one that was sure to sweep him up in its infinite possibilities.

"You okay?" Sam asked quietly as Charlie drove us to the grad party, the three of us wedged into the front bench of his pickup.

"Yeah. Just thinking about how fast this summer's going to go by," I replied, watching the bush grow thick around the road we were headed down. "At least we still have two more months." I gave him a small smile as Charlie coughed something under his breath.

"What did you just call me?" I snapped.

"Not you." He looked at Sam from the corner of his eye, but neither said anything more.

We had been driving for almost twenty minutes, when Charlie turned down a dirt road that cut through the brush and then, without warning, opened onto giant rolling fields. The sun had already set, but it was bright enough to make out the old farmhouse and barns perched at the top of the driveway. Dozens of cars were parked in lines on the grass, and there was a small stage with lights and a DJ booth set up at the edge of one of the pastures. Charlie pulled up in front of the farmhouse, where two girls sat behind a folding table with a cash box and a stack of red plastic cups. Twenty bucks bought you entrance and a cup to fill at the keg.

"I'll pick you up at one right here," he said as we climbed out, then peeled away in a cloud of dust.

The air smelled of fresh grass and Axe body spray. There were way more people milling about the fields than the students that made up Sam's small graduating class. As promised, the girls wore flip-flops or sandals with their dresses, some of them in floor-length prom-style gowns and others in more casual summer cotton. Most of the guys were in dress pants and button-down shirts, but a few, like Sam, wore jackets. We filled our cups and then tried to find Jordie and Finn, but the only lights were the ones on the stage, and unless you were standing in front of it, you had to squint to make out faces in the fading blue light.

Every few minutes, someone would come up to Sam to tell him how fantastic his speech was. We made our way to the stage, watching other drunker people dancing with their arms linked around each other's shoulders. Several beers in, I noticed that there were no porta potties and that girls were sneaking away to squat in the bushes. I slowed down my drinking after that, but eventually was forced to break the seal among the leaves like everyone else.

"That was a unique experience," I said to Sam when I got back. The red lights of the stage illuminated his four-beer grin and hooded eyes.

"Dance with me," he said, circling his arms around my waist, and we swayed together slowly even though the music was a pounding club song.

"I know a million people have already told you this tonight," I said with my fingers twisted in the hair at the nape of his neck. "But your speech was kind of incredible. I thought *I* was the writer in this relationship. What other secrets are you keeping from me, Sam Florek?" The smile slipped from his face.

"What?" I asked. He pressed his lips together, and my stomach dropped. "Sam, what? Is there something you're keeping from me?" I stopped moving.

"Let's go somewhere quieter," he said, taking my hand to lead me away from the stage and toward a clump of boulders. He pulled me behind the rocks and ran his hand through his hair.

"Sam, you're really freaking me out," I said, trying to keep my voice steady. The beer was making my head fuzzy. "What's going on?"

He took a deep breath and shoved his hands in his pockets. "I got accepted into this intensive workshop for premed students."

"A workshop?" I parroted. "You didn't tell me you had applied."

"I know. It was a long shot. They only accept twelve first-years. I really didn't think I'd get in."

"Well, that's great," I said, my words slurring. "I'm proud of you, Sam."

"The thing is, Percy," he hesitated, shifting on his feet. "It starts early. I have to leave in three weeks." Battery acid dripped down my spine.

"Three weeks?" I repeated. Three weeks was no time at all. When would I see Sam after that? Thanksgiving? I shut my eyes—everything was starting to spin. "I'm going to be sick," I groaned.

"I'm sorry I didn't tell you sooner. I should have, but I knew how much you were looking forward to spending the summer together," he said, taking my hand.

"I thought you were, too," I murmured. Then I threw up all over his new dress shoes.

Charlie took one look at me when I climbed into the truck, cheeks stained with mascara tears, and said to Sam, "Finally told her, huh?" Sam shot him a dark look, and no one spoke for the rest of the drive.

Three weeks went by as if they were seconds, and my dread formed roots in my feet and grew branches that spread to my shoulders and arms. Sam spent much of our time together with his nose in various textbooks, as if he was cramming for a major exam. He refused to break our annual lake-crossing tradition, and insisted I do the swim on his last day before heading to school. It was a gorgeous sunny morning, and I went through the motions of stretching and warming up. Since I started competitive swimming, paddling across the lake wasn't a challenge for me like it used to be. I felt almost numb when I made it to the far shore, pulling my knees up to my chest and gulping down the water Sam had packed for me.

"Your fastest time yet," he said happily when I was done, throwing an arm around me and pulling me against his side. "I thought I might not be able to keep up." I let out a bitter laugh.

"That's funny," I said, hating how resentful I sounded. "I feel like I'm the one being left behind."

"You don't really think that, do you?" I wouldn't look at him but could hear the worry in his voice.

"What am I supposed to think, Sam? You didn't tell me that you applied to this course. You didn't tell me when you were accepted." I swallowed back tears. "I understand why you want to go. It's amazing that you got in. And I one hundred percent think it's going to be great for you. But you keeping all this from me until the *very last minute* hurts. A lot. It makes me feel like this is a one-sided thing we've got going on."

"It's not!" he said, his voice cracking. He pulled me onto his lap so I was facing him and took my head between his hands so I couldn't look away. "God, of course it's not. You're my best friend. My favorite person." He kissed me and pulled me against his bare chest. It was warm with sweat and he smelled so much like summer, so much like Sam, that I wanted to curl up inside him.

"We'll talk all the time."

"It feels like I'm never going to see you again," I admitted, and then he smiled at me with pity, like I was being truly ridiculous.

"It's just university," he said, kissing the top of my wet head. "One day, you won't be able to get rid of me. I promise."

~~~~

SUE AND SAM left early the next morning while Charlie and I waved from the porch, tears streaming down my face.

"C'mon," he said after the car had driven out of sight, throwing his arm around my shoulders. "Let's go for a boat ride."

It turned out that Charlie was a lot less of a jerk without Sam around to harass. Much to my parents' confusion, I decided to pick up extra shifts at the Tavern. Even when Charlie wasn't working, he would give me a ride. Most days, he'd swim over when I was down at the lake to see how I was doing.

I was not doing well. More than a week had gone by without me hearing from Sam, even though he had finally got a cell phone before he left for Kingston. I knew he wouldn't be big on texting, but I couldn't fathom why he hadn't responded to any of my HOW R U, I MISS U, and CAN U TALK??? messages. And when I called his dorm landline, he didn't answer.

Charlie kept giving me questioning looks whenever I came into the kitchen to pick up an order. On the way home one night, he cut the motor in the middle of the lake and turned to face me.

"Spill it," he ordered.

"Spill what?"

"I don't know, Pers. You tell me. I know you're bummed that Sam's gone, but you've been moping around like Miss Havisham."

"You know who Miss Havisham is?" I grumbled.

"Fuck off."

I sighed. "I still haven't heard from him. Not an email. No phone call."

Charlie rubbed his face. "I don't think he's got his internet set up yet. And Mom told you he called home. He's fine."

"But why didn't he call me?" I whined, and Charlie laughed.

"You know how expensive those long-distance calls are, Pers."

"Or text?"

Charlie sighed, then hesitated. "Okay, you want to know what I think?"

"I don't know, do I?" I narrowed my eyes. You never knew what you were going to get with Charlie.

"Honestly, I think my brother was a coward to keep the course a secret." He paused. "And if it were me, I would have called you as soon as I got to Kingston."

"Thanks," I said, my face hot.

"Sam has it in his head that you belong to him. Not in a creepy possessive way, but it's more like he has this belief that everything is meant to work out between you two in the end. And I think that's pretty much bullshit."

I blanched. "You don't think it's meant to work out?" I whispered.

"I don't think anything is meant to be," he said flatly. "He already screwed things up when you got that hockey player boyfriend. I hope he fights harder this time," he said, starting the engine. "Or someone else will."

15

Now

I SNEAK OUT TO THE CAR TO REAPPLY MY MAKEUP AND HAVE a few minutes alone. It's bad enough having an attack in front of Sam and Charlie, but Jordie and Finn seeing me on my hands and knees is a special kind of humiliation. I'm frustrated with myself for not recognizing the signs early enough to find a quiet place to fall apart instead of what I did: jump to the conclusion that my heart was about to peace out on me, amping my panic up to one thousand.

I'm dotting on another round of concealer when my phone buzzes. The name on the screen is one I can't ignore any longer.

"Hello?" I answer.

"P!" cries Chantal. "Are you okay? I've been calling you all day."

I wince, remembering the message I sent her this morning. "Sorry. I, um, got a little caught up here. I'm . . ." I trail off, because I'm not sure what I am.

"Persephone Fraser, are you serious right now?" she screeches. "You can't send me a text that says you need help, that you need to talk *ASAP* and then not answer your phone. I've been going nuts trying to reach you. I thought you had a panic attack and passed out in the woods somewhere and got eaten by a bear or a fox or something."

I laugh. "That's not far from the truth, actually." I can hear her rummaging around in the kitchen and then a glass being filled. Red wine, no doubt. She drinks red wine when she's stressed.

"Do not laugh," she huffs. Then adds more softly, "What do you mean that's not far from the truth? *Are* you lost in the woods somewhere?"

"No, of course not. I'm in my car." I hesitate.

"What's going on, P?" Her voice has returned to its natural velvety texture.

I bite the inside of my cheek, then decide to rip the bandage off: "I had a panic attack. A little while ago at the wake. It's not a big deal."

"What do you mean it's not a big deal?" Chantal erupts so loudly I lower the volume on my phone. "You haven't had a panic attack in years, and now you see the love of your life for the first time in a decade at his mom's funeral—a woman, who if I recall correctly from the handful of times you've told me about her, was kind of like a second mom to you—and now you're having panic attacks at her wake, and it's not a big deal? What about this isn't a big deal?"

I splutter.

"P," she says at a lower decibel but with no less force. "You think I don't see you, but I do. I see how you keep almost everyone around you at a distance. I see how little you care about the pompous douchebags you date. And even though you've buried your shit with Sam under more piles of shit, I know this is a big fucking deal."

This stuns me. "I thought you liked Sebastian," I murmur.

She lets out a low laugh. "Remember when the four of us went to brunch? The server had been ignoring us, and you had to use the bathroom? You told Sebastian to order for you if she came by?"

I tell her I remember before she continues.

"He ended up ordering you a huge stack of chocolate-chip pancakes while you were gone. You hate sweets at breakfast, and you didn't say a thing. You just thanked him. You ate, like, half a pancake, and he didn't even notice."

"It was just breakfast," I say quietly.

"There is nothing *just* about food," Chantal replies, and I can't help but laugh. Sue and Chantal would have gotten along. Then she sighs deeply. "My point is that he didn't really know you, even months and months into the relationship, and you didn't help him get to know you. I didn't like that."

I don't know what to say.

"Just tell me what's going on," Chantal says after a moment of silence. Chantal, who figured out my entire relationship strategy with one brunch order. So I do. I tell her all of it.

"Are you going to tell him?" she asks when I've finished. "The whole truth?"

"I don't know if it's worth it, bringing up the past again, just so I don't feel guilty anymore," I say.

Chantal makes a humming sound that means she doesn't agree. "Let's not pretend this is just about making yourself feel better. You've never moved on."

~~~~

BY THE TIME I head back inside, most of the guests have gone home, Dolly and Shania have been shut off, and Sam, Charlie, their grandparents, and a small group of aunts, uncles, and cousins are sitting around a row of pushed-together tables with glasses of wine and brandy. Sam and Charlie look tired, but mostly they seem relieved, not so bunched up in the shoulders. I leave the Floreks to reminisce, find a spare red apron in the linen closet and a serving tray behind the bar, and start clearing the dirty plates and glasses, bringing them to Julien, who's hunched over the dishwasher in the kitchen.

We've been working mostly in silence for almost an hour and finishing up the last of the cutlery when Julien says, "I always wondered where you went to," his eyes still on the silverware.

"I didn't really go anywhere. I just didn't come back," I tell him. "My parents sold the cottage." A few long seconds go by.

"I think we both know that's not why you disappeared," he says, and I pause. I dry off the last fork, and I'm about to ask Julien what he means, when he speaks. "We all thought you should come." He turns to me, his eyes boring into mine. "Just don't vanish again."

"What do you mean we . . ." I start to say, when the door swings open and Sam steps in, holding a half-dozen dirty glasses. He stops when he sees us and the door swings shut, bumping him in the shoulder. He eyes the apron and the tea towel I'm holding.

"Déjà vu," he says with a lazy half grin. He seems a little blurry around the edges. He's removed his jacket and loosened his tie. The top button on his shirt is undone.

"Still got it," I say, sticking my hip out and motioning to the apron, feeling Julien's eyes on me. "You know where to come if you're short-staffed."

Julien scoffs. "She's only a little less shit than you at dishes," he tells Sam just as Charlie walks in with a few empty snifters.

"Everyone's cleared out. This should be the last of it," he says, putting the glasses in a rack. "Thanks so much for cleaning up, both of you. And for putting this all together, Julien. It was exactly what Mom wanted." He brushes by me to give Julien a hug, smelling of the brandy and cigarettes he's been indulging in. Sam follows suit, then pulls me into an embrace, whispering a thank-you in my ear that feels like a warm towel wrapped around damp shoulders.

"You kids get out of here," Julien says. "I'll finish and lock up."

Charlie looks around at the spotless stainless steel surfaces. "Everything seems done to me. Why don't we all head out and go back to the house? We can grab a pizza on the way—I didn't eat anything."

Julien shakes his head. "Thanks, but you go ahead," he says, adding in a gruff voice, "And get Percy to drive. You two jack-asses are in no state."

~~~

WE PICK UP a couple of Pizza Pizza pizzas on the way to the Floreks' since none of us ate at the reception. I'm relieved Julien asked me to drive the boys home. I'm not ready to say goodbye.

I feel calmer after talking to Chantal. She didn't offer any advice—just listened to me talk about the last few days, then told me not to feel so bad about what happened with Sam in the truck, that people cope with grief differently.

And maybe that's all this morning was for Sam, comfort in his darkest hour. I could be okay with that, I tell myself, if that's all it is, if that's all he needs from me.

"This is weird," says Charlie from the back seat of the car. "You two up front and me in the back. It used to be me driving you around."

"It used to be you driving us nuts," Sam replies, and our eyes meet. He's smiling and now I'm smiling, and for a second it feels like there's no one but us, and that it's always just been us. And then I remember Charlie in the back seat and Taylor in wherever the heck she's gone.

"So tell us about these panic attacks, Pers. You a head case or what?" Charlie asks.

"Charlie." Sam's voice is hard as concrete.

When I look in the rearview mirror and meet Charlie's eyes, there are no sparkles of mischief, only soft concern.

"They let me out just for the funeral," I tell him, and he laughs but the lines between his eyebrows have become canyons. "I have a bit of an anxiety thing," I say, looking back out at the road. I wait for the pressure to build up in my lungs, but it doesn't, so I keep going. "I can usually manage it. You know—therapist, breathing exercises, mantras—the basic self-care practices of a privileged white girl. But sometimes the anxious thoughts get a bit out of control." I find Charlie in the mirror again and smile gently. "I'm okay, though."

"That's good, Percy," Sam says, and I glance at him expecting pity but I don't find it. I'm surprised how easy it is to tell them both.

Once we get to the house, they change out of their suits and we each grab a beer from the fridge, taking the pizza out to the deck and eating it straight from the box with squares of paper towel in lieu of plates. We scarf down the first slices without talking.

"I'm glad all that's done with," says Charlie when he comes up for air. "Just the ashes now."

"I don't think I'm ready for that," Sam replies, taking a sip of his beer and gazing out over the shore, where a boy and girl are climbing onto the Floreks' raft.

"Me neither," Charlie replies. Squeals and splashes carry up from the lake.

"The kids from next door," Sam says, noticing me looking at them. "At your cottage." They're both dark-haired, the boy a bit taller than the girl.

"Don't you dare!" she shouts just before he pushes her off the raft. They break into a fit of giggles when she climbs back on.

"How much longer will you be here for, Charlie?" I ask.

"About a week," he says. "We have a few loose ends to tie up." I assume he's referring to the house and the restaurant, but I don't ask—the idea of them selling this place is almost as heartbreaking as losing the cottage, but it's none of my business. "And what about you, Pers? When are you heading back?"

"Tomorrow morning," I say, peeling the label off the beer bottle. Neither one of them replies, and the silence feels dense.

"Did Taylor go back to Kingston after the funeral?" I ask to change the subject, and because I can't shake the feeling that she should be the one sitting here right now. Sam murmurs a yes, but Charlie's frowning. "That's too bad," I say, reaching for another slice.

"Are you fucking kidding me, Sam?" Charlie growls, and I jerk my arm back, knocking a half-full beer onto my lap.

"Shit!"

"It's none of your business, Charlie," Sam snaps as I stand, trying to brush the liquid off my dress. But it's as though they've forgotten I'm here.

"I can't believe you!" Charlie bellows. "You're doing the same thing all over again. You're a goddamn coward."

Sam's nostrils flare with each deliberate breath before he speaks. "You have no idea what I'm doing," he says quietly.

"You're right. I don't," Charlie replies, pushing back his chair so hard it tips over.

"Jesus, Charlie," Sam shouts. "She knows Taylor and I aren't together. Not that it's your business."

"You're right, it's not," Charlie snaps, his chest rising and falling with heavy breaths, anger radiating from him.

"Charlie?" I take a step forward. "Are you okay?"

He looks at me with a stunned expression, like he's surprised to find me standing there. His eyes soften.

"Yeah, Pers. I'm fine. Or I will be after I roll a joint and take a long walk," he says, and heads toward the house. "Get her some dry clothes," he tells Sam over his shoulder, and then he's gone.

I start grabbing the dirty paper towels and empty bottles with unsteady hands, not looking at Sam.

"Here," he says, taking the empties from me and bending down to my eye level. If it were anyone else, I'd say he was strangely calm for someone who was just told off by his brother, but it's classic Sam, and I can see the scarlet streaks staining his cheeks.

"Will he be all right?" I ask.

"Yeah," he sighs and looks toward the sliding door that Charlie disappeared through. "He doesn't think I've changed much since we were kids. He's wrong about that." He looks at me carefully, slowly, and I know he's deciding whether he should say more. "But you do need something dry to put on."

"I can't wear her clothes, Sam," I tell him, my voice as wobbly as my hands.

"Agreed," he says, gesturing toward the house with his head. "You can wear something of mine."

In some ways, this whole trip has been a time warp, but I'm still not ready for the wave of nostalgia that bashes against me when I follow Sam into his old bedroom. The dark blue walls. The anatomical heart poster. The desk. The twin bed that seems so much smaller than it once did.

He hands me a pair of sweatpants and a T-shirt. "I'll let you change," he says and steps outside, closing the door behind him.

Sam's clothes are about six sizes too big. I fold up the sleeves of the shirt and tie it in a knot at the waist, but there's not much I can do about the pants, except to tighten the drawstring and roll up the legs.

"You're going to laugh when you see me," I call as my eyes catch on a yellow-and-red box on the top of the bookshelf. It's no longer standing upright on display, but it's there nonetheless. I'm reaching for it when Sam walks back into the room.

"I can't believe you still have this," I say, holding the *Operation* box out to him.

"You know, that dress was hot, but this is a much better look on you." He smirks and motions to the pants. "Especially the saggy crotch."

"Leave my crotch alone," I tell him. One of his eyebrows quirks up in response. "Shut up," I mumble. He takes the box from me and puts it back on the shelf.

"Unless you want to play?" he asks, and I shake my head.

"What else do you still have?" I wonder aloud, leaning closer to the shelves.

"Pretty much everything," Sam says from beside me. "Mom didn't pack up my stuff, and I haven't touched it since I've been back."

I squat down in front of the Tolkien novels and sit cross-legged on the carpet.

"I never finished this." I tap *The Hobbit* and look up at him. He's watching me with a tight expression.

"I remember," he says quietly. "Too much singing."

He kneels beside me, his shoulder touching mine, and I nervously adjust my hair so it falls over my face, putting a barrier between us. I run my fingers over the thick medical tomes. I stop on the anatomy textbook, remembering what happened in this room when we were seventeen.

The thought enters my head unbidden and leaves my mouth at the same time: "That was the hottest thing that's ever happened to me." And then: "Shit." I keep my sight clamped to the shelf, wanting to die in an avalanche of out-of-date science books. Sam lets out a breath that sounds a little like a laugh, and then moves my hair behind my shoulder.

"I've picked up one or two moves since then," he says, his voice low and close enough that I can feel the words on my cheek. I put my hands on my thighs, where they're safe.

"I'm sure," I say to the books.

"Percy, can you look at me?" I close my eyes briefly but then I do, and I immediately wish I hadn't because his gaze drops to my mouth, and when it returns to my eyes, his are dark and wanting.

"I'm sorry about this morning," I blurt. "It should never have happened." I fidget with the drawstring on the pants.

"Percy," he says again, framing my face with his hands so I can't look away from him. "I'm not sorry."

"What did you mean when you said you've changed since we were young?" I ask, partially because I want to know but also because I'm stalling for time. He takes a deep breath and runs his hands down the sides of my face to grasp my neck, his thumbs tracing the curve of my jaw.

"I don't take things for granted anymore. I don't take people for granted. And I know time is not infinite." He smiles softly, sadly maybe. "I think Charlie always understood that. Maybe because he was older when Dad died. He thought I was wasting time with Taylor. But I think it's more like I've been following the path of least resistance."

"Isn't that a good thing?" I ask. "To have as little friction as possible in a relationship?"

His answer is quick and sure. "No."

"Why did you break up with her?"

"You know why."

Instead of relief, I'm sticky with panic. I can feel my heart picking up its pace. I try to shake my head in his hands, but he holds it firmly and then slowly brings his face down to mine, pressing his mouth so gently to mine it's barely a kiss, barely a whisper. He pulls back slightly.

"You drive me crazy, you know that? You always have." He kisses me again with so much care I can feel my heart relax a little, like it thinks it's safe, and my lungs must agree because I let go of a sigh. "And I never laughed with anyone like I laughed with you. I've never been friends with anyone like I was with you." He takes my hands and puts them around his neck, pulling me up so we're both kneeling. I want to tell him we need to talk before we head down this path, but he hugs me tight to his chest, and my bones and muscles and all the bits holding them together liquefy so that I melt into him.

He releases me enough to brush the hair back from my ear and whisper into it, "I've tried to forget about you for more than ten years, but I don't want to try anymore." I don't have time to reply because his lips are on mine and his hands are in my hair, and he tastes like pizza and movie nights and resting on the sand after a long swim. He sucks on my bottom lip, and when I moan, I feel him smile against my lips.

"I think I drive you crazy, too," he says against my mouth. I want to climb him, and consume him, and be consumed by him. I slip my hands under his shirt and over the two indentations on his lower back, bringing him harder against me. I feel his groan rather than hear it, and he pulls off his shirt, then mine, throwing them both on the floor while I stare at the expanse of tanned skin. I move my hands through the light hair on his chest and then over his stomach, memorizing every ridge.

"Not bad, Dr. Florek," I breathe. But when I peer back up at him, the slant of his grin and sky-blue of his eyes are so familiar, so much like home, that I know I have to tell him, even if it means losing him again. I drop my hands to my sides.

"What's wrong?" His eyes flit across my face.

"We need to talk," I say, then look at the ceiling, but not before two fat tears roll down my cheeks. I brush them away.

"You don't have to tell me anything," he says, taking my hand. But I shake my head.

"I have to." I squeeze his fingers tight. "Twelve years ago, you asked me to marry you," I whisper. Breathe.

"I remember," he says with a sad smile.

"And I pushed you away."

"Yeah," he rasps. "I remember that, too."

"I need you to know why I said no, when I loved you so much, when all I wanted was to say yes."

Sam wraps his arms around me and draws me to him, his warm chest against mine. "I wanted you to say yes, too." He presses his lips to my shoulder and leaves a kiss behind.

"I overheard you talking with Jordie and Finn earlier today," I say into his skin, and I can feel his body tense. I look up at him. "It sounded like you were talking about us."

"We were."

"What did they mean when they said you were messed up after what happened?"

"Percy, do you really want to talk about this now? Because there are other things I'd rather be doing." He kisses me softly.

"I want to know. I need to know."

He sighs, and his brows knit together. "I went through a tough time after, that's all. The guys knew. Jordie went to university with me, remember? He saw it all firsthand—lots of partying, drinking, that sort of thing. They're just overprotective."

This doesn't sound like the full truth, and Sam must see my suspicion.

"It's in the past, Percy," he says. And even though I know it's not, at least not for me, when he pulls my hair off my neck and sets a kiss just above my collarbone, I tilt my chin back and put my hand in his hair, holding him against me.

"Sam, stop," I manage to say after several seconds, and he does, leaning his forehead against mine.

"I'm not good enough for you," I tell him. "I don't deserve you. Or your friendship. And especially not anything more than friendship." I'm about to go on, but he puts two fingers over my mouth and looks at me with wide eyes.

"Don't do this, Percy. Don't shut me out again," he pleads. "I want this." He's breathing rapidly, his forehead creased in question. "Don't you want this, too?"

"More than anything," I tell him, and one corner of his mouth ticks up. He brings my hands up to his lips and kisses each, not taking his eyes off mine.

"Then let me have you," he says. And I don't know if he means right now or for good, but as soon as the yes leaves my mouth, he's kissing me.

~~~~

THE KISS IS fierce and clumsy, and when our teeth knock together, we both laugh.

"Fuck, Percy. I want you so much," he says, biting at my bottom lip. The sharpness sends a shudder through me, and he moves his mouth down, nipping at my collarbone along the way.

"I used to lie awake at night thinking about these freckles," he murmurs, kissing the constellation of brown dots on my chest. I don't notice him unhooking my bra, but when he pushes the straps off my shoulders, the whole thing falls away. He brings his hands to my breasts, moving the nipples between his thumbs and fingers, and when they tighten at his touch, he leans down, circling his tongue around one, then sucking it into his mouth, and pinching hard on the other. My hands fly to his shoulders to steady myself. When his name moves across my lips, he kisses me wetly before moving his mouth back down to my breasts.

I reach for the fly of his jeans and fumble with the button, distracted by what his tongue and his teeth are doing and the needy pulses between my legs. I conquer the button, then the zipper, and work the jeans past his hips. I feel his hardness through his briefs and he inhales sharply. The sound sets off something within me—an old need to push Sam, to make him come undone, to make him make more noises like the one he just made. It's fireworks of lust and longing and humid summer nights. I run my nails up his back and then bring his face to mine.

"Just so we're clear," I tell him, unblinking, "I want this. I want you. You can have me, but I want to have you, too." When I kiss him, it's with every last drop of every bit of myself that I have. I move my hand down his chest, his stomach, slipping it inside the waistband of his underwear, wrapping my hand around him, moving it over his length. He looks down and watches for a second, then back to me with a smile, pulling my hand away and leaning me back on the carpet.

"Remember the first time you did that?" he asks, smiling down at me and taking his jeans off.

"I was so nervous," I say. "I thought I was going to hurt you." He curls his fingers over the top of the sweatpants and pulls them down my legs, leaving them around my ankles.

"You got the hang of it," he says, kneeling between my legs. "We had quite a bit of practice," he says, looking up at me with a slanted grin.

"We did," I say, smiling back.

"But you didn't let me practice this." He bends and kisses me over my underwear.

"I was too self-conscious," I breathe.

"And what about now?" he asks, moving my underwear to the side. My legs twitch. "Are you still too self-conscious?"

"No," I gasp, and he smiles up at me, but his eyes are stormy with hunger.

"Good." He hooks his fingers around the edge of my panties and pulls them down around my ankles, then pins my wrists by my hips so I can't move my arms. "Because I have a lot of time to make up for." He buries his tongue inside me, then brings it up over my clit, flicking and swirling and sucking, telling me how many times he's thought of this, how good I taste. I cry out, and he sucks harder. I try to spread my legs, but my ankles are restrained by the fabric around them.

"You like that?" he asks softly, and I lift my hips closer to his mouth in response. He lets go of my wrists, gets rid of the clothes around my ankles, and grabs the flesh of my ass, holding me up to his mouth, while my fingers grab at his hair. He moves his tongue inside me again, his moan vibrating through me, his fingers tracing lightly where I need them. I squeeze my thighs around him, and he bites my inner thigh while he reaches up to my nipple, squeezing and pinching. His mouth follows, his tongue hot on my breast, while his fingers work the swollen flesh between my legs. I whisper his name over and over, and he presses his finger inside me. My body is hot and damp with sweat, and I ask for more. He looks up at me, his eyes burning as he adds another finger and another, until I'm full of him. My legs start shaking and he moves down my body, sucking on me, hard and long, and then he grazes his teeth against me, and I scream and fall into tiny little jagged pieces.

He kisses his way back up my limp body, and I wrap my arms and legs around him.

"Just think of all the time you wasted being self-conscious," he says with a grin.

"Shut up." I squeeze him with my legs and he laughs and kisses me more, brushing my bangs off my damp forehead.

"Told you I had a few new moves," he says, kissing me again.

"I'm worried about your ego," I say, a goofy smile on my face. He nips at my shoulder, then my ear, and then Sam is above me. Pressing against me. Looking down at me. I'm not sure I've been this happy in more than a decade, so I push aside the nagging voice in the back of my head, even though I know I can't ignore it much longer. I feel frantic for him. We've never had sex, and I want to erase all the others, so that it's only ever been him.

I bring my face to his and kiss him slowly, rolling my hips against him. I work his underwear down and feel him hot and hard against my hip. He reaches up behind my head and pulls a condom from his nightstand drawer, rolling it over his length, and with his forearms beside my head, he lies back over me, holding my eyes with his.

"Are we really doing this?" I whisper. He pushes into me and

I inhale sharply. He holds still, and we look at each other for several seconds.

"Yeah, we are," he says, and pulls out almost all the way, and then thrusts in again, and we both groan. I capture his waist with my legs and raise my hips to meet him, following the unhurried rhythm he sets, my hands on his shoulders, his back, his ridiculously firm ass, and his eyes never leave mine. He hikes my knee up, pushing himself deeper inside me and moving his hips in infuriatingly slow circles that inch me toward release but don't take me there. I growl in frustration and pleasure and ask him to please keep going, to please not stop, to please go faster. I'm very polite, but he only grins and pulls on my lip with his teeth.

"I've waited a long time for this. I'm not in a hurry," he says.

And he's not in a hurry, not at first, not until his back is slick and his muscles are taut and he's shaking from restraint. He holds back until I grow impatient and needy and bite on his neck and whisper, "I've waited a long time for this, too."

After, we lie on the floor facing each other, the early evening sun glowing golden over us. Sam's eyes are heavy, a tired smile on his lips. He's running his fingers up and down my arm. I know I have to tell him. The words run in a loop in my mind. I just have to say them out loud.

"I love you," he whispers. "I don't think I ever stopped."

But I barely hear what he says, because at the same time, the words I should have said twelve years ago bubble up my throat and out of my mouth.

16

Summer, Twelve Years Ago

BY THE TIME I FINALLY HEARD FROM SAM, IT WAS TWO WEEKS after he'd left for school, and I was furious. He was apologetic and full of *how are you*s and *I love you*s and *I miss you*s, but he was also off. He evaded my questions about the workshop, his dorm, and the other students, or gave one-word answers. Five minutes into the call, a knock sounded in the background and a girl's voice asked if he would be ready to leave soon.

"Who was that?" I asked, the words tight.

"That was just Jo."

"A girl Jo?"

"Yeah. She's in the workshop," he explained. "Most of us are on the same floor. We're having a potluck, and, well, I should go."

"Oh." I could hear the blood rushing through my ears, hot and angry. "We haven't even done three updates."

"Listen, I'll email you later. I finally got my internet working this week."

"You got your email working this week? Like, earlier this week?"

"A couple days ago, yeah."

"Oh."

"I didn't write because there really wasn't much to say. But I will, okay?"

True to his word, Sam did email, dashing off quick, unsatisfying notes, promising fuller updates in the future. He even sent a couple of texts. I relayed everything to Delilah—who promised to keep an eye on him when she got there and report back on any "skanky-ass losers" she saw him with—and to Charlie, who listened but didn't offer much feedback.

"You need to start swimming again," Charlie said as we pulled up to the restaurant one drizzly evening after I told him about Sam's latest message. He would be switching to a two-person dorm room so Jordie and he could bunk together in September. "Like you did with Sam," Charlie continued without a look in my direction. "Get out of that head of yours. We'll start tomorrow. If you're not at the dock by eight, I'll come drag you there." He hopped out of the truck, not waiting for a response, and swung open the back door to the kitchen, while I watched him with my mouth open.

The next morning, he was waiting for me on the dock, in sweats and a T-shirt, a mug of coffee in hand. I'd rarely seen Charlie awake so early in the morning.

"I didn't know your species could function before noon," I said as I walked up to him, noticing the pillow creases on his face as I got closer.

"Only for you, Pers," he said, and it sort of sounded like he meant it. I was about to say thank you—because as much as swimming was a thing Sam and I did together, it was also my thing, and I had missed it—but Charlie nodded his head to the water, his message obvious. *Get in.*

We met every morning. Charlie rarely joined me in the water, and sat watching at the edge of the dock, sipping from his steaming mug. I quickly learned that he was basically nonfunctional until he'd gotten halfway through his first cup of coffee, but once it was drained, his eyes would spark up, fresh as spring grass. On the hottest mornings, he'd dive in and swim laps beside me.

After a week of mornings at the water, Charlie decided that I was going to swim across the lake again before the end of summer. "You need a goal. And I want to see you do it up close," he'd said when we were heading up to the house from the lake. I thought back to the summer Charlie suggested that I take up swimming and offered to help me train, and agreed without argument.

Sometimes we'd have coffee and breakfast with Sue after the swim. At first she seemed uncomfortable with our friendship, looking between us with a slight frown. I'd mentioned it to Charlie once, but he'd brushed me off. "She's just worried you're going to figure out who the better brother is," he said, and I'd rolled my eyes. But I wondered.

One thing Charlie was right about: I did get out of my head when I swam, but the vacation only lasted as long as I was in the water, focusing on my breath, moving forward. And by mid-August, I had picked up what some may describe as crazy-girlfriend behavior, calling Sam from the cottage landline when I got home from shifts, no matter how late and despite my parents' limiting long-distance calls to twice a week. I would have used my own cell if the reception at the lake hadn't been so shoddy. I knew Sam was waking up extra early to squeeze in a run before he had to be in the lab at eight, but I also knew he would be at home alone, in bed, and couldn't avoid me.

But the calls didn't make me feel any better. Sam was often

distracted, asking me to repeat questions, and offered so little information about the workshop, seemed to not even be enjoying it, that I became bitter not just about his keeping it a secret from me in the first place but that he'd even gone at all.

"You gave up our summer together for this. You could at least pretend to be getting something out of it," I'd snapped at him one night when he was particularly monosyllabic.

"Percy," he'd sighed. He sounded exhausted, worn down by me or the program or both.

"I'm not asking for much," I told him. "Just a modicum of enthusiasm."

"A modicum? Are you sleeping with your thesaurus again?" It was his attempt at lightening the mood, but it didn't improve mine. And so I'd asked the question that had been gnawing at me from the moment he told me he'd be leaving for school early.

"Did you apply to this thing so you could get away from me?"

The other end of the line was silent, but I could hear my heart pumping in my ears, my temples throbbing with its angry supply of blood.

"Of course not," he replied eventually, quietly. "Is that what you really think?"

"You barely say anything when we talk, and you seem to hate it there. Plus, the whole *Surprise, I'm leaving in three weeks!* thing doesn't exactly instill confidence in our relationship."

"When are you going to get over that?" He said it with a harshness I'd never heard from him before.

"Probably as long as you spent keeping it a secret from me," I shot back.

I could hear Sam take a deep breath. "I didn't come here to leave you," he said, calmer now. "I came to start building something for myself. A future. I'm just adjusting. It's all new."

We didn't stay on the phone much longer after that. It was past midnight. I lay awake most of the night, worried that what Sam was building for himself wouldn't have room for me in it.

~~~~

I GREW IRRITABLE with everyone around me. I was short with Sam on the phone and sometimes I avoided replying to Delilah's texts, annoyed with her excitement about going away to school. It seemed unfair that she and Sam would be sharing the same campus. My parents didn't seem to notice my sulking. I often walked into the cottage to find them speaking in hushed tones over stacks of paperwork.

"We're not going to be able to make it all work," I heard Dad say to Mom on one of these occasions, but I was too wrapped up in my own teen angst to concern myself with their grown-up problems.

The only intermissions from my anxiety were the mornings with Charlie in the water. I hadn't bothered telling my parents that I was going to swim across the lake again. Mom and Dad had gone back to the city early—something involving the house, I hadn't paid much attention—and wouldn't be here for the last ten days of summer. On the day of the swim, I met Charlie on the dock like any other morning, gave him a nod, dove in, and took off. I didn't even wait for him to get in the boat, but soon enough I could see the oar hitting the water beside me.

That long, steady swim across the lake was a reprieve from everything that had been nagging at me, and when I'd made it to the beach, my limbs burned in a way that felt pleasant, that felt alive.

"Thought you'd forgotten how to do that," Charlie called over to me as he pulled the boat up onto the shore next to me. He was wearing a bathing suit and a sweat-soaked T-shirt.

"Swim?" I asked, confused. "We've been training every day for almost a month."

Charlie sat down beside me. "Smile," he said, nudging me with his shoulder.

I reached up and felt my cheek. "It felt good," I said. "To move . . . To escape."

He nodded. "Who doesn't need to escape from Sam every now and then?" He wiggled his eyebrows as if to say, *Am I right? Or am I right?*

"You're always so hard on him," I said, still grinning into the sun and catching my breath. I was almost giddy from the endorphin rush. I wasn't looking for a response, and he didn't give me one. Instead, I asked, "So did it meet your expectations?"

He tilted his head.

"You said you wanted to watch the swim up close. Was it everything you dreamed of?"

"Absolutely." He threw in a dimpled smile for emphasis. "Although in my dreams you were wearing that little yellow bikini you used to strut around in." It was the kind of classic Charlie line that I'd once shrugged off, but today it hit me like jet fuel. I wanted to bask in it. I wanted to play.

"I didn't strut!" I cried. "I have never strutted in my life."

"Oh, you strutted," Charlie said with a perfectly straight expression.

"You're one to talk. I am fairly certain your photo is under the word 'flirt' in the dictionary."

He laughed. "A dictionary definition joke? You can do better than that, Pers."

"Agreed," I said, laughing now, too. "Did you know you were my first kiss?" The question tumbled out of me—not intended to carry any weight, but Charlie's dimples disappeared.

"Truth or dare?" he asked. I'd sometimes wondered if he'd forgotten. He clearly hadn't.

"Truth or dare."

"Huh," he said, looking out at the water. I don't know what reaction I was expecting, but it wasn't that. He stood up suddenly. "Well, I'm hot as balls. I'm going for a dip."

"Figures the one time you decide to wear a shirt is the only time you really shouldn't have," I quipped as he stood up and yanked it over his head. I usually tried to keep my focus squarely on Charlie's face when he was shirtless. It was too much—the expanse of skin and muscle—but here it all was, deeply tanned and coated in sweat. He caught me staring before I could scrape my eyes away, and flexed his bicep.

"Show-off," I muttered.

I lay back in the sand, eyes closed to the sun while Charlie swam. I'd almost dozed off when he sat beside me again.

"You still writing?" he asked. We hadn't really talked about writing before.

"Umm . . . not much," I said. I hadn't felt particularly creative this summer. *Not at all*, was the truth.

"They're good, your stories."

I sat up at this. "You read them? When?"

"I read them. I was looking for something in Sam's desk the other day and found a stack of them. Read them all. They're good. You're good."

I was looking over at him, but he was staring out over the water.

"You're serious? You liked them?" Sam and Delilah were always so effusive, but they *had* to like them. Charlie wasn't in the habit of doling out compliments that didn't involve body parts.

"Yeah. They're a bit weird, but that's the point, right? They're different, in a good way." He looked over at me. His eyes were a pale celery in the sun, bright against his browned skin. But there was no hint of teasing in them. "Might help with the escaping, to write something new," he said.

I hummed a noncommittal sound in response, suddenly fully aware of all the ways Charlie had been trying to help me get out of my funk this summer. Even though I had been a troll. And if it hadn't been obvious to me then, it would have been later that evening.

We had pulled up to the back of the Tavern, my legs too wobbly for the walk from the town dock to the restaurant, and Charlie turned off the engine and turned to face me. "So I've got an idea, and I think it might cheer you up a bit." He gave me a hesitant smile.

"I already told you three-ways are a hard limit for me," I told him with a straight face, and he chuckled.

"Whenever you get sick of my brother, let me know, Pers," he said, still laughing. I went still. I'd never spent so much time with Charlie. And the thing was, I enjoyed it. A lot. Some of the time I even forgot how mad I was at Sam and how much I missed him. Charlie didn't have a girl hanging off him that summer, and he was a surprisingly good listener. He bulldozed over my bad moods, either ignoring them completely or calling me out. "Being a bitch doesn't suit you," he told me the last time I snapped at him after receiving another painfully short email from Sam. Now the air in the truck was as thick as caramel sauce.

"The drive-in," Charlie blurted, blinking. "That's the idea. They're playing one of those cheesy old horror movies you like, and I thought it might be a good distraction. Your parents are in the city this week, right? I figured you might be a bit lonely."

"I didn't know there was a drive-in in Barry's Bay," I said.

"There's not. It's about an hour from here. Used to go all the time in high school." He paused. "So what do you think? It's playing Sunday, and we're not working." It felt dangerous in a way I couldn't quite put my finger on. Horror movies were mine and Sam's thing, but Sam wasn't here. And I was. And so was Charlie.

"I'm in," I said, hopping out of the truck. "It's exactly what I need."

<p style="text-align:center">~~~~~</p>

I GOT SAM'S email on Saturday. I had trudged up from the lake after a hectic shift, my skin still sticky despite the cool wind on the boat trip home. Practically every order was for pierogies, and we'd run out halfway through the night. Julien had been foul, and the tourists weren't too happy about it, either.

The cottage was completely empty. I showered and fixed myself a plate of cheese and crackers while I booted up my laptop to check my email. This was my usual post-work, pre-call-with-Sam ritual. What was unusual was the unread message from him waiting in my inbox, sent a couple of hours earlier. Subject line: *I've been thinking.* Sam's emails usually came in the morning, before his seminar, or in the afternoon, right afterward. One- or two-sentence updates, and they never had subject lines. My limbs went numb with dread as I opened it and saw the paragraphs of text.

Percy,

The last six weeks have been hard. Harder than I thought. I'm still not used to this room or the bed. The school is huge. And the people are smart. The kind of smart that makes me realize how growing up in a small town gave me a false sense of my own intelligence. I look around during a lecture or a lab and everyone seems to be nodding along and following instructions without need for clarification. I feel so behind. How did I even get accepted into this workshop in the first place? Is this what all of school will be like?

I know I spent our last bit of time together studying, but it wasn't enough. I should have worked harder. I need to work harder now if I want to succeed here.

And I miss you so much. I can't concentrate sometimes because I'm thinking about you and what you might be doing. When we talk, I can hear your disappointment in me—for not telling you about the workshop and for how unhappy I seem here. I don't want it all to have been a waste. I will work harder. I will succeed here. I have to.

And that's why I think we need to establish some boundaries. I love hearing your voice on the other end of the phone, but I hang up and feel nothing but loneliness. Soon you'll be starting school too, and you'll see what I mean. We owe it to ourselves and each other to immerse ourselves—you in your writing and me in the lab.

What I'm proposing is a break from constant communication. Right now, I'm thinking a phone call every week. We can make it the same time—like a date. Otherwise, you'll be all I think about. Otherwise, I won't be able to do this thing that I've wanted for so long, I won't be the person I want to be. For you, but also for me. Just a little space—to build a big future.

What do you think? Let's talk about it tomorrow—I was thinking Sunday could be our day.

Sam

I read the whole thing three times, my cheeks wet with tears, a wad of crackers lodged in my throat. Sam wanted space. From us.

From me. Because talking to me made him feel lonely. I was a distraction. I was holding him back from his future.

Sam was kidding himself if he thought I'd wait till tomorrow to talk about this. To fight about this. This was not how you treated your best friend, and it was absolutely not how you treated your girlfriend.

His phone rang three, four, five times until he picked up. Except it wasn't Sam who yelled hello over the music and laughter in the background. It was a girl.

"Who is this?" I asked.

"This is Jo. Who is this?" Was this why Sam didn't want me calling? He wanted to have other girls over?

"Is Sam there?"

"Sam's busy at the moment. We're cheering him up. Can I take a message?" Her words slopped together.

"No. This is Percy. Put him on."

"Percy." She giggled. "We've heard so . . ." Suddenly she was gone, the music went quiet, and there was muffled laughter before a door closed. Then silence until Sam spoke.

"Percy?" From the one word, I could tell Sam was drunk. So much for needing space to work harder.

"So was this whole email bullshit? You just want more time to get drunk with other girls?" I was yelling.

"No, no, no. Percy, look, I'm really wasted. Jo brought over raspberry vodka. Let's talk. Tomorrow okay? Right now, I think I'm gonna . . ." The line went dead, and I curled up on the couch and cried till I passed out.

~~~~

CHARLIE PICKED ME up a bit before eight the next evening. By that time, I was all out of tears. I had sobbed through a long conversation with Delilah and then again when Sam sent a short apology for hanging up on me to puke. He wrote that he wanted to talk tonight. I didn't reply.

I didn't think it would be possible to laugh, but the mountain of snacks Charlie had assembled on the front seat was truly insane.

"There are burgers, dogs, and fries there if you want something more substantial," he said as I eyed the packages of chips and candy.

"Yeah this probably won't be enough," I joked. And it felt nice. Light. "I usually go through at least four party-sized bags of chips a night, and there's only three in here, so . . ."

"Smart-ass," he said, glancing my way as he headed down the long driveway. "I didn't know what flavor you like. I was covering my bases."

"I've always wondered what happens to all those girls you date," I said, holding up a box of Oreos. "Now I know. You fatten them up and eat them for dinner."

He shot me a mischievous grin. "Well, one of those things is true," he said in a low drawl. I rolled my eyes and looked out the window so he couldn't see the blush spreading from my chest to my neck.

"You scare easily," he said after a minute had gone by.

"I don't scare easily. You like to provoke people unnecessarily," I told him, turning back to study his profile. He was frowning. "What? Am I wrong?" I barked, and he laughed.

"No, you're not wrong. Maybe 'scare' is the wrong word, but it's easy to get you worked up." He looked over at me. "I like it." I could feel the flush move down through my body. He turned back to the road wearing a big enough smile that a hint of a dimple appeared on his cheek. I had a strong urge to run my finger over it.

"You like to make me mad?" I asked, trying to sound indignant, but also trying to flirt. He glanced over again before answering.

"Sort of. I like how your neck gets red, like you're hot all over. Your mouth gets all twisty, and your eyes look dark and kind of wild. It's pretty sexy," he said, his eyes on the empty stretch of highway. "And I like that you stand up to me. Your insults can be pretty savage, Pers." I was shocked. Not by the sexy part—that was just Charlie being Charlie, at least I thought so—but by the fact that he'd so obviously been paying attention to me. Spending time with him had been the only thing keeping me halfway sane, but I was getting the impression that he'd started paying attention before he'd taken pity on me this summer. At least I thought it had been pity. Now I wasn't so sure.

"When it comes to insults, you deserve only the best, Charles Florek," I replied, trying to sound easy.

"Couldn't agree with you more," he said. And then added after a beat, "So what's with these puffy eyes of yours?"

I looked out the window again. "Guess the cucumber slices didn't work," I mumbled.

"You look like you've been swimming with your eyes open in a chlorinated pool. What's he done now?" he asked.

I sputtered a bit, not sure how to get the words out quickly enough that I wouldn't start to cry again. "He, umm." I cleared my throat. "He says I'm distracting him and wants to take a break." I looked over to Charlie, who was watching the road, his jaw tight. "He needs more space. From me. So he can study and be important one day."

"He broke up with you?" The words were quiet, but there was so much anger behind them.

"I don't know," I said, my voice cracking. "I don't think that's what it was, but he only wants to talk to me once a week. And when I called last night, there were people in his room, and this girl he's been hanging out with. He was drunk." A muscle twitched in Charlie's jaw.

"Let's not talk about it," I whispered, even though we had both been silent for seconds. Then I added with more certainty, "I want to have fun tonight. There's one week left of summer and one of the best horror movies of all time ahead of us."

Charlie looked over at me with a pained expression.

"Please?" I asked.

He looked back out the windshield. "I can do fun."

The movie was *Rosemary's Baby*, one of my favorites from the sixties, and not exactly the cheesy slasher film Charlie had expected. As the credits rolled, he stared at the screen, mouth hanging open.

"That was some messed-up shit," he murmured and turned slowly to me. "You like this stuff?"

"I *looove* it," I cooed. We had gone through a bag of salt-and-vinegar chips, a bunch of gummy worms and licorice and two slushies from the concession stand. I was amped from the sugar. It was the most fun I'd had all summer, which was shocking since I'd spent most of the day in the fetal position.

"You're one disturbing girl, Pers," he said, shaking his head.

"And that's saying something coming from you." I grinned, and when he grinned back, my eyes dropped to his dimples before noticing that his were on my mouth. I cleared my throat, and he quickly looked at the clock on the dash.

"We better get you back," he said, starting the truck.

We spent the drive home talking, first about his economics program at Western and the rich kids he was sharing a house with in the fall, and then about how I felt like everyone was moving on to bigger and better things while I stayed in Toronto, following the path my parents laid for me. He didn't try to make me feel better or tell me I was overreacting. He just listened. There weren't more than a few seconds of dead air the entire hour drive back. We were cracking up over a story about his first school dance when he pulled up to the cottage. His dad had taught him the "proper" way to dance beforehand, which ended up with Charlie two-stepping a thoroughly freaked-out Meredith Shanahan across the gymnasium floor.

"You wanna come in?" I asked, still laughing. "I think there are a few of Dad's beers in the fridge."

"Sure," Charlie said, cutting the engine and walking me to the door. "If you play your cards right, I might ask you to dance."

"I only tango," I said over my shoulder as I turned the key in the lock.

"I knew it would never work between us," he said in my ear, scattering goose bumps down my arm.

We kicked off our shoes and Charlie took in the small, open space. "I haven't been in here in ages," he said. "I like that your parents have kept it as a real cottage. Well, other than that," he said, pointing to the espresso machine that took up way too much of the kitchen counter. I walked to the other side of the room and flicked on the floodlight that shone up into the towering red pines.

"It's my favorite place in the world," I said, watching the swaying boughs for a moment. When I turned around, Charlie was studying me with a strange expression on his face.

"I should probably get home," he said hoarsely, pointing over his shoulder.

I tilted my head. "You literally just got here." I moved by him to open the fridge. "And I promised you a beer." I passed him a bottle.

He scratched the back of his neck. "I'm not really in the habit of drinking alone." I rolled my eyes and pulled the sleeve of my sweatshirt over my hand so I could twist off the cap. I took a long drink, then handed him the bottle.

"Better?" I asked. He took a sip, eyeing me warily.

"You really made an effort tonight, huh?" he said, gesturing to my outfit, a pair of ripped jean shorts and a gray sweatshirt. I'd thrown my hair up into a ponytail. It was only then I registered that he was wearing nice dark jeans and a new-looking polo shirt.

"Left my ball gown in Toronto," I replied.

He smirked, his eyes dropping to my legs. "My dates don't wear ball gowns, Pers," he said, his gaze returning to mine. "But usually they wear clean clothes." I looked down and, yep, there was an orangey stain on the leg of my shorts. "You know, as a sign of a basic level of hygiene," he added. I could feel myself heating, and his smile split open.

"Told you," he said, his voice deep and low. He put his bottle down and took a step toward me. "Red neck. Twisted-up mouth. And your eyes are even darker than usual." We stood like that, neither of us breathing, for several long seconds.

"It's sexy as hell," he rasped. "You're so fucking sexy I can't stand it."

I blinked once and then threw myself at him, slinging my arms around his neck and bringing his mouth down to mine. I wanted to be wanted so badly. He met me just as eagerly, grabbing my waist and pulling me against his hard body. He held my hips against him with one hand and wrapped the other around my ponytail, pulling my head back and then sucking on the exposed flesh of my neck. When I moaned, he cupped my butt and lifted me off the floor, guiding my legs around his waist, parting my lips with his tongue and backing me up so I was sitting on the counter. He spread my legs wide and stepped between them, trailing a hand up my calf.

"I didn't shave," I whispered between kisses, and he laughed into my mouth, sending vibrations through me. He crouched down, holding my ankle, then ran his tongue from my shin up over my knee to the edge of my shorts, eyes on mine the entire time.

"I really don't care," he growled, then stood and captured my face between his hands. "You could go a month without shaving, and I'd still want you." I squeezed my legs around him and kissed him hard, then bit down on his lip, making him groan. The sound was catnip to my ego.

"Let's go upstairs," I said, then pushed him away so I could jump down, and led him up to my bedroom.

His hands were on me as soon as we passed through the doorway. I walked backward until my knees hit the bed, and reached for his shirt at the same time he reached for mine. We took them off in a tangle of arms and then he unhooked my bra in seconds, throwing it onto the floor. My hands flew to the buttons of his jeans, desperate to feel him against me, to erase all the sad parts, to feel wanted. He watched me take them off, then unzipped my shorts, sliding them over my hips so they hit the ground. We stood in front of each other, breathing heavily, and then I pushed my underwear down my legs and moved closer to him, brushing my fingers over his shoulders. I didn't realize they were shaking until Charlie put his hands on top of mine.

"Are you sure?" he asked gently. In reply, I pulled him down onto the bed on top of me.

~~~

I MUST HAVE fallen asleep immediately after because when I woke, pink morning sky glowed through the windows. Still groggy, I felt breathing on my shoulder before I realized there was a thigh thrown over me. The box of condoms my mom had given me last year sat open on the nightstand.

"Good morning," a gravelly voice rasped in my ear. It sounded so much like Sam. I squeezed my eyes shut, hoping it was a bad dream. He shifted his weight over me and kissed my forehead, nose, then my lips, until I opened my eyes and stared up into a pair of green eyes.

The wrong eyes.

The wrong brother.

I inhaled raggedly, seeking oxygen, feeling my pulse, fast and uncomfortable, all over my body.

"Pers, what's wrong?" Charlie moved off me and helped me into a seated position. "Are you going to be sick?"

I shook my head, looked at him wild-eyed, and gasped, "I can't breathe."

~~~

I MOVED THROUGH the final days of summer in a fog of self-loathing, trying to figure out why I'd done what I'd done and how I could possibly tell Sam about my betrayal.

After the panic attack subsided, I kicked Charlie out of the cottage, but he'd come back in the afternoon to check on me. I yelled and screamed at him through hot tears, telling him it was a huge mistake, telling him I hated him, telling him I hated me. When I started hyperventilating, he held me tightly until I'd calmed down, whispering how sorry he was, how he didn't mean to hurt me. He apologized once I had, looking pained and flattened, and left me alone feeling even worse for having hurt him as well.

Charlie apologized again when he picked me up for my last shift at the Tavern a day later, and I nodded, but that was the last we spoke of what had happened between us.

When I returned to the city, my parents immediately broke the news that they would be putting the cottage up for sale in the fall. I should have seen it coming, paid more attention to the way my parents had been sniping at each other about money. I burst into tears when they explained how our Toronto home needed renovations and, besides, I could always stay with the Floreks. It felt like punishment for what I'd done.

Sam and I had only exchanged emails since the night with Charlie, but he called me as soon as he read my message with the news, saying he was sad but was sure I could spend the next summer at their house.

"I know how upset you must be," he said. "You won't have to say goodbye alone. We can pack your things together over Thanksgiving and move a bunch of it to my place. The *Creature from the Black Lagoon* poster can go in my room."

Neither of us mentioned his email. And I said nothing of what had happened with Charlie.

What I needed was to talk to Delilah, but she had already shipped out to Kingston. I wanted to confide in her, I wanted her to give me a plan for how to make everything better, but I couldn't do that via text, and I didn't want to do it on the phone, to hear her voice but not see her reaction.

I don't remember much about those first weeks of school. Only that Sam began to write longer emails between our scheduled Sunday calls. Now that Jordie and he were rooming together and he was getting used to the campus and the city, he was feeling more settled. Also, while his workshop wasn't graded, he had received a glowing review from the supervising professor and an offer to work part-time on his research project. He hadn't yet bumped into Delilah, but he was keeping his eyes open for a head of red hair.

He explained how lonely he'd been when he first got to school, how he kept his notes short so as not to worry me. He apologized for the drunken state he'd been in when I called him, and told me that when he thought of building a future, it was always a future with me in it. He also apologized for not making that clear. He told me I was his best friend. He told me he missed me. He told me he loved me.

Sam's classes ended early on Fridays and he wanted to take the train to Toronto to see me on weekends, but I pushed him off, telling him my professor had asked for a twenty-thousand-word short story to be completed in a matter of weeks. It wasn't a lie, but I also finished the assignment well ahead of time without letting Sam know. By the time Thanksgiving rolled around, I was humming with nervous anticipation. I still hadn't told Delilah what had happened, but I had talked myself into telling Sam the truth. I would do anything I could to make it right between us, but I couldn't lie to him.

I drove up Friday, not even stopping to pee, so I could make it to the cottage by the time Sue got back to Barry's Bay with Sam. My parents had already moved most of our knickknacks out of the cottage and weren't coming back for the holiday. They left my room for me to take care of. The Realtor would be there the following week to stage the place and start the showings.

I had emailed Sam that I had something important to talk to him about as soon as he got home. *That's funny, I have something I want to talk to you about too*, he wrote.

I kept myself busy waiting for him, my stomach in knots and my hands shaking as I untacked the *Creature from the Black Lagoon* poster from over my bed. I cleared out my desk, flipping through the clothbound notebook Sam had given me, and running my fingers over his slanted inscription on the inside cover, *For your next brilliant story*, before packing it in a box. I set the wooden box with my initials carved on its lid on top. I knew without having to peek inside that it still contained the embroidery floss I made our bracelets with.

He has to forgive me, I thought to myself, over and over, willing it to be true.

I was just getting started on the nightstand when I heard the back door open. I flew down the stairs and threw myself into Sam's arms, knocking him backward and against the door, his laugh reverberating through me, our arms tight around each other. He felt bigger than I remembered. He felt solid. And real.

"I missed you, too," he said into my hair, and I breathed him in, wanting to climb inside his ribs and snuggle up beneath them.

We kissed and hugged, me through tears, and then he led me over to the middle of the room and leaned his forehead against mine.

"Three updates?" I whispered, and his eyes crinkled with a smile.

"One, I love you," he replied. "Two, I can't stand the idea of leaving again, of you not coming back to this cottage, without you knowing how much I love you." He took a shaky breath, then knelt on one knee, taking my hands in his. Three"—he looked up at me, his blue eyes serious and wide and hopeful and scared—"I want you to marry me."

My heart exploded in a burst of happiness, molten pleasure seeping into my bloodstream. And just as fast, I remembered what I'd done and who I'd done it with, and the color drained from my face.

Sam rushed to go on. "Not today. Or this year. Not until you're thirty, if that's what you want. But marry me." He reached into the pocket of his jeans and held out a gold ring with a circle of small diamonds surrounding a center stone. It was beautiful, and it made me feel violently ill.

"My mom gave me this. It was her mom's ring," he said. "You're my best friend, Percy. Please be my family."

I stood in silent shock for five long seconds, my mind racing. How could I tell him about Charlie now? When he was down on one knee, holding his grandmother's ring? But how could I accept without telling him? I wouldn't. I couldn't. Not when he thought I was good enough to marry. There was only one option.

I knelt down in front of him, hating myself for what I was about to do. What I had to do.

"Sam," I said, closing his hand over the ring and biting back tears. "I can't." He blinked, then opened his mouth and closed it again, then opened it, but still nothing came out.

"We're too young. You know that," I whispered. It was a lie. I wanted to say yes to him and *screw you* to anyone who questioned us. I wanted Sam forever.

"I know I said that before, but I was wrong," he replied. "Not many people meet the person they're meant to be with when they're thirteen. But we did. You know we did. I want you now. And I want you forever. I think about it all the time. I think about traveling. And getting jobs. And having a family. And you're always there with me. You have to be there with me," he said, his voice cracking and his eyes moving over my face for a sign that I'd changed my mind.

"You might not always feel that way, Sam," I said. "You've pushed me away before. You kept the course from me, and then I spent most of the summer wondering why I barely heard from you. And then that email . . . I can't trust that you'll love me forever when I don't even know if you'll love me next month." The words tasted like bile, and he jerked his head back like I'd hit him. "I think we should take a break for a while," I said softly enough that he wouldn't be able to hear the agony in my voice.

"You don't really want that, do you?" He croaked out the words, his eyes glassy. I felt like I'd been punched in the stomach.

"Just for a while," I repeated, holding back tears.

He studied my face like he was missing something. "Swear on it." He said it as though he was issuing a challenge, as if he didn't quite believe me.

I hesitated, and then I wrapped my index finger around his bracelet and tugged.

"I swear."

17

Now

"I SLEPT WITH CHARLIE," I SAY TO SAM, BARELY REGISTERING that he's just told me he loves me.

He's silent.

"I'm so sorry," I tell him, tears already streaming down my face. I say it over and over. And still he says nothing. We're facing each other on the floor. He's looking over my shoulder, his eyes dull and unfocused, his fingers frozen on my arm.

"Sam?" He doesn't move. "It was a mistake," I tell him, my voice shaking. "A huge mistake. I loved you more than anything, and then you left. And then you wrote that letter, and I thought you were done with me. I know that's no excuse." The words spill out in a sopping mess. "And that's why . . . why I broke us. I loved you, Sam. I did. So much. But I wasn't good enough for you. I'm still not . . ." I trail off because Sam is opening and closing his mouth, like he's trying to say something, but nothing comes out.

"I'd do anything to take it back, to make it better," I say. "Tell me what to do." He looks at me, blinking in shutter-fast bursts. He shakes his head.

"Sam, please say something, anything," I plead, my throat dry. His eyes narrow and his cheeks darken. His jaw is moving back and forth, like he's grinding his teeth.

"How was it?" he asks in a voice so low I think I must have misheard him.

"What?"

"You fucked Charlie. I asked you how it was." It's venomous and so unlike Sam that I flinch. I lie completely still, a prickly feeling spreading across my chest and down my arms like his words really were toxic. I've imagined what it would be like to tell Sam, what his reaction would be—hurt or anger or maybe indifference now that so much time has passed—but I didn't ever think he'd be cruel.

He's staring at me intensely, and I'm suddenly aware of how naked I am. I need to get out of here. I thought I could handle this, but I was wrong.

I sit up, covering myself with one arm while I reach for my clothes with the other, my hair falling around my face. I dress as quickly as possible, facing the bookshelf, trembling and numb, and then rush to the door.

"I can't believe you," Sam says from behind me, and I pause. "You're just going to leave." I wipe my tears away roughly. When I turn, Sam's standing completely naked, his arms folded across his chest, his feet planted wide apart. I want to respond, but my thoughts have congealed.

He shakes his head once. "You're running away just like before." Every word is sharp and acrid. Six poison darts. "I left for school, but you left and never came back."

I stammer, searching for something solid among the mush,

but I'm confused by the subtle change in topic. The only thing that seems to be working is my heart—and it's in overdrive. I can feel my pulse in my fingertips.

"I didn't think you'd want to see me," I finally manage. "We sold the cottage . . . there was nothing to come back to." His eyes flash with hurt.

"I was here to come back to. Every holiday. Every summer. I was here."

"But you hated me. I wrote to you. You never wrote or called back."

He puts his hands on his head, and I shut up. He sucks in air through his nose, and then he explodes.

"How did you expect me to react?" he yells, the tendons in his neck bulging. I can only look at him, my mouth open. "You slept with my brother!" He roars the final word, and I cringe.

Something in my brain isn't working right, because I can't process what he's just said. The time lines are all mixed up. *I slept with Charlie. I broke up with Sam. We never spoke again.* My chest is tight. I rub my face and try to focus again. I slept with Charlie, but that's not why Sam didn't speak to me. He stopped speaking to me because I turned down his proposal. And then the pieces start clicking together, and I have to gasp for air. My head feels like it might float off my neck. Tiny spots race across my vision like ants, and I squeeze my eyes shut. I need to get out of here now.

I spin on my heels, fling the door open, and bolt down the hallway, then the stairs, to the entrance. Sam is calling my name, and I can hear him following behind me. I grab my purse from the hook by the door and run outside, down the porch steps, and then stop suddenly.

My car is gone. *Where the hell is my car?* I turn around wildly, as if I'm in a parking lot and maybe I've just got the wrong row. But there's nothing. Just grass and trees and Sam, standing naked in the doorway. I could swear I drove here after the funeral, but now I'm not so sure. *What is happening?* There's a loud wheezing noise coming from my mouth. *I must be dreaming*, I think. *This is all a dream.*

I charge up the gravel to the road. Sam is yelling and swearing, but I keep going, the sharp pebbles digging into my feet. It's like my body has turned on autopilot while my lungs struggle to find oxygen, because without thinking, I head toward my cottage. I don't stop when I come to the top of the long driveway.

This is just a bad dream.

All I want is to curl up in my bed and sleep until it's tomorrow. I'll wake up, have breakfast with my parents, and Sam will be there a little while later, sweaty from his run, to take me swimming. And everything will be back to the way it should be. Me and Sam and the lake.

When the cottage comes into view, I almost don't recognize it. An entirely new section juts out from the back, and the pines have been cleared from around the building. There's a firepit that never used to be there and a red minivan parked beside the door. It's not my cottage, and this isn't a dream. Somehow I stumble back to the road but my legs buckle at the top of the driveway and I drop onto the ground, gulping for air, closing my eyes against the sting of tears.

I don't hear Sam approaching. I don't notice him at all until his sneakers are right in front of me.

"Two panic attacks in one day is a little excessive, don't you think?" he says, but there's no bite to his words. I can't reply. I can't even shake my head. I can only keep trying to breathe. He squats down in front of me.

"You need to slow down your breaths," he says. But I can't. It feels like I'm running a marathon at a sprinter's pace. He sighs. "C'mon, Percy. We can do it together." His hands come around my face so his thumbs are on my cheeks and his fingers are in my hair.

"Look at me," he says, and tilts my face up to his. He starts breathing slowly, counting the breaths, like he did earlier, his forehead creased. It takes me a minute to focus, but eventually I can breathe a little easier, then a bit slower, and my heart follows not long after.

"Better now?" he asks. But it's not better, not even close, because now that the fog has started to clear, I remember what stirred this tornado of anxiety in the first place.

"No," I croak. I look at him, my chin trembling, his hands still around my face, and force myself to say the words. "You already knew."

He swallows and presses his lips together. "Yeah," he rasps. "I knew."

I close my eyes and collapse into a heap on the dirt, silent sobs shaking my body. I hear him say something, but all I can focus on is how long he's known and how deeply he must have hated me all that time.

First I feel his hands on my back and his arms coming around me, and then everything goes black.

18

Winter, Twelve Years Ago

DELILAH TOOK A TAXI FROM THE TRAIN STATION STRAIGHT
to my house as soon as she got home for Christmas break,
dragging her suitcase behind her. She threw her arms around me
as soon as I opened the door. I can still remember the smell of
her as I pressed my face into her shoulder—a mix of her wool
coat, damp from the heavy snowfall, and her Herbal Essences
shampoo.

"You look like a piece of shit," she said when she released me.
"We're not supposed to let men do this to us."

"I did this to myself," I replied, and her face crumpled with
sympathy.

"I know you did," she whispered, and then hauled her suitcase up to my room and lay with me on my bed while I recounted
everything I had already told her on the phone, including the
many messages I had left for Sam that he never returned.

"I haven't spotted him on campus," she told me when I'd
asked. "But I promise I won't keep it from you if I do."

Having Delilah back in Toronto for those short weeks of winter break was the first slice of normal I'd had since summer. She and Patel had gotten back together (for the hundredth time). Delilah said it was a purely casual hookup relationship, but I wasn't sure I believed her. They had plans to get together over the holiday, but Delilah spent almost all her time with me. We took the subway downtown and bummed around the mall, eating poutine in the food court and sprawling out in the movie theater when our feet got sore.

We sat together on my bedroom floor one day, digging into a whole cheesecake with our forks, and I told her how I'd been struggling at school, how the words weren't coming to me as easily as they used to when I wrote.

"I miss his feedback," I told her through a chocolaty mouthful. "I don't know who I'm writing for anymore."

"You write for you, Percy, just like you always did," she said. "I'll be a reader for you. I promise to keep sex-related requests to a minimum."

"Is that even possible?" I asked, feeling a rare smile creep across my mouth.

"For you, I'd do anything," she said with a wink. "Even give up erotic literature."

On New Year's Eve, we went to the big concert and countdown in the square outside city hall, huddling against the icy wind and taking covert sips of vodka from her dad's flask. We didn't talk about Sam, and when we were together, I felt like I could see past the haze I'd been stumbling through for months. But when she left for Kingston, the fog descended again, draining me of my energy, my appetite, and any ambition I'd once had for excelling at school.

Delilah kept her promise. She called me in early March.

"I saw him," she said when I picked up. No hello. No small talk.

I was walking between buildings at the university, and sat down on the nearest bench.

"Okay." I said, exhaling loudly.

"It was at a party." She paused. "Percy, he was really drunk."

There was something un-Delilah about the way she spoke. Something too gentle.

"Do I want to hear the next part?" I asked.

"I don't know," she said. "It's not good, Percy. You tell me if you want to hear it."

I put my head down so my hair fell around my face, protecting me from the bustle of students.

"I have to hear it."

"Okay." She took a deep breath. "He hit on me. He told me I looked good and asked if I wanted to go upstairs." The world stopped moving. "I didn't, obviously! I told him to go screw himself and left."

"Sam wouldn't do that," I whispered.

"I'm sorry, Percy, but Sam did do that. But he was really, really wasted, like I said."

"You must have done something," I cried. "You must have flirted like you always do or told him how cute he was or something."

"I didn't!" Delilah said, sounding angry now. "I didn't do or say anything to make him think I was interested. How could you think that?"

"You can't blame me for thinking that," I said crisply. "You know you're a bit slutty. You're proud of it."

The shock of what I said stretched between us. Delilah was silent. I only knew she was there because I could hear her breathing. And when she spoke again, I could also hear that it was through tears.

"I know you're upset, Percy, and I'm sorry about Sam, but never speak to me like that again. Call me when you're ready to apologize."

I sat with my head bent and the phone pressed to my ear long after she hung up. I knew I shouldn't have said what I did. I knew how ugly it was, and I hadn't meant it. I thought about calling her back. I thought about saying I was sorry. But I didn't. I never did.

19

Now

I WAKE UP IN SAM'S BED WITH A POUNDING HEADACHE. There's a faint bluish-pink light coming in the window. How long was I asleep for? I push the sheet back, hot. I'm still wearing his T-shirt and sweatpants, the knees covered in dirt. I lie there listening, but the house is quiet. On the nightstand are a glass of water and a bottle of Advil. Sam must have put them there.

After popping two pills and drinking all the water, I sit on the edge of his bed, my feet on the carpet, and my head in my hands, taking inventory of the wreckage I've caused. I bulldozed Sam with the truth at the worst possible moment. On the day of his mother's funeral. I didn't think about him; I only thought about getting the ugliness off my chest. And he knew. He knew, and he hadn't wanted to talk about it, at least not then.

Sam has put my purse on the floor beside the bed. I dig around for my phone. Determined not to push anyone else out of my life, I call Chantal.

"P?" she says, groggy with sleep.

"I still love him," I whisper. "I screwed everything up. And I love him. And I'm worried that even if I can get him to forgive me, I'm still not good enough for him."

"You're good enough," Chantal says.

"But I'm such a mess. And he's a doctor."

"You're good enough," she says again.

"What if he doesn't think so?"

"Then you come home, P. And I'll tell you why he's wrong."

I close my eyes and let out a shaky breath.

"Okay. I can do that."

"I know you can."

When we hang up, I cross the dark hallway to the bathroom. I turn on the light and grimace at my reflection. Underneath the streaks of mascara, my skin is blotchy and my eyes bloodshot and puffy. I splash some cold water on my face and scrub at the black makeup stains until my cheeks are red and raw.

The smell of coffee hits my nose as I tiptoe down the stairs. There's a light on in the kitchen. I take a deep breath before I have to face Sam again. But it's not Sam. It's Charlie. He's at the table in the same spot where Sue used to sit. He has a mug in his hand, and he's looking right at me like he was waiting for me.

"Good morning," he says, lifting his coffee my way.

"You took my car," I say, standing in the doorway.

"I took your car," he replies, then takes a sip. "Sorry about that. I didn't realize you would be needing to leave in such a hurry." Clearly Sam has filled him in on a couple of details. "He's down at the water," he says before I ask.

I look in the direction of the lake and then back to Charlie. "He hates me."

He gets up and walks over to me, smiling kindly as he tucks a strand of hair behind my ear.

"You're wrong," he says. "I think his feelings for you are basically the exact opposite." His eyes move over my face and his smile fades. "Do you hate me?" he asks quietly.

It takes me a moment to figure out why he would ask me that, but then I realize: Charlie's the only other person who would have told Sam about what happened between us.

"Never," I say, my voice cracking, and he pulls me into a tight hug. "I didn't hate you then, either. After what happened. You were good to me that summer."

"I had ulterior motives, but I didn't ever plan to make a move," he whispers. "Until that night."

"That night was my fault," I tell him. Charlie squeezes me and then lets go.

"Can I ask you something?" I say when we separate.

"Sure," he rasps. "Ask me anything."

"Did your mom know?" His face wilts a little, and I close my eyes, swallowing back the lump in my throat.

"If it makes you feel better, she was mostly mad at me."

"That doesn't make me feel better," I croak.

He nods, his eyes flickering like fireflies. "I tried to tell her how *you* seduced *me* with candy and hairy legs, but she wasn't convinced."

I huff out a laugh, and a little of the heaviness lifts.

"She told me to call you," he says, serious again. I stop breathing. "Before she died. She said he'd need you after."

I hug him again. "Thank you," I whisper.

~~~

SAM IS SITTING at the edge of the dock, his feet in the water. The sun hasn't risen above the hills yet, but its light casts a halo around the far shore that promises it will soon. My footsteps shake the wooden planks as I walk toward him, but he doesn't turn around.

I sit beside him, putting two steaming cups of coffee down, then roll my pants up over my knees so I can dip my legs into the lake. I pass him one of the mugs, and we drink in silence. There aren't any boats out yet, and the only sound is the distant, mournful call of a loon. I'm half-finished with my coffee—trying to figure out where to begin—when Sam starts talking.

"Charlie told me about the two of you over Christmas break when we came home from school," he says, looking out over the calm water. I want to cut in and apologize, but I can tell he's got more to say. And, at the very least, I owe him the chance to tell his side despite how afraid I am to hear it—to hear about what it was like for him to know what I'd done all this time, to hear him get to the part where he never wants to see me again.

His voice is husky, like he hasn't spoken yet this morning. "I was in rough shape after we broke up. I didn't understand what had gone wrong and why you would shut down like that. Even if you weren't ready for marriage or to even talk about getting married, breaking up didn't make sense to me. I felt like maybe I had experienced our entire relationship completely differently from how you had. I felt like I was going crazy."

He pauses and looks at me from the corner of his eye. I can feel the shame tighten its grip on my throat and my heart beating harder, but instead of fighting it, I accept that this is going to be uncomfortable and focus instead on Sam and what he needs to say.

"I think Charlie thought if I knew what had really happened, it might somehow make it better, explain why you pushed me away." He shakes his head like he still can't believe it. "He told me that you did still love me, that you had immediately regretted it and completely freaked out."

"I had a panic attack," I whisper.

"Yeah, I kind of figured that part out at the wake," he says, looking at me straight on. He's so much calmer than he was yesterday, but his voice sounds hollow.

"I did regret it," I tell him, hesitating before putting my hand on his thigh. He doesn't move away or tense up under my touch, so I keep it there. "It's the biggest regret of my life. I wish it hadn't happened, but it did, and I'm so sorry."

"I know," he says, looking back at the lake, his shoulders slumped. "I'm sorry I lost it yesterday. I thought I had moved past it years ago, but hearing you say the words, it felt like hearing it for the first time all over again."

I take his hand in mine and shake it. "Hey," I say so he looks at me, and when he does, I squeeze his hand tighter and look him in the eye. "You don't have anything to apologize for. Me, on the other hand . . ."

He smiles sadly and runs his hand through his hair.

"The thing is, Percy, I do." I can feel my face scrunch in confusion. He brings one leg on the dock, twisting so he can face me. I take my feet out of the water and tuck them under me so I can do the same.

"You always thought I was perfect."

"Sam, you *were* perfect," I reply, stating the obvious.

"I wasn't!" he says, adamant. "I was obsessed with getting out of here, and then when I went away to school, I was so terrified I was going to mess it up, that I had only seemed smart because I'd grown up in such a small town. It felt like any day they'd figure out I was a fraud. I was paralyzed with fear. I was homesick, too. I missed you like crazy. I didn't want you to know how bad it was, to think less of me, so I didn't call."

"You were eighteen, and it was totally normal to feel that way. I was too immature to realize that."

He shakes his head. "I was always jealous of Charlie. I think you knew that. He barely studied in high school and would just kill every test. Girls loved him. Everything seemed to happen so easily for him. And then you did, too." My stomach feels like it just dropped forty stories.

"I felt like my future exploded when you said you couldn't marry me," he goes on. "But I thought one day you would change your mind. I thought we both needed a bit of time. But then . . . I didn't take it well, hearing about you and Charlie." He rubs his face. "I was angry. With you. With Charlie. And with myself. The way I felt about you was always so clear to me—even when we were young I knew you and I were meant for each other. Two halves of a whole. I loved you so much that the word 'love' didn't seem big enough for how I felt. But I realize now that you didn't know that. You wouldn't have turned to Charlie if you knew that. And for that I'm sorry." He reaches toward me, pulling my bottom lip out from under my teeth with his thumb. I hadn't realized I'd been biting it.

I start to reply, to tell him he doesn't need to apologize, that I'm the one who should be explaining herself, but he stops me.

"When I went back to school after Christmas, I just wanted to forget you and us and everything that happened," he says. "I wanted to get you out of my system, but I think I also wanted to hurt you the way you hurt me. I studied like crazy, but I also drank a lot. I'd go to these big house parties—there was always a keg, and there were always girls." He pauses. The muscles in my stomach seize at the mention of the other girls. He squints, as if he's asking my permission to continue, and I take a deep breath and wait.

"I can't remember most of them, but I know there were a lot. Jordie tried to keep an eye on me. He was worried I was going to catch something or screw around with some psychopath's girlfriend, but I was relentless. It didn't make a difference, though. All I could think about every day was you," he says, his voice scratchy. "Even when I was with other girls, trying to erase you from my mind, you were still there. I'd wake up, sometimes I didn't even know where I was, so full of shame and missing you so much. But I'd just do it all over again, trying to forget. And then one night at some party in a frat house basement, I saw Delilah." My breath hitches at her name, and I rub my chest as though I can soothe the ache beneath my breastbone.

Sam waits until I meet his eyes again.

"You don't need to tell me this part," I say. "This part I'm pretty sure I know."

"Delilah told you?"

I nod.

"I thought she would. She was a good friend to you." I wince, remembering how terribly I'd treated her. I'd been mad and then when I got over my anger, I was too ashamed to apologize.

"I was out-of-my-mind drunk, Percy. And I made a pass at her. She told me off and stormed out of there. I think I puked all over myself, like, two minutes later."

Exactly what Delilah had told me.

He lets out a bitter laugh. "I stopped sleeping around after that. I just ate, went to class, and studied. I was kind of a robot, but after a while I stopped being so angry with you and Charlie—and myself."

"I'm so sorry," I whisper. "I hate that I did that to you." I watch the ripples radiating from where a fish has jumped. We're both quiet. "I deserved it," I say after a little while, turning back to him. "The other girls. You hitting on Delilah. You yelling at me yesterday. For what I did to you, I deserved it all."

Sam leans forward like he didn't hear me correctly. "Deserved it?" he repeats, his eyes ferocious. "What are you talking about? You didn't deserve it, Percy. Just like I didn't deserve what happened with Charlie. Betrayals don't cancel each other out. They just hurt more." He takes my hands and rubs them with his thumbs. "I thought about telling you," he says. "I should have told you. I got all the emails you sent, and I even tried writing back, but I blamed you for a long time. And I thought maybe you'd keep writing if you still cared about me, but eventually you stopped."

His head is bent, and he's looking at me through his lashes. "When I found that video store with the horror section in fourth year, I almost reached out to you. But it felt too late by then. I figured you would have moved on." I shake my head forcefully. Of everything he's just told me, this is what hurts the most.

"I didn't move on," I croak. I squeeze his fingers, and we stare at each other for several long seconds. And then they come to me—three words from yesterday, echoing in my head in tentative bursts of happiness.

I love you.

Sam has known about Charlie and me for years, for the entire time I've been back. He broke up with his girlfriend despite what I'd done.

I love you. I don't think I ever stopped.

The words didn't break through my panic before, but now they stick to my ribs like molasses.

"I still haven't," I whisper. He's perfectly still, but his eyes dance frantically across my face, his head tilted slightly, like what I've said doesn't make sense. Now that it's getting lighter, I can see how red his eyes are. He can't have slept much last night.

"I thought I'd never see you again." My voice hitches, and I swallow. "I would have given anything to sit on this dock with you, to hear your voice, to touch you." I run my fingers over the stubble on his cheek, and he puts his hand over mine, holding it there. "I fell in love with you when I was thirteen, and I never stopped. You're it for me." Sam closes his eyes for three long seconds, and when he opens them, they are glittering pools under a starry sky.

"Swear on it?" he asks. And before I can answer, he puts his hands on my cheeks and brings his lips to mine, tender and forgiving and thoroughly Sam. He takes them away all too soon, and rests his forehead against mine.

"You can forgive me?" I whisper.

"I forgave you years ago, Percy."

He looks at me for a long time, not speaking, our eyes locked.

"I have something for you," he says. He shifts and reaches for something in his pocket. I look down when I feel him fiddling with something at my hand.

It's not as bright as it once was, the orange and pink have faded and the white has turned gray, and it's too big for me. But there it is, after all these years, Sam's friendship bracelet tied around my wrist.

"I told you I'd give you something if you swam across the lake. I figured you earned a consolation prize," he says, tugging on the band.

"Friends again?" I ask, feeling the smile spreading across my cheeks.

The corner of his mouth lifts. "Can we have sleepovers as friends?"

"I seem to remember sleepovers being part of the deal," I say, and then add, "I don't want to mess this up again, Sam."

"I think messing it up is part of the deal," he replies, giving my waist a little squeeze. "But I think we might be better at cleaning it up the next time."

"I want that," I tell him.

"Good," he says. "Because I want that, too."

He pulls me onto his lap, and I run my hands through his hair. We kiss until the sun has risen high above the hill, wrapping us in a blanket of bright morning heat. When we eventually part, we're both wearing big, dorky grins.

"So what do we do now?" Sam says in a gravelly voice, running his finger over the freckles on my nose.

I'm supposed to check out of the motel later this morning, and I have no idea what will happen after that. But right now? I know exactly what we're going to do.

I pull his shirt off over his head and run my hands down his shoulders and smile.

"I think we should go for a swim."

EPILOGUE

One Year Later

WE SPREAD SUE'S ASHES ON A FRIDAY EVENING IN JULY. IT'S taken a full year for Sam and Charlie to work themselves up to letting her go. We choose this time of day because on the extraordinarily rare occasion that Sue was home with the boys on a summer evening, she'd serve dinner on the deck, right as the sun began to cast its light on the far side of the lake, and sigh in weary delight.

"I don't know if it's more beautiful because I hardly ever get a chance to see it this time of year, or if it's always this special," she once said to me as we set the table. "It's the magic hour."

And it does feel magical as Sam and I, hand in hand, follow Charlie down the hill to the lake. How the golden glow illuminates all the details of the tree line and shore that you can't see when the sun is high overhead. How the water seems to still as if it, too, is taking a break from the day's activities for cocktail hour and a family barbecue. How we're walking across the wooden plans of the Floreks' dock and climbing into the Banana Boat.

Both Charlie and Sam agreed the boat needed to be part of today, that we would take a trip in their dad's boat to say goodbye to their mom. They had tried to fix it up together on the few weekends in the spring when we were all up from the city. I had been skeptical of this grand plan, but Charlie insisted that they'd done it once before and could do it once again. Sam had declared that he was a lot handier than he used to be. Neither of which turned out to be true.

On the long weekend in May, I found them in the garage, covered in grease, half-drunk and walloping the side of the boat in frustration. They hauled it into the marina the next day.

Now, Charlie takes the driver's seat and Sam sits in the chair beside him, and we head out to the middle of the lake. I watch them from the bench in the front, the bench I sat on all those years ago when I first realized that I had a crush on my best friend. Today Sam is wearing a suit—another thing he and Charlie agreed on was that this was an occasion that required jackets and ties, despite how they both hated them. Sam looks so grown-up, something that still occasionally takes me by surprise, and also so much like that skinny science nerd I fell in love with.

He sees me staring, and gives me a lopsided smile, mouthing the words *I love you* over the roar of the engine. I mouth them back. Charlie catches our exchange and belts Sam on the arm as he turns the motor to idle. We're the only ones out on the water.

"This is no time for flirting, Samuel," Charlie says with a wink in my direction.

We all live in Toronto now. Sam and I in a little rental condo downtown and Charlie in another, swankier one he owns in a posh neighborhood five stops north on the subway line. Between Charlie's long hours at work, Sam's shifts at the hospital, and my writing (which Sam convinced me to *try, just try*, and I now wrestle with it in the predawn hours before heading into the office), we don't have as much time together as we'd like. And we do like having time together. It's a revelation and a relief—one that has come with uncomfortable moments and a couple of arguments, especially during those early get-togethers—but here we all are, wind in our hair, sun on our faces, zipping out to the center of Kamaniskeg Lake in the Banana Boat.

It's taken a lot of work for Sam and me to get here as well—for us to find our footing as a couple, to trust each other, and for me to fight off the persistent voice that tells me I'm not good enough, that I don't deserve him or my happiness. We've snapped at each other, we've flung accusations around, and we've yelled, but we've both stuck around and cleaned up the mess. We've also been friends. And that's the part that's been easy—laughing, teasing, rooting for each other. We can still speak to each other without speaking. And we've made good use of Sam's collection of horror movies.

Sam is holding on to the urn, a smoothly polished teak vessel that seems too small to contain everything that was Sue. Her smile. Her confidence. Her love.

"So?" he asks his brother. "Are you ready?"

"No," Charlie replies. "Are you?"

"Not at all," Sam says.

"But it's time," Charlie tells him.

And Sam agrees. "It's time."

Sam heads to the rear while Charlie stays in the driver's seat, watching his brother remove the lid and brace his legs against the back of the boat. Sam looks at us over his shoulder, first at me and then at Charlie, and nods.

"Hit it," he says.

Charlie pushes the throttle down, and the boat takes off

across the water. Sam raises the urn up and out, tipping it so
Sue's ashes fly through the air behind the boat, a faint gray streak
across the bright blue water. And in seconds, she's gone.

We head back to the house in silence, Charlie leading the way
and Sam beside me, his arm around my shoulders. We can hear
the music and laughter before we've made it halfway up the hill.

There will be a few dozen people inside the Floreks' home—
a big party, just like Sue would have wanted. There will be Dolly
and Shania over the speakers. There will be an excess of food
and beer and wine. There will be pierogies made by Julien, who
bought the Tavern at a "family discount" from Charlie and Sam.
There will be dozens of guests—all the people who loved Sue,
including my parents, and some who didn't get the chance to but
would have, like Chantal. And there will be a flash of red hair.
Because one of the hardest things I did over the last year was
apologize to Delilah. I expected her to be polite but unaffected
when I met her at a coffee shop in Ottawa—it was all so long ago.
I didn't expect her to circle her arms around me and ask what the
hell took so long.

And later tonight, when everyone has left and it's just Sam
and me in our pj's in the basement, there will be popcorn and a
movie playing in the background and a ring in an old wooden
box with my initials carved on top. It will be made from twisted
threads of embroidery floss that match the faded bracelet on my
wrist. And I will get down on one knee and ask Sam Florek to be
with me. To be my family. Forever.

Acknowledgments

In July of 2020, I decided to write a book. This had long been an ambition of mine, but one I shoved deep in the caverns of my heart and mind. I didn't think I'd ever get around to doing it, and I was convinced that if I did try, I wouldn't be able to finish it. Besides, I was an editor—my job for fifteen years had been to help make other writers' words shine. But that summer the pandemic had me asking Big Life Questions, and I decided not to put it off any longer. I gave myself two goals: to draft a novel by the end of the year and to make it good—not perfect but something I was proud of. I didn't know that writing *Every Summer After* would be the most satisfying project I'd ever undertaken. I didn't know that it would bring me such joy during difficult times. And I didn't know that it would become an actual book and myself an author along with it. For that, I have many people to thank.

The first is Taylor Haggerty, my dream agent. I fought back tears when Taylor offered to represent me. She is a true superhero, one who comes equipped with sharp instincts, impeccable editorial judgment, and endless patience for a rookie novelist with a lot of questions. There is no one I'd rather partner with on this journey. Taylor, thank you for believing in me and this book.

From our first conversation, I felt Amanda Bergeron was meant to be my editor. I will be forever grateful (and a little gobsmacked) because that's exactly what happened. Amanda and I were both pregnant while we worked on *Every Summer After*, and I love that we brought it into the world along with two tiny new humans. Amanda, thank you for your bottomless passion for Percy and Sam's story and for everything you've done to bring it to life.

I was gifted with the talent and guidance of a second brilliant editor, Deborah Sun de la Cruz. Deborah, thank you for your whip-smart line edits and for rallying the Canadian troops around the book. I am incredibly fortunate to have you on my team.

To Sareer Khader, Ivan Held, Christine Ball, Claire Zion, Jeanne-Marie Hudson, Craig Burke, Jessica Brock, Diana Franco, Brittanie Black, Bridget O'Toole, Vi-An Nguyen, Megha Jain, Ashley Tucker, Christine Legon, Angelina Krahn, and the sales team at Berkley, as well as Jasmine Brown and the Root Literary team: Thank you for your enthusiasm for this book and for your hard work in putting it out into the world.

Thank you to Nicole Winstanley, Bonnie Maitland, Beth Cockeram, Dan French, and Emma Ingram at Penguin Canada for giving both myself and *Every Summer After* a loving home in Canada. Thank you also to Heather Baror-Shapiro for making *Every Summer After* a truly global book. And to Anna Boatman and the team at Piatkus for bringing the novel to the UK, New Zealand, and my other homeland, Australia.

To Ashley Audrain and Karma Brown, thank you for your astonishing kindness, support, and invaluable words of wisdom in navigating the publishing world and life as an author.

Meredith Marino, Courtney Shea, and Maggie Wrobel: Thank you for being my earliest readers and for your insightful feedback (on my two-week deadline, no less!). I am lucky to count such brilliant, encouraging women as friends. In the early stages of writing, I sent Meredith the first ten pages of the manuscript, and she promised to be honest with me about what she thought. Very soon after, I got a text from her that read: "I think you're going to be a real author!!!!!!!!!!!!" Meredith, you were right, as usual. Thank you for giving me the confidence to carry on.

I was terrified to let my husband see my first draft. I didn't think I could live in the same house while he read the thing beside me, hating every word. Marco spent several days convincing me to get over myself and give him a copy. When I finally did, he read it at breakneck speed and deemed it to be "a real book" that he very much enjoyed. He also said it was full of typos. Thank you, Marco, for copyediting the manuscript before I sent it out into the world. Thank you for not balking when I suddenly announced that I was going to write a book and devote time to the task every single day. Thank you for taking care of Max while I got my words in. And thank you most of all for helping me find the courage not to let fear stand in my way.

EVERY SUMMER AFTER

Carley Fortune

Behind the Book

I moved to the lake the summer I was eight. In my parents' own whirlwind love story, my mom, a Canadian, and my dad, an Aussie, met in Scotland, got engaged three months after that, and settled in Toronto to start a life together. When I was three, we moved to Australia; when I was eight, we came back. But instead of buying a home in the city, they decided to put down roots in Barry's Bay—a tiny town in Eastern Ontario—where they owned a small cottage on Kamaniskeg Lake.

I grew up on the water, down a narrow dirt road in the bush. I spent summers in damp bathing suits, reading on the dock, and when I was older, working at my family's restaurant in the evening. (Although the inspiration for the Tavern in this book comes from the beloved Wilno Tavern, one town over from Barry's Bay.)

My parents sold our home on Kamaniskeg well over a decade ago, but because a lake is my happy place, my husband and I have continued renting a cottage just outside Barry's Bay for a couple weeks every August. The owner is an American and in 2020, when the border between Canada and the United States closed to travelers, he let us squat there for the summer.

In mid-July that year, I had a very strong and sudden desire to write a book. I'm not a spiritual person at all (even the *om* in a yoga class makes me feel weird), but the force at which this urge hit me was unlike anything I've felt before or since. It was an epiphany, my one and only Oprah Winfrey–worthy Aha Moment.

I think you'll be able to tell after reading *Every Summer After* how nostalgic I was feeling when I wrote it. It's no coincidence that I was living by the lake in the corner of the world where I grew up when I began the manuscript. I wanted to pay tribute to shimmering water and dense bush, to skies that stretch endlessly and the storms that light them up in the dark. I wanted friendship bracelets and drippy ice cream cones. I wanted to escape 2020 and retreat into the best of my childhood summers.

I'm mildly embarrassed to admit that for a long stretch of my adulthood, reading seemed more like a chore than a break from reality. As an editor, I read for work all day, and the idea of looking at more words in my slivers of downtime was completely unappealing. I could barely stand to pick up a book. I wish I could remember precisely which one started me on a roll of reading women's fiction and romance and young adult novels a few years ago. I'd like to know so I could track down the author and thank her with all of my heart. It could have been Christina Lauren or Colleen Hoover or Jenny Han or Angie Thomas or Emily Henry or Tahereh Mafi or Sally Thorne or Nicola Yoon or Helen Hoang. Or many, many others. What I do know is that once I started, I couldn't stop. I went from reading a handful of books a year to downing several a week.

I didn't realize it at the time, but I think the editor part of my brain was figuring out how these books worked— what the narrative beats were and where they fell in the story, what kinds of characters I find intriguing, how authors keep a reader engaged from beginning to end. I had been studying the elements of a novel without realizing how hard I'd been cramming. I have a journalism degree, not a formal background in creative writing, but I consider the time I spent—and continue to spend—as a deeply engaged reader as my education.

Before I set fingers to keyboard, I knew I wanted to tell a love story, and I knew I wanted it to have a happy ending. (In 2020, a happy ending was the only kind I could stomach.) I wanted the central relationship to span many years and capture all the hormone-fueled angst and excitement of being a teenager, and the heaviness we live with as adults. I wanted to explore the incredible feeling of finding your person, that friend who gets you like no one else does, who makes you feel seen and safe and sparkly.

I also wanted to write about people who screw up but who ultimately try their best to do better. The characters in this book are all flawed. (Except maybe for Sue. I'm pretty sure Sue is perfection.) I hope that makes them all the more compelling. I'm personally drawn to protagonists like Percy and Sam, who grapple with their own shortcomings, who face obstacles both external and internal. For some readers, Percy's betrayal will be unforgivable. And yet Sam does forgive her. But this acceptance doesn't come easy; their happy ending is hard-earned.

Most of all, I wanted to write the kind of book I like to devour, the kind of book that gave me back my love of reading several years ago. Writing *Every Summer After* was an escape for me. I hope reading it was for you as well.

Discussion Questions

1. Sam and Percy are fast friends. What do you think each gets from their relationship?

2. Have you had an important relationship—either platonic or romantic—that ended in a way that you wish you could get a do-over?

3. Sam and Percy's romantic relationship began when they were very young. Do you think it would have survived had they not broken up? Did they need the time apart to ultimately end up together?

4. How do you think Charlie feels about Percy in the past and present?

5. What did you think of Delilah and her friendship with Percy? Do you see Delilah as a good friend? What about Percy?

6. How did Percy's betrayal change your opinion of her? Do you sympathize with what she did? Do you think her act is forgivable?

7. As a teenager, Percy looks up to Sue, perhaps even more so than her own parents. Why do you think that is?

8. The story is told from Percy's point of view. What moments do you wish you could have peeked inside Sam's head?

9. In the final chapter, Sam tells Percy, "Betrayals don't cancel each other out. They just hurt more." Do you agree with him? Or do you think "getting even" has merit?

10. The lake is Percy's happy place, where she feels the most creative and alive. What's yours?

Carley's Reading List

1. *28 Summers* by Elin Hilderbrand
2. *Beach Read* by Emily Henry
3. *Carry On* by Rainbow Rowell
4. *Everything After* by Jill Santopolo
5. *Forever, Interrupted* by Taylor Jenkins Reid
6. *Get a Life, Chloe Brown* by Talia Hibbert
7. *Hana Khan Carries On* by Uzma Jalaluddin
8. *Summer Sisters* by Judy Blume
9. *Love Lettering* by Kate Clayborn
10. *Words in Deep Blue* by Cath Crowley

Carley Fortune is an award-winning Canadian journalist who's worked as an editor for Refinery29, *The Globe & Mail*, *Chatelaine*, and *Toronto Life*. She lives in Toronto with her husband and two sons. *Every Summer After* is her first novel.

CONNECT ONLINE

CarleyFortune.com

CarleyFortune

CarleyFortune